The Kingfisher Secret

By Anonymous

CENTURY

1 3 5 7 9 10 8 6 4 2

Century
20 Vauxhall Bridge Road
London SW1V 2SA

Century is part of the Penguin Random House group of companies
whose addresses can be found at global.penguinrandomhouse.com.

Penguin
Random House
UK

First published in Great Britain by Century in 2018
Published simultaneously in Canada by McClelland & Stewart, an imprint of
Penguin Random House Canada, a Penguin Random House Company

www.penguin.co.uk

A CIP catalogue record for this book is available from the British Library.

Hardback ISBN 9781529123722
Trade Paperback ISBN 9781529123739

Typeset in 12.25/17.75 pt Times New Roman by Jouve (UK), Milton Keynes
Printed and bound in Great Britain by Clays Ltd, Elcograf S.p.A.

Penguin Random House is committed to a sustainable future
for our business, our readers and our planet. This book is made
from Forest Stewardship Council® certified paper.

FSC
www.fsc.org

MIX
Paper from
responsible sources
FSC® C018179

A commonly known type of sexpionage is a honey trap operation, which is designed to compromise an opponent sexually to elicit information from that person. A man who is the seducer in a honey trap operation is known as a raven. A female seductress is known as a swallow.

– Wikipedia entry on 'Sexpionage'

The Kingfisher Secret

1

MONTREAL, 2016

Grace Elliott sat on a stained purple sofa in the cheapest hotel in downtown Montreal. The junior suite had not been updated since the 1980s, when washed-out photographs of surfers standing on beaches counted as art. There were holes in the wall and in the carpet, blobs of mold on the ceiling, and neon pink stripes on the hazy mirror. The ninth was a smoking floor. Room 927 smelled the way a generation of cigarette-and-beer breath, body odor, and failure ought to smell.

To Grace, it was beautiful. She noted every detail so she could return to it again and again, this afternoon that was sure to relaunch her career.

Her digital recorder was running and so was an app on her phone, as a backup. The devices captured the raspy voice of

1

the tall woman on the corner of the bed, whose screen name was Violet Rain. Part of the agreement to secure the interview was to supply Violet with thin Davidoff cigarettes, Juicy Fruit gum, and a forty-eight-dollar bottle of Rioja. Now Violet was smoking, chewing, and drinking at the same time. Despite this onslaught, her teeth were bleached white. Her soft yellow flip-flops were faintly discolored but her hair and toenails were as impeccable as her teeth. To Grace, Violet's artificial breasts seemed a miraculous but painful burden to carry.

'So he never gave you money?'

'What kinda question is that? Why would he?' Violet looked around, like there were other people in the room who might be insulted along with her. 'I'm not a whore. I'm an actor. Was Julia Roberts a whore when she banged that old fart in *Pretty Woman*? No. She was just playing a whore in the movie.'

This directly contradicted Grace's source. 'Sorry.'

'Whatever. You're not the only one. My parents and my good Christian brother who stopped speaking to me when I was nineteen, they couldn't figure it out either. You've had real sex. All that moaning and calling out? That's acting. I'm an actor like any other actor. When I'm with a man off-set in my regular life, a gentleman friend, I'm just me and he's just him.'

'Did you always want to be an actor, Violet?'

'I did drama in junior high and high school. I played Juliet once! It's like: *Parting is such sweet sorrow that I shall say goodnight till it be morrow.* Living here in this filthy, Frenchy capital of porn for twenty years wasn't my choice. It just happened. But I'm finally gonna make the transition to TV and, Grace, you're gonna help me.'

As an American, Grace had trouble thinking that Montreal could be the capital of anything, least of all pornography. She was not even aware of this instinct until she'd been forced to move here. Back home, it was a key component of the emotional education system: everything modern and powerful and neat and naughty had been born in the USA.

Grace leaned forward, her elbows on her knees, close enough that the smoke from Violet's cigarette twirled into her hair. She would need a shower, but not here. 'If he didn't give you money, what did he give you? I mean, he's a lot older than you. You're stunning and he's . . . well, he's him.'

'Age doesn't matter. Most men are gross, when you get right down to it.' Violet sighed, put out her cigarette and lit another. 'I guess I might as well tell you. When you wanted to talk to me I blew you off for the first week because I don't want to be some narc. It just isn't me, to get someone in trouble. He didn't do anything illegal or even weird, unless cheating on your wife is weird. You know the reason I finally texted you back? Because the man is a liar. He said, I swear he said, that he was going to bring me down to New York and LA and introduce me to some producers. He was going to make my transition to TV.'

'He didn't follow through?'

'Ghosted my ass. We were together five times and it was all about to happen, maybe reality TV, maybe the soaps, and then . . . nothing. You can't do that to me.'

Half an hour earlier, Violet had talked about her strict parents. She had dropped out of high school and moved to Montreal from Northern Ontario when she was seventeen. The plan was to begin as a model, leap to New York or London or Paris, make some money, meet the right people, and break into the movies. Now, at the end of a career in pornography, she was thirty-six. She had been dating a married actuary but the relationship had recently collapsed in a financial dispute.

It occurred to Grace, listening to Violet, that a porn star and a supermarket tabloid journalist could have a lot in common. Both of them had come to Montreal for professional reasons, thinking it would be temporary. Both of them hoped these ninety minutes in Hotel Clementine would put them back on the path of their dreams, that this story would change everything.

When she was in seventh grade, Grace had won a writing competition in her hometown of Bloomington, Minnesota. Part of the prize was lunch in Minneapolis with a city hall reporter from the *Star Tribune*. She still remembered every moment. The idea that she could order anything from the menu, an appetizer *and* a main course, was wizardry. A new world had opened.

But 1998, the year she graduated in the middle of her class with a master's in journalism, had been a lean one for newspapers. Or at least for Grace Elliott in newspapers. She sent her résumé to every large daily paper in the country including the *Star Tribune*. Then, when she heard nothing back, to medium-sized dailies and magazines. It broke her heart a little, and then a lot. She had not cultivated a mentor in school, and the city hall reporter who had taken her to lunch in Minneapolis had died. The only response she received to her job applications was for an unpaid internship at *Esquire*. She was not in the financial position to accept an unpaid internship in one of the most expensive cities in the world, so one dark weekend she responded to an oblique ad on the college bulletin board that did not specify the *National Flash* or its location. The tabloid's parent company had just moved from New York to Canada because the chair of the board had secured a thirty-year lease on a stone warehouse in Old Montreal for one dollar a year. The free space had something to do with economic development, after a dalliance with Quebec separation, but Grace never understood what value the locals received for their money. The *Flash* employed a total of three Canadians.

'When are we doing the photo shoot?' said Violet, when they were finished. 'If you don't know anyone, I know a guy. He used to shoot ads for Guess jeans.'

'I had a pair of those.' Grace was on the verge of giddy. Violet had gone into grim, humiliating detail about her affair with the man some hoped and many feared would become the next president of the United States. They would both be in New York soon enough, doing interviews on CNN. When she turned off the recorders, Violet had emptied the bottle of Rioja into two plastic glasses and now they were celebrating what would come next. 'I'll text you with dates right away. But we'll make sure the photos are sexy and strong.'

'To girl power.' Violet lifted her wine.

'Girl power.' Grace tapped the rim of her plastic glass to the rim of Violet's and they drank. At almost six feet, Violet was a few inches taller than Grace and far more voluptuous. The last man Grace had dated had called her 'sinewy in a good way', which made her feel as seductive as a male marathon runner. It was quiet enough, as they drank their wine, to hear a couple having sex in the adjacent room.

'She's definitely faking,' Violet whispered. 'So what comes next?'

'I go back to the office and get working on your contract. You can't tell anyone else about this, not until the issue comes out.'

'When do I get paid?'

'As soon as it gets through legal. I'll make sure they rush it. When my editor hears your story . . .'

'Do you think he'd pay two hundred thousand? Instead of one-fifty? I need a new car.'

'I'll say you insist on two-fifty. He'll want to negotiate, so maybe we can land at two hundred.'

This did not bother Grace, the notion of advocating for Violet. The man who owned the *National Flash* funded most of the worst things that happened in America. It would horrify her professors, back in Austin, to know she paid sources for stories. But nothing about journalism was as she had imagined it back in the 1990s.

Outside, it was a cool but sunny dusk. The last of the October leaves in a churchyard whirled off the trees and landed in her hair. Walking east and south from downtown to Old Montreal, lightly buzzed from the wine, Grace loved everything she usually hated: pawnshops and fast food chains, cigarette butts in the gutter, graffiti, multiply pierced young punks in black leather who sat on cardboard with filthy dogs and begged for money. It was, she thought, all so human. Nothing could ruin this feeling because she was about to break the biggest – well, actually the first – story of her career. She was forty-three, divorced and childless by choice, the owner of a one-bedroom condominium and a cat, with three unfilled prescriptions for antidepressants in her purse. She spent an average of five evenings a week alone, with romantic comedies on Netflix and wine that did not come close to the bottle of Rioja she had bought for Violet. Violet Rain! For two months she had pursued Violet. Even the esteemed professors of journalism at the University of Texas at Austin would agree it's not easy to contact a porn star, to win her trust, to convince her over several coffee meetings to tell her story publicly.

The *National Flash* would always be a joke to her classmates who ended up at legacy publications before they hit thirty, but they would all agree that what Grace had achieved here was dogged, patient, ethical investigative journalism. After this story popped, if she found an editor with a bit of imagination and an appetite for risk, she too would *make the transition*. She would do what she had wanted to do since she was a twelve-year-old girl: be a real journalist.

Grace smiled at strangers. She stopped to give a bit of love to a golden retriever. In a boutique that smelled of vanilla a block from her office, she tried on a three-hundred-dollar cashmere scarf she had admired for months. Until today, she had been afraid to touch it. When you're writing cutlines for photos of out-of-shape celebrities on Mediterranean beaches, you don't deserve to touch cashmere. In the mirror she stood with her shoulders back, messed her brown hair so it fell properly over the scarf and jacket, took off her glasses, put them back on again, took them off.

'Very sophisticated,' said the shopkeeper.

She bought the scarf because the old Grace, the pre-Violet Grace, would not buy the scarf. This was the pivot, the moment of her reinvention.

At the warehouse she said hello to the main floor concierge and took the stairs instead of the elevator. Her boss, the editor in chief and publisher of the *National Flash*, Steadman Coe, was on the telephone in his glassed-off office. He sat back in his chair with his loafers on his desk, his big voice and booming courtesy laugh leaking through the windows. Despite the chilly temperatures, Coe was sockless. His suit was baby blue and his tie was black. He shaved his head in the mornings and by this time of day he already had a ring of stubble above his ears. It was the day after production day, so the office was otherwise empty apart from the video game designers who sub-leased the northwest corner. Grace turned away from Coe and practiced what she would say. She could see herself as she said the words, with the new scarf, reflected in the window.

She was slouching. Why was she always slouching? She stood up straight and pulled her shoulders back again. This is going to be *the biggest story of my career – and yours.*

Sunset came early this time of year. The clouds over the St Lawrence River were pink and purple. She kept touching her new scarf, which still carried the vanilla smell of the boutique. The last three times she had visited her doctor, with the usual fears of a middle-aged woman – something funny about her left breast, a lumpy mass behind her right knee, headaches unrelated to wine – the tests had resulted in nothing, nothing, and nothing again. But the subsequent question-and-answer session, about her mental health, had not gone terribly well. Grace would not call herself depressed, though the doctor had determined she was. It was not until she arrived on the third floor of the nearly empty warehouse, with Steadman Coe barking and bellowing behind his glass, that she arrived at a self-diagnosis: she was simply unfulfilled. She had not reached her potential. She had felt sorry for herself, as though journalism, her ex-husband, and the global economic order had chosen this life for her. How had she missed this, this deep truth? It was her choice.

'It's my choice.'

'You're talking to yourself, Gracie.' Coe stood in his office with the door open, an unlit cigar in his mouth.

Stand up straight, shoulders back.

Coe sat down again, put his shoes back up on the desk, and before Grace had a chance to tell her story he related the insignificant advertising-related victory of his just-finished phone call. Other newspapers were losing ad revenue. They were only gaining, thanks to the upcoming presidential campaign.

'Well, that'll be over soon.'

'Not if he wins,' said Coe. 'These polling firms, they under-value and misunderstand our people, your people, Gracie . . .'

The slouch was creeping into her shoulders. 'Steadman.'

'It's almost six o'clock. Why are you still here?'

'For the last two months, I've been working on—'

'You need to get out more, take a holiday. Do yoga or some shit, join a board.'

'I *do* do yoga. Now listen.'

'I'm listening.'

'I just finished a long interview with a porn star named Violet Rain.'

'Nice. Did you get me an autograph?'

'Who had an affair, four years ago, with Anthony Craig.'

Coe removed his feet from the desk and put his cigar in an empty coffee cup. The smile departed from his face, along with what remained of his tan.

Grace told the story, right up to her celebratory glass of Rioja in the Hotel Clementine. Yes, $250,000 was a lot of money, but the election was in less than a month. This would be, ever so briefly and gorgeously, the biggest story in the world.

His voice was unusually small when he spoke. 'Everyone knows he has affairs. His divorces—'

'With porn stars? You want a president who has affairs with porn stars?'

Coe shrugged. The look on his face was not remotely what she was expecting. There were bottles of Veuve Clicquot in the little fridge that hummed in the corner of his office. She thought by now he would have opened one. This would be the biggest issue of the year. There could be an online component. Violet had pictures on her phone: nasty proof!

'Can you give me a minute? I'll call Jack.' He stood up slowly.

'Steadman, I know he's our guy. "Our people's guy." But this . . .'

'Just give me a minute. Close the door.'

She left his office and went back to her chair, watched his face on the other side of the glass. Jack Dodson owned the *National Flash*, along with casinos and hotels and an ascendant hamburger chain with evangelical Christian roots. He was a major donor to the party and to Anthony Craig's presidential campaign. But Dodson was a former journalist himself. He would get this.

It took less than a minute, then her boss waved her back in. 'Sit down,' Coe said, when she opened his door.

'I'll stand. Tell me.'

'Who did you hear this from?'

Grace was not obliged to tell him. A real editor of a real newspaper would know not to ask. She sighed. 'Why?'

'It could compromise your relationship with Elena.'

Grace had considered this many times, especially since Elena *was* her source. The story had come out accidentally, after a few glasses of champagne, but a real journalist doesn't lose sleep over such things. 'It could, but—'

'We'll buy the story.'

'Really?' She clapped her hands. 'I was thinking the worst, Steadman, I have to say.'

'We'll pay her two hundred thousand.'

'She'll be thrilled. I'll have the story written by end-of-day tomorrow. We have to book a photo shoot, and the art department—'

'We're buying the story, Gracie. But we aren't publishing it. Give me her details. Jack's lawyer will take care of it.'

'What? Why?'

'It's too close to the election. It's unseemly.'

'Our cover art on Friday is of Roseanne Barr in a bikini.'

He shrugged. 'Not my call.'

'You can't, Steadman. We often do the wrong thing but this is *wrong*. We need to run the story. People need to know about Violet, about him—'

'I'm sorry, Gracie.'

This was the moment to resign. It had to be! There was no other choice. But her mother's monthly bill, at her home in Florida, ate up a third of her paycheck. Then she had her own mortgage payments. She had no money saved. It went hot just behind her eyes but she was *not not not* going to cry in front of Steadman Coe. So she reached over the desk and pulled his

Cuban cigar from the coffee cup, wet on one end – disgusting – and tore it in half and threw it at the wall.

'I do have something that will make you feel better.'

Rather than look at his Botox-frozen face one moment longer, Grace walked out of Coe's office.

'You haven't been to Europe, have you?' He followed her across the wooden floor, his leather-soled loafers clacking. It was otherwise silent in the office now. Even the video game designers had gone home.

Grace dropped her new scarf in the empty garbage bin at her desk. It was tainted with failure now, like the ironic Barry Manilow picture on the side of her cubicle and the single gerbera daisy in a champagne flute she had bought herself – *bought herself.*

What was she thinking? Of course this wouldn't work out. Nothing worked out for Grace Elliott or any of the Elliotts. She was cursed, like her blind mother and her dead father and her poor and forgotten grandparents and great-grandparents before them. She would stop on the way home and fill a prescription. That and a bottle of cheap Australian wine would take care of this.

Coe leaned over and placed a thick piece of paper on her desk, with a familiar logo on top: La Cure Craig. At the bottom, Elena's loopy signature came with a personal note. 'Change of plans. Join me, *duše moje.*'

'You're flying somewhere far more exotic than New York for your next session with her. She isn't running for president but she might have something to say about her ex-husband.

13

Gracie, think about it. If he wins, if we help him win in our small and seemly way, you could have exclusive access to one of his dearest confidantes. Elena Craig has a nickname for you. You could even write a book.' He paused, and pointed to the paper. 'You didn't take a holiday in the summer because you said you couldn't afford it. Well, here you go, all expenses paid. Gracie: go to Prague.'

2

NEW YORK, 2014

On her first night in New York since her twenty-first birthday weekend, Grace Elliott had stayed in a small hotel on a noisy corner near Times Square. It wasn't the sirens and the screaming maniacs of the night that robbed her of sleep. She had earplugs for that. Grace did not sleep because at nine o'clock the next morning she would meet Elena Craig.

When Elena divorced her famous husband in the early 1990s, it was a Manhattan scandal and a global story. She was on every local news channel and in every newspaper in the world. Rather than waste an opportunity, she launched her own business: La Cure Craig.

For sixteen years, Grace had written about famous people for the *National Flash* but she had never spent the morning

15

with one. She had worn her sleeveless black dress with red dots from the Gap, the best in her closet. At breakfast, reading through her list of questions one final time, she had sloshed a bit of coffee on the dress, turning one of the red dots brown.

Her appointment with Elena Craig was in La Cure Craig's flagship location, just off Central Park West. Grace had decided to walk, to calm her heart and to see a bit of the city, but it was an unusually gusty March day. The wind blew her hair in every direction. By the time she arrived, her Taylor Swift bob had transformed into a day-at-the-beach cut. The hostess, who could have modeled Viking robes, wore a lot of black eyeshadow. It seemed far too much eyeshadow, but Grace knew this was an incorrect feeling. A Midwesterner is born to assume that in New York the only fashion error possible is her own.

La Cure Craig was made of glass. The chandeliers were crystal, the staircase was crystal, the furniture was crystal with flawless white leather for cushions. The grand piano in the lobby was crystal, and on her first visit to the spa, on the second day of spring in 2014, it automatically played a Chopin sonata. In La Cure Craig if it wasn't crystal, it was white.

Why crystal? Grace had learned, from the Elena Craig episode of a Netflix series about rich people, that Czech crystal makers were the finest crystal makers. Beer and glass were key parts of their culture, like sushi and sake in Japan or maple syrup and unnecessary apologies in Canada. The lobby of the spa smelled of hot, sweet herbs. To calm herself, waiting for Elena Craig to appear for their introductory meeting, she focused on the Chopin. There was a word for these sorts of pianos, which played themselves, but Grace could not remember it. She was so tired and so nervous her brain was failing her. Her left eyelid twitched.

At precisely nine o'clock Elena Craig walked down the crystal staircase in a dress suit so white it worked as camouflage. Grace stood to meet her, and felt profoundly small. The women were about the same height, but there was something giant about Elena. She filled a room with herself, which was something that did not come through on television. There were two kinds of media stories about Elena Craig. In one, she is the ex-trophy wife with the funny accent who never earned her position in the upper caste of New York society. In the other, Elena is an intelligent and formidable woman who designed iconic luxury vehicles, launched one of the most successful spa chains in America, and remained one of her ex-husband's most important advisors. Grace's instinct was that the second was true and the first was constructed and reinforced by men who were intimidated by Elena Craig and did not enjoy the feeling.

'Ms Elliott?'

'You can call me Grace.' She extended a hand.

Elena took it and squeezed. Her eyes seemed to be everywhere upon Grace as she took in the coffee stain on her dress, her cheap mall shoes, the remains of a pimple on her forehead. Grace tried to block the stain with her notebook but somehow Elena could see through it. In the moments before she spoke,

Grace was sure Elena would send her away. She was not smart enough, not fashionable enough, *not enough* to be in this woman's presence let alone write from her point of view.

'When did you arrive, Grace?'

'Yesterday.'

'Steadman Coe is putting you up at a decent hotel, I hope, with the money I am giving him?'

'Oh fine. Yes.'

'Really?'

'No, Ms Craig. It's a terrible hotel.'

'We'll choose something better next time.' Elena smiled, just slightly, and took Grace's hands in hers. 'You are nervous. Not familiar with New York?' Elena led Grace to a private lounge with a view over the park. 'I remember my first time in this city, all those years ago. It is like nowhere else. Yes? You feel like a bug. Yes?'

'Yes.' Grace nearly said *yes, thank you*. She wondered how Elena knew all this about her, knew everything, despite all she had done to seem worldly and confident.

'You are a Midwestern woman?'

'I am. How did you know?'

Instead of answering the question, Elena encouraged Grace to sit and asked what she would like to drink, or eat. Would she like a tour of La Cure Craig now or later? After their conversation would she like a massage or perhaps a manicure?

Elena Craig was the opposite of what Grace had first imagined; her power was in noticing other people, in making them feel important and worthwhile and comfortable. Ten minutes later, after revealing details of her own childhood in Minnesota, her journalistic ambitions dashed by the realities of a tough industry, and her utter cluelessness about fashion, Grace realized Elena knew everything about her and she understood even less about Elena.

The job was a weekly advice column in the *National Flash*, sponsored by La Cure Craig, under Elena's byline. It was to be about fashion, food, glamor, divorce, motherhood, remarriage, and what Coe referred to as 'affordable fabulousness'.

Every six months Elena Craig and Grace Elliott would meet in person to come up with twelve questions and answers. They would invent the name of a woman for each question and give her a banal place to live. Elena would pay for the airfare and the hotel, and provide Grace with a $120 per diem Coe never knew about.

In their first meeting, Grace realized she did not know how to be a ghostwriter. It was different from journalism. The first three questions she asked were too general, about Elena's overall philosophy.

'No one really cares about that sort of thing, do they?' said Elena. 'Do they not want something quite specific?'

Grace laughed.

'What? Am I wrong, Grace?'

'No. It's funny but you're right about everything.'

'Now *that* is funny. And a bit sad, too, to consider. Now, duše moje, before we really begin, would you like a mimosa?'

Grace had never tasted a mimosa. 'Okay. And what did you call me?'

'It's Czech. Something like "my soul". In *Pinocchio*, I watched it with my daughter, the lying boy's soul is a cricket.'

'Jiminy Cricket.'

'That is you.' Elena called for two mimosas. 'Now, imagine yourself an average woman of a certain age in Nebraska.' It seemed to delight Elena, saying *Nebraska*. 'What do you want to know from me?'

'Well, you were married to Anthony Craig.'

'For many years.'

'He's . . . famous.'

'To say the least.'

'Why did you keep his name, after the divorce? It was so public. I just watched a documentary about it. He was awful to you.'

A waiter arrived quickly with the mimosas, and Elena made meaningful eye contact when she thanked her. The flutes filled with juice and champagne were pretty on the crystal table. 'Duše moje, thank you for your concern. But it was mostly theater, yes? Life is a performance. Tell me, would you remember the name Elena Klimentová?'

'Maybe.'

'Do not be polite right this moment. Be honest. You would forget. You have already forgotten, yes? I am a businesswoman. A name is a brand.'

Five minutes later, Grace had arrived at this:

Dear Elena,

I caught my husband cheating with one of my friends who isn't even that pretty. We're divorcing, of course. But should I keep his name?

Heartbroken in Hackensack

After this first meeting, they always worked in the late afternoon with a bottle of champagne unsullied by orange juice. Grace would listen to Elena, to Elena playing Elena. She would quote key phrases, to sound authentic. From these notes she would fill ten inches of copy.

For Coe, it was a cynical maneuver: a lucrative advertorial project. For Elena, it was a way to remain relevant, to stay in touch with a certain kind of woman who genuinely interested her: the kind who bought tabloids at the supermarket checkout, imagining a different sort of life. For Grace, even if the columns were not in her name they were a way to reach millions of readers every week with something she had created. Unless there was a genuine scandal, *Ask Elena* was the best-read feature in the *National Flash*.

'The divorce, it was painful and humiliating. But Anthony and I are friends, partners in our child's life and in our business interests and in our ambitions.' She took a long drink. 'You cannot put this in my column, but there is another reason. My Tony will become the most powerful man in the world.'

'I'm sorry.' Grace stopped writing. 'I don't know what you mean.'

Elena Craig leaned over the crystal table. Below her, the champagne fizzed and pipped in the flutes. There was no smile on her face or in her eyes. She tapped her Cartier watch. 'Just you wait, duše moje.'

3

PRAGUE, 2016

Grace Elliott was pleased she had plucked her new cashmere scarf from the garbage, in the warehouse in Old Montreal. Even in the airport, walking with her bag, it made her feel more European. This was her first time away from North America. In high school there had been a class trip to Germany, but her parents could not afford the $1,500 price tag at the time. Grace was one of only three kids in junior year who stayed home, and the shame of it was fresh almost thirty years later.

Her best friend, Manon, who had an aunt and uncle in France, advised her the best way to fight jet lag was to stay awake until nighttime in your destination. The advice was not necessary. Though it was noon when she arrived, and it turned out she could not sleep on airplanes, Grace was so thrilled to be in Europe she couldn't imagine napping.

Her Uber driver could not speak English, but that did not stop Grace from pointing out all the European things: cars and buses and ambulances, trees, road signs, billboards, roundabouts.

'Is that the communist stuff?' Grace pointed at a complex of concrete buildings. 'When we want to complain about ugly architecture in America, we call it communist.'

The driver, who wore a black Yankees cap, shrugged and grunted.

When they entered the old part of Prague, Grace had to force herself not to take poor quality photographs from the back seat of a moving car. How else to express delight and wonder in 2016?

Elena had paid for Grace's flight and for a room in the Four Seasons Hotel where she was launching her new line of perfume. The room would not be ready for an hour so Grace wandered through the miniature topiary garden behind the hotel. On October 25, there was a cold wind and the few yellow leaves that had clung to the branches of the aspen trees swirled down to the inky Vltava River below.

A flock of birds flew over the red rooftops of *Malá Strana*, the 'little side' of the river. The preferred colors of paint in central Prague were various shades of sunshine. Tourists, undaunted by the wind, gathered on the Charles Bridge with their smartphones out. The plan was to meet with Elena after a four o'clock press conference, for a drink. Grace's jacket was packed and in the hotel storage so instead of exploring the old town she read a book by a local author in the elegant hotel lounge, to better understand the spirit of Prague: *The Castle* by Franz Kafka. She found it hard to concentrate. In the hotel lobby, wine and spirits sat in a massive wooden armoire with a mirror in the center. Grace sneaked looks at herself, her blue scarf and red sweater.

Twenty minutes before the press conference, swarms of stylishly untidy men and women made their way through the lobby and down the stairs into the basement ballrooms: writers, photographers, miniature film crews. When the press conference was scheduled to begin, Grace signed her drink to the room she had not yet seen and walked down the stairs.

In the ballroom, packed with journalists, a young man in a double-breasted suit was reading from notes, making the introduction. Grace took one of the last chairs three rows from the back. The flamboyant young man with a refined British accent spoke of renaissance and rebirth, and when he said Elena's name she emerged from a door to his left. Journalists being journalists there wasn't much applause, which made the theatrical entrance seem a bit silly.

Elena's face had a fresh tightness about it, from the last mini-surgery at the beginning of the summer. Her dress was red, with Asian embroidery, and her hair was bright blonde. At this distance, Elena at sixty-six could be mistaken for images from the documentaries of Elena at thirty-six. She retained the athleticism and control that came from the gymnastics training of her youth.

'Oh God,' said one of the journalists, a man, behind Grace, as Elena paused and looked out over her audience. There was a snottiness in his tone. She wanted to turn and ask what he meant by it. What was his objection to her? Was she too beautiful? Too glamorous? Too strong?

'When I decided to relaunch my line of perfume I knew I did not want to put my name on a fragrance anyone could create. What you will experience this afternoon is derived from the fruits and herbs and seeds and flowers of my two homes, Bohemia and America.' She took a breath and made eye contact with a few of the journalists again before looking down at her prepared notes. 'This is the birth of a new era and it needs a new line of fragrances. Introducing, reintroducing: Elena.'

A white-haired man in the back of the room led the applause, a little too enthusiastically. Grace turned and recognized him from somewhere. At first she thought television and then she remembered: Montreal.

The MC replaced Elena at the microphone. 'There will be samples for everyone.' Then he repeated himself in Czech. 'Any questions about the fragrances?'

Two hundred arms went up at once.

'Lester Allan, *New York Times*. As a foreign-born American yourself, Ms Craig, how do you feel about your ex-husband's proposals on immigration?'

'Fragrances?' The young MC looked about the room. A number of hands were still up. 'All right, you.'

'Anna Rocard, Agence France-Presse. As a feminist, and a

woman in business, do you take exception to Monsieur Craig's words about women and the most recent harassment allegations against him? I mean, you yourself, during the divorce proceedings—'

'Fragrance questions?' The young moderator tapped the podium with his pen.

When Elena smiled, Grace could tell it took genuine effort. The man in the row behind Grace snorted. 'We wouldn't be here, not her, not us, if it weren't for her goddamn ex-husband. It's perfume, for Christ's sake.'

There were only a few hands up now. 'Garrick O'Byrne, BBC. Will you be taking a role in the White House if your ex-husband wins? He calls you one of his most trusted advisors. What exactly do you advise him on?'

A man near the front shouted, 'Deodorant!' The journalists laughed and applauded.

Agence France-Presse, BBC, *New York Times* : in university, and even in her twenties and early thirties, these were the sorts of companies where Grace had most wanted to work, terminal destinations for serious journalists. Despite just about everything she had done since graduation, this was still how she saw herself. She was still on her way.

The episode in Montreal, with Violet Rain, had kicked her to the gap between her ambitions, what she still considered her truest and finest self, and what she actually did for a living. The *National Flash* was supposed to be a brief bridge to a better future. But soon it would be twenty years. Twenty years! It was a long time to feel temporary, to feel ashamed. Whenever she was in the States now, and someone asked what she did and where she lived, Grace lied.

She looked around the room. A few of the journalists were still pleasing one another by repeating, 'Deodorant.' There were no more hands up. Some of the reporters were standing to leave. There was probably a million dollars' worth of travel budget in the room, all of it wasted on 'no comment'.

'Grace Elliott, *National Flash*.'

More laughter. A trickle of sweat eased down her spine.

'Can you elaborate a little bit more, Ms Craig, on why you think now is the right time for a renaissance in the perfume industry?'

'Thank you. Thank you, Grace. Do any of you get a headache when you walk into the fragrance section of Saks Fifth Avenue? I do! And let me tell you . . .'

By the end of her long answer about organic herbs only a few of the journalists remained. The moderator asked if there were any other questions about the new fragrance line, in English and Czech, but by then it was clear the party was over. He led Elena out the side door.

Grace smiled at the last four women who remained in the room, as they gathered up their recorders and notebooks and phones and bags. None of them smiled back. The hallway had a coffee stand and some biscuits, but by the time Grace made it out the coffee was gone, the biscuits were gone, the perfume samples were gone.

In the women's restroom, a large group of journalists in line for the toilets made fun of Elena: her clothes, her accent, her hair, her enhanced eyes and lips, the way she referred to herself in the third person. But mostly her ex-husband. When she couldn't take it anymore Grace ditched the lineup and returned to the lobby where the handsome white-haired man from the back of the room stood waiting for her.

'Ms Elliott. Let me escort you upstairs.'

She remembered his name: Josef Straka. He had been on the symphony orchestra board with Steadman Coe, and he came to the *National Flash* Christmas party every year. Both men were powerful outsiders in Québécois culture. 'Monsieur Straka. I didn't know you were Elena's friend.'

They stepped onto the elevator. He wore a navy suit with a crisp, exceedingly white shirt and smelled faintly of La Cure Craig. His top two buttons were undone. He held eye contact longer than a normal person would in an elevator, though Grace could not decide if it was unsettling or fatherly. She wondered if it was Straka who had made the original introduction to Steadman Coe, in 2014, to get their *Ask Elena* column going.

He just stared. Definitely unsettling. He reached into his jacket and pulled out a calling card, handed it to her.

When Kafka had seemed too much, in the lobby, Grace had read a brochure about the hotel. The Four Seasons was a marriage of four architectural eras that matched the great eras of the city: Baroque, Renaissance, Neo-Classical, and modern.

Grace tried to figure out which eras they were passing through, on the way to the presidential suite.

Elena stood at the large window, overlooking the river. Like Josef Straka, she stood with perfect posture and it was easy for Grace to see them together, these two aristocratic Central Europeans. Through the window, Grace could see the castle, the Charles Bridge, and Petřín Hill. A few streaks of afternoon sun made it through the clouds and lit up the red roofs of Malá Strana. Classical piano music played quietly from an elegant Bose speaker in the corner of the room. On the table a bottle of vodka was open and half finished, with a can of tonic and a quartered lemon. Elena held a glass, took a sip. She did not turn around. 'Duše moje.'

'I'm sorry about that, what happened down there.' Grace spoke freely, but she wished she were alone with Elena. They weren't quite friends but she wanted to be. This was the upside of the Violet Rain story falling apart; she had not betrayed Elena's trust. Instead of fussing in the suite's kitchen or at least looking at his phone, Straka stared at them.

'Thank you, darling. I feared it would be terrible and it was. They are right. I want to have it both ways, to be my own woman but also to be *that* woman. This is what is wrong with me.'

Straka said something in Czech.

'No, Josef, I do mean it. The correct word is *wrong*.' Elena turned to face them. Grace was expecting tears, or at least sadness – disappointment – but her eyes were not wet, they were defiant.

Their last meeting had been in the Hamptons that spring. Anthony Craig had just become the presumptive nominee of the Republican Party and Elena was staying away, 'for the integrity of the campaign'. Together they worked on their six months' worth of *Ask Elena* columns on a balcony overlooking the ocean with a bottle of Gosset Grand Blanc de Blancs champagne. It was warm but cloudy, with a hint of drizzle over the beach. The six-bedroom blue-shingled beach house was in a compound owned by people who spoke Slavic languages, wore matching sweat suits, smoked cigarettes, and drove Range Rovers and Porsches, who played techno from the late 1990s and drank and danced until late at night.

Grace had never seen her somber. She had assumed Elena wanted to be a bigger part of the presidential campaign, that she felt cruelly excluded by the professional machine, but after the bottle of Gosset was finished, Elena admitted they had invited her to the convention. They had invited her to speak, but she had turned them down, which seemed unlike her. The people who owned the compound annoyed Elena, but when Grace asked who they were Elena changed the subject. She talked about Anthony Craig's current wife and about Violet Rain. Grace could not decide if Elena was jealous or if it was something else.

It was, by far, their strangest day together.

Dear Elena,
    Your ex-husband is the presumptive nominee for the Republican Party and will run for president in the fall.

31

He could, as you once predicted, become the most powerful man in the world. He remains your business partner and something like a friend. Why are you acting as though your dog just died?

Wondering in Westhampton Beach

Now, in the presidential suite of the Four Seasons, Elena pulled Grace to the window and together they looked out in silence, the piano music a perfect soundtrack to the melancholy scene before them: dusky, autumnal Prague. She wanted to ask about the campaign, but enough people had asked about it today.

In the background, Straka cleared his throat. 'Ms Elliott knows me.'

'From Montreal,' said Grace. 'He's friends with Steadman Coe.'

Elena shook her head. 'I worry our Mr Coe is trying too hard, loving Tony. What do you think? Is it too much?'

'He thinks their audiences intersect.'

Elena took Grace's hand. 'I had hoped to work with you this afternoon and evening on *Ask Elena*, with vodka and tonic, and something delicious and fattening from room service. But I do not have it in me. Today was a mistake.' She sighed. 'When he wins, Tony will rip those satisfied smiles from their faces.'

Straka topped up Elena's glass with vodka. He did not bother with the tonic or lemon or offer one to Grace.

'Tomorrow, duše moje, I go to my hometown.'

'Mladá Boleslav?'

'Very good, you remember. You will come with me. In the car we will work on *Ask Elena*. Yes?'

'I would like that.'

Straka put his left hand on Grace's back and with his right hand motioned toward the door of the suite. It did not feel right to leave Elena alone with him, but she could not say why.

'Are you okay, Ms Craig?'

'Ten o'clock in the morning, duše moje. I will have recovered.'

Grace had no choice. She allowed the man to lead her out. 'If you need anything, I'm in room—'

'She knows where to find you, Ms Elliott,' he said, at the threshold. 'Good evening.'

Grace waited and watched Elena in the near-dark of the presidential suite as Josef Straka closed the door.

4

MLADÁ BOLESLAV,
CZECHOSLOVAKIA, 1968

The instant she began to fall off the balance beam at the national championships Elena Klimentová knew her life had already changed. She would not finish in the top three. She would not finish in the top thirty. For her vault she had lacked confidence on the springboard, and then she had botched her routine on the uneven bars.

It had been her dream for years to travel the world in gymnastics tights. Now that a regular Czech, Věra Čáslavská, had won six medals in Mexico City, Elena's dream felt possible. She stands on podiums in France, in America, in Korea with bouquets of yellow flowers. She lifts an arm, humbly. '*Kde domov můj*' plays from giant black speakers. Someone opens a bottle of champagne and the crowd says, 'Oooh!' and the Czech flag is a shawl over her shoulders.

Driving north now, back to Mladá Boleslav, the wind was so fierce Elena thought the little blue Škoda would fly into the ditch on an icy road. Sleet pounded the windscreen. Her dream, the hundreds of hours, thousands of hours she had spent on it, was now a humiliation.

It nauseated her. Go ahead, she thought, fly into the ditch.

Coach Vacek spoke only to her companion, Josef, who had finished in the top ten in all of his events. Josef leaned back in the front seat and recounted his triumphs in the competition: a boy from Prague, one of his longtime rivals, had fallen off the uneven bars and had cried.

'Aha!' Coach Vacek punched the steering wheel, laughed at the roof of the Škoda, shook his fist.

When they arrived in Mladá Boleslav, the city was dark. December was different now. The new soldiers, who did not speak Czech, had confiscated the Christmas lights because they were signs of Western imperialism, signs of resistance and therefore treason. There were only two market stalls in front of the old town hall and a grim statue of Ded Moroz, 'Old Man Winter', with his Russian staff.

Josef lived north of the city so Coach Vacek stopped first at Elena's little house in what her mother called the *train station ghetto* along the muddy Jizera River. Tonight, filtered through failure, their gray, small, sad house seemed even grayer and smaller and sadder. Elena opened her door before the car came to a full stop.

'Let me help you,' said Josef.

'I can do it.' Elena pulled her bag from the back seat.

Coach Vacek lit a cigarette. 'I will come in.'

'No.'

'You were not feeling well. Your balance was off.'

She had felt perfectly well before the competition. She had trained for weeks, all summer and all autumn. There were no excuses that were not lies and in the darkness of the three-hour drive home she had vowed to tell the truth. Elena had turned eighteen. Her chance had come and now it was gone. It was not so bad to have regular dreams. Like her mother, and her grand-mother, she would work in the factory.

Coach Vacek followed her to the door. So did Josef.

Elena turned to them. 'Please. Go home.'

Coach Vacek and Josef understood what this meant for Elena and for her parents. A daughter who brings glory to Czechoslovakia and the Communist Party also brings comfort to her parents: better food, better jobs, better doctors.

A better home. A place her mother deserved.

Elena shut her eyes for a moment, sighed, and opened the door. Her coach and Josef followed her inside. She was about to turn and order them, again, back to the car to talk about their magnificent success when the temperature in the house, the smell, the electricity stopped her.

'Sweetheart.' Her mother, Jana, wore a red dress and lipstick. She was almost a foot shorter than Elena, she had gone thick around the middle, and her hair – once black as olives – was now streaked with gray. In her day, she told Elena, she had been the most popular and the most beautiful girl in Mladá Boleslav. She was secretly descended from Charles IV, the Holy Roman Emperor and King of Bohemia, and the beautiful Blanche of Valois, but the communists could not know the truth of this because they would be jealous and make their lives even worse.

Now she took the bag from Elena and dropped it on the kitchen table, which was against every house rule. Gymnastics equipment went in the closet immediately. Jana ignored Coach Vacek and Josef, who stood waiting for a greeting, and whispered into Elena's ear. 'We have a visitor. A wonderful visitor.'

There was something in the oven: meat and dumplings. Elena was hungry, but why were they having a special dinner at eight o'clock on a Sunday night?

She turned back to Coach Vacek and Josef whose faces showed the same bewilderment she felt, and silently they moved from the kitchen into the small salon.

A young man in a prim suit was sitting next to her father, who looked as though half the blood had been drained from him. The young man stood up and extended his hand. He was slim and handsome, with the confident air of a young professor, and Elena immediately felt childlike and ridiculous in her faded blue tights and team jacket.

'Elena.' He spoke with a Russian accent.

'Good evening.' She took his hand, its skin soft and smooth.

'I am Sergei Sorokin. I have come here from Prague to meet you and your parents.'

Stepping past Elena, he shook Coach Vacek's and Josef's hands. He knew their names too. 'How did it go today?'

Elena wanted all of these people out of the house so she could speak to her parents and, possibly, cry. 'Josef got seventh overall,' she said.

Sergei Sorokin clapped and so did her mother. It took some coaxing to get her father on his feet and clapping too.

'And you?' Sergei asked.

Elena had a feeling he already knew the answer. 'I did not have a good day.'

'She has a cold,' said Josef.

'It can affect one's inner ear, the balance,' said Coach Vacek.

'Nonsense. I felt fine. I simply performed miserably. I came in thirty-ninth overall. I'm sorry, Mother. Father.'

There had been two hundred and fifty female gymnasts in the competition. This was not a disastrous result for a mediocre athlete but Elena was not a mediocre athlete. Up until this point, her life had been powered by the belief – the certainty – that she was an exceptional gymnast, one of the best not only in Czechoslovakia but the world. But she had felt a change as she had run up the hills of Mladá Boleslav earlier that autumn, preparing for the national championships. The younger girls had more power in their legs. They were stronger and more elegant.

The Kliment family lived on the main floor of the house. Another family, the Novaks, who had a temperamental five-year-old boy, lived upstairs. There was a bedroom for her parents and an office or closet that had enough room for a single bed and a desk. Her bedroom.

Elena sighed. Was this finished, whatever it was? Could she go in her little room now, so her parents could continue discussing whatever it was they had to discuss with the young Russian?

'I knew I had come to the right place.' Sergei Sorokin smiled. Russians were not supposed to smile. Hundreds of thousands of them had arrived in the country a few months ago with tanks and guns to 'normalize' the country. Many young people had died. Elena knew her father was worried, and that he had wanted to flee to the Austrian border.

Now it was too late. There were soldiers in towers with guns; they had put up electric fences and patrolled the border with trucks and German shepherds trained to tear you apart. Elena knew that if you somehow made it over the fence you entered the minefields.

They were not allowed to speak of it. Any of it. Not here at home, where someone could be listening, and not in school and not in the mountains and not in the town. The police heard everything. They knew.

Yet Sergei smiled. 'It takes enormous courage to admit and own our defeats. You do not comfort yourself. You face hard realities.'

Elena looked down at the thin, frayed carpet.

'I have come here to tell you, Elena Klimentová, that what happened today does not matter.'

'What is this?' Josef took an aggressive step toward Sergei, who ignored him.

'You see, darling.' Her mother took both of her cold hands in hers. 'It's a new beginning for us.'

Sergei Sorokin shook Coach Vacek's hand and thanked him for taking such good care of Elena. He did not shake Josef's hand.

'Who are you?' Coach Vacek stood up straight.

Sergei pointed to the door. 'Good evening,' he said.

Coach Vacek did not move. 'I asked: who are you?'

Sergei stepped close to him and spoke softly. 'Leave. Or I will make you leave.'

'Petr. What is this?' Coach Vacek looked at Elena's parents.

'Go,' said her father, weakly.

When the front door closed and they were alone, Elena drew a shaky breath. She was sure something terrible was about to happen. This man, Sergei Sorokin, would take her father away and put him in a work camp. Somehow he knew what her father had been thinking since the Russians had arrived in Prague. He knew her father had cheered for Věra Čáslavská at the Olympics when she protested against the Soviet occupation at the awards ceremony. Sergei Sorokin was going to pull a gun from the inside pocket of his suit jacket and shoot her father in the head with that mysterious, crooked smile still on his face.

Outside, the Škoda roared away from the little house.

It took a moment to realize Sergei Sorokin was speaking to her. 'Your grandmother, I understand, was the foreman of the Laurin & Klement factory.'

'Yes, sir,' Elena whispered.

'You are Škoda royalty.'

Elena watched her mother smile. This was always Jana's contention, that communism had eroded all the natural and good hierarchies of Mladá Boleslav. They belonged at the top of the hill, in the suite of rooms Jana herself had grown up in. Piano ought to play in the evenings. They ought to dress for dinner, to have a maid.

Royalty.

'I like this about Czechoslovakia. You have these matriarchal tendencies.' Sergei Sorokin smiled again, at Jana this time. 'Yes?'

'Oh yes,' said Jana.

Was that a flower in her mother's hair? Elena realized it was an old piece of fabric, an artificial rose clipped with a bobby pin.

'And you, Elena Klimentová, you are so astonishingly beautiful.'

Elena looked at the carpet again. Was this a threat?

'You must be wondering why I am here, Elena Klimentová. Can I call you Elena?'

'Yes, sir.'

How old was he? Not much older than her, yet he carried so

41

much more intelligence and experience in the way he spoke, the way he stood, the way he mastered the room.

There were four glasses on the table. He reached down and filled the empty one with Becherovka and handed out the glasses.

Elena smelled hers. The bitter smell of Becherovka reminded her of Christmas, and the Old Man Winter statue in the town square. This was a nightmare. The Russians had ruined everything. Yet this young man with the cunning smile had not drawn a gun to punish them – yet.

'To Elena.'

They lifted their glasses and toasted her and drank.

'But I fell off the balance beam. Today was a disaster.'

'In three weeks, Elena, you will move to Prague. You have been accepted into a special program at Charles University, one of the oldest and finest universities in the world.'

'A very special program, darling,' said Jana.

'But I applied to no program.'

'And your parents: they will be moving up the hill, to a much larger apartment. There will be a lovely room for you, when you visit.'

'You see?' said Jana.

Elena's father, Petr, looked at the wall. He had already finished his glass of Becherovka.

'What sort of program, Mr Sorokin?'

'I know you're a brilliant student, Elena. I spoke to your teachers here in Mladá Boleslav. In Prague you will learn languages and culture. You will learn about economics and finance, philosophy, political philosophy, what we sometimes call statecraft. You will learn how it is to live in other countries, even Western countries. Do you know the French word *étiquette*? You will learn etiquette. Manners for any room, any audience. Fashion, even. And you will continue with your gymnastics, if you like. With the best coaches in Czechoslovakia. How does that sound?'

Why me, Elena was thinking. What have I done?

'There is only one thing you must remember, and it is important.'

'This is very important,' said Jana. 'Listen carefully to this part.'

Sergei Sorokin turned to her father and watched him for a moment before he addressed Elena again. 'It is life or death, I'm afraid.' He paused, his pale face stern. 'You must never speak of this.'

'Of Charles University?'

'Oh yes, of course you will talk about *that*. You will be officially enrolled in the physical education department, given your sporting prowess. Yes?'

'Yes.'

'You can talk about this. Your parents can boast about you, their scholar. But the special program, the special opportunities, the special life all this will afford you: you can never speak of it.'

'But why?'

For a moment Sergei Sorokin looked at her the way he had looked at Coach Vacek, and Elena shivered. This man would reach into your mouth and tear your tongue out. 'That will become clear later.'

'Must I say yes, Mr Sorokin? What if I . . .'

For the second time, her father spoke. They all turned to him.

'I am so sorry, darling.' Her father's eyes had filled with tears. 'It is my most important job, to protect you. But you must say yes to this program. You cannot refuse.'

5

PRAGUE, 2016

The next morning, there was a knock on Grace's door. A man of about twenty, in a cheap black polyester suit, introduced himself as Gabriel the chauffeur. He led Grace down to the lobby and out to a long silver Craig sedan, not quite a limousine. Once she was settled, he went off to get Elena. The seats were black leather with wood trim and there was a tiny cooler between the front and back. Inside there were soft drinks, water, and a bottle of Perrier-Jouët champagne.

Grace spoke French but not as well as Elena, who, as she entered the car, was already arguing on the phone about a new distribution deal for her fragrances in the Galeries Lafayette in France. The woman on the phone had wanted to wait until after the election, but Elena disagreed and was gently accusing the woman of discriminatory practices.

It was a gray morning, with rain threatening to fall. Grace watched out the window as the cobblestones of old Prague turned to pavement and the carved stone buildings turned to precast concrete. Curves and flourishes of art and beauty became hard rectangles. There were few pedestrians around, and no cyclists.

Grace leaned forward with her notebook. 'Gabriel, is there a name for the architectural style of communism?'

He pointed to a typically ugly set of concrete towers. 'You mean for this?'

'Yes.'

Next to her, Elena had apparently achieved a victory, and was praising Madame for her intelligence and courage.

'These are *paneláky*. It was a very fast and efficient way to build. Many families lived in the same apartments exactly. We in Czech Republic are the world champions of concrete.'

They reminded Grace of public housing projects on the outskirts of New York and Minneapolis. 'It's so depressing. Sorry.'

Gabriel looked at her through the rear-view mirror. 'You are a happy woman?'

'I'm in the back seat of a Craig with a bottle of champagne in Prague. How could I not be?'

'This is not the Czech way. Maybe someday my children or the children of my children will be *happy always* like Americans.'

Elena ended her call. '*Bien*. Shall we get started, duše moje?'

On the flight to Prague, Grace had come up with eighteen

questions from eighteen potential women in flyover states, none of them terribly interesting. 'How do you speak so many languages?' she asked, instead.

'Not so many.'

'Surely it wasn't normal for a Czech girl, growing up, to be so proficient in languages?'

Elena reached over for her notebook. 'This does not sound like a question for a woman in Ephraim, Utah.'

They were out of the city, but now and then a hollow mini-metropolis would appear in a valley. There were rural versions of concrete housing projects: a tower with a factory beside it, both now abandoned, a rusted swing set.

Steadman Coe had ruined Grace's planned transition to serious investigative journalism, but he had been right about one thing: she had unique access to Elena Craig. Last night, Grace had thought of Elena, alone in the darkness of the presidential suite. She was much more than the owner of a chain of spas. Elena was a complicated, successful, intriguing woman one step away from enormous power. In her small but perfect hotel room, Grace had played with the idea of writing her life story. She went through her own notes from their five meetings, but there wasn't much outside the *Ask Elena* material. She had flipped through everything she could find online about Elena's childhood in Mladá Boleslav, about her marriage to Anthony Craig, about the divorce. Most of it came from New York gossip magazines in the 1990s and it wasn't terribly interesting.

She pulled a book out of her purse, the book she had bought

at the airport in Montreal: Anthony Craig's 1988 memoir of business success, *Make It Big or Don't Bother*. It was a best-seller again, now that he was running for president. That morning, over a bowl of granola and yogurt in the Four Seasons restaurant, she had underlined the Elena sections. Now, in the back of the Craig, she flipped to page seventy-nine and read aloud.

Elena Klimentová was on the 1972 Olympic gymnastics team for Czechoslovakia, she was a top model in Europe and in Canada, she had a degree from the best college in Prague, she came from this family of car engineers, and she was tough as nails. And here she is, without a date, at my party, the most important day of my life until that moment. Talk about a perfect woman!

Elena pulled the book from her and flipped through it herself. There were pictures in the middle. 'Anthony was exaggerating. I was merely an alternate.'

'What does that mean?'

'If a better gymnast was sick, I would compete.'

'You didn't compete?'

'No.'

It was the sort of *no* that did not invite follow-up questions. Grace pretended nonchalance but she wanted to open her notebook and begin writing. 'Was Josef Straka your boyfriend?'

Elena laughed. 'Yes and no. In the end he was like a brother. But you know how it is when you are young.'

Grace thought of her strange elevator ride as Straka had led her up to the presidential suite. 'I didn't have a boyfriend-brother.'

Elena gently whacked Grace over the head with *Make It Big or Don't Bother*. 'We must work on our questions for the *Flash*. My time is precious.'

Gabriel said something in Czech and Elena gave him directions. He turned off the highway and they eased down a secondary road into a deep valley with a small river running through it. There was a large stone house at the end of a long driveway lined with gnarled and twisted, leafless fruit trees.

The Craig stopped at the end of the driveway and Elena waited for Gabriel to come around and open her door. Grace exited on her own and walked over to Elena's side of the car. Birds called out but otherwise it was silent here. No one could see them or what they were doing for miles and miles. Elena inhaled and opened her arms. 'You smell that?'

To Grace it smelled like outside.

'This should be in every bottle of my perfume. Nature, childhood, hope, family, safety.'

The large stone house was closed up and the shutters were down. Grace described the place in her notebook and took some photos. 'Is this your house, Ms Craig?'

Elena did not respond for a while. She walked away from the house, to the muddy banks of the river. The water was brown. 'When I was in university, I visited my parents here. My father and I went on such beautiful walks. After Anthony

and I married, every summer my daughter and I would visit.
I would return to America and she would stay with her
grandfather.'

'Before the end of communism?'

'Oh yes.'

'What was that like?'

Elena looked at Grace's notebook.

'I mean, your daughter must have found it strange to move
from the global center of capitalism to a communist country.'

'Why?'

'It's so different. I guess you could say she lived a double
life.'

'Oh it was not a *double life* at all. My father taught her
things. To fish, to garden, to live on the land in a traditional
European way. She learned to take care of herself whether she
is a billionaire like Anthony or . . .' Elena looked at the river
again. 'My father died too young. I was not here for him when
he needed me.'

'Your father? He believed in communism?'

'My father believed in his family. He believed in order and
safety. There are compromises we make, sacrifices we make.
We all do! It does not matter where we live. We protect our
children.'

'How about your mom? You don't talk about her much.'

'Oh, she very much adores her life in New York and in Florida.' Elena put her arm around Grace, led her back toward the
car, and pulled the notebook from her hand. She opened it and

looked at what Grace had been scrawling. Gabriel walked ahead, to open the door.

'Communism doesn't sound so bad for your family. This is a pretty nice place.'

'We were lucky. But I will show you something else.'

Fifteen nearly silent minutes later, they arrived on the flat outskirts of a hilltop town: Mladá Boleslav. Grace wanted to describe it but Elena had not returned her notebook. In Czech, Elena directed Gabriel to an unloved collection of two-storey concrete houses, stained by weather. The trees in the front were neglected. Dusty plastic garbage had gathered in the corners of the yard.

They stopped in front of a house with two apartments, one up and one down.

'Does this seem nice to you?' Elena did not look at her as she spoke. 'Do you still say communism was not so bad? This is where I lived as a girl. It did not matter that my grandmother was foreman of Laurin & Klement car factory. It did not matter that my parents were educated, my mother an engineer and my father an optician. We lived here, like everyone else. This is communism. Pretty nice, you think?'

It was difficult to imagine Elena anywhere near this building.

Grace took a picture of the house and they climbed back into the car. Elena had left the notebook on the seat so Grace took it again and opened it to a new page. She asked what it was like inside the little house, about Elena's daily routine as a girl. She spoke again of her father and seemed to be on the verge of crying.

Gabriel drove up a switchback road, toward the hilltop where they passed empty, boarded-up storefronts. Young men and women stood on the sidewalks, drinking beer from cans and smoking cigarettes.

'What changed?'

Elena did not answer.

'How did you and your family go from that house to the beautiful land you showed me?'

'Like I said, we were lucky.'

'But what does that mean? Was there a house lottery or something?'

At the top of the hill there was a hairpin curve and Mladá Boleslav opened into a plaza. There was a statue and a grand old town hall with a clock tower and a cupola shaped like an onion. There were a few industrial-looking pieces of art in the plaza, dark twisted tubes.

Elena had not answered so Grace continued. 'I don't know much about communist Czechoslovakia. When you were—'

With a flash of anger Grace had never seen, Elena turned to her and ripped the notebook out of her hands. She opened it and began to tear out the pages Grace had written on. 'Get out,' she whispered.

'What? Why?'

'This is not for *Ask Elena*.' Elena continued to rip the pages out and to stuff them in the side of her door. 'I do not know what you are doing, why you are writing these things. For what?'

'I was . . . I was going to ask if I could write a book about you. I'm sorry, I should have mentioned it earlier. You're such an amazing and inspiring woman, to go from that house at the bottom of the hill to your life now, and I think a lot of women would—'

'Get out of the car.' Elena's voice was louder.

'Ms Craig, please. It's just an idea. Obviously, if you don't want me to write it I won't write it.'

'A secret book? An exposé? You have abused my trust. Gabriel!' Here Elena switched to Czech, barked some orders. Now that she had ripped out all of the pages with writing on them, she tossed the notebook back to Grace. Gabriel looked in the rear-view mirror, met Grace's eyes. By the time he had made it around the car Grace had already opened her door.

Grace stuttered an apology and asked for another chance, but Elena would not look at her. It was raining now and Grace did not have an umbrella or a jacket.

Without a word, Gabriel moved Grace out of the way, closed the back passenger door, returned to the front seat, and got in. A moment later, the long Craig sedan was rumbling over the cobblestones, past the town hall and down the hill.

At first it seemed so preposterous Grace wanted to laugh. In all their time together she had never seen Elena react that way to anything. Then she realized it was over: *Ask Elena*, or at least her role in it. The rain was cold and the wind was unpleasant. There were five or six people in the narrow plaza, walking with bags or leaning against a storefront and smoking. A big black dog wandered through the industrial art, without a leash or even an owner. She was alone in an apparently un-touristed city an hour from Prague.

Her heart pounding, she scanned the locals for the kindest face and went for a stout, elderly woman standing under the awning of a pet food store with a cigarette in her fingers and a blue beanie on her head.

'Hello, excuse me.'

The woman did not return her smile but she lifted the cigar-ette in greeting.

'Do you speak English?'

Apparently not. After a beat the woman pointed her cigar-ette at a building across the plaza.

'Over there? That store? Someone speaks English there?'

'English,' said the woman.

Grace ran over the gray cobblestones of the plaza to a sport-ing goods store across from a restaurant. It was a short but discouraging journey. She imagined calling Steadman Coe to tell him their most popular feature was in jeopardy and it was entirely her fault.

Far worse was losing someone she had hoped would become a friend. She did not have many, and in the minutes since Elena had blown up at her in the back of the Craig she had come to see her reaction as extreme but possibly justified. Grace could not imagine what it must have been like to divorce Anthony

Craig, to be drawn into his election campaign twenty-four years later, and to have your own efforts as a businesswoman dismissed. Like the journalists in the basement ballroom of the Four Seasons, she had been trying to use Elena to enter Anthony Craig's orbit of fame and power. With Violet Rain, and now with the notion of a book.

In the window of the sporting goods store, mannequins were decked out for winter fun: hockey and figure skating, alpine and Nordic skiing, snowshoeing. Grace entered and a fit, muscular woman about her age, wearing black tights and a yellow T-shirt, looked up from a rack of down jackets. She carried a clipboard in one hand and a pencil in the other.

'*Dobrý den.*'

'Hi there. I'm sorry.' Grace took a deep breath, to slow her heart. 'I don't speak Czech, and I'm a bit lost.'

'You've come to the right place.' The woman smiled. She spoke English with a North American accent. 'How can I help you?'

'I need to get back to Prague. Is there a bus or a train?'

'Of course. The train runs every hour, I believe, to Prague central station. The express runs less often but if you have a bit of time even the slow train will get you there. It's about a twenty-five-minute walk to the station. Car trouble?'

'Sort of.'

The woman had short red hair and freckles. 'Just a moment.' She walked through the shop and behind the cash desk, where she bent down and re-emerged with a small box. 'I knew these would come in handy someday.' She pulled out a thick transparent poncho that said *Praha 2016* on it, with a laurel leaf logo. 'Prague bid for the Olympics a long time ago. They didn't make the shortlist but they did make a lot of stuff.'

'How much?'

'Oh I can't sell it. I'm not even sure why I kept it around.'

Grace pulled the poncho over her head. It knocked her glasses off and the woman picked them up. Grace thanked her and introduced herself.

'I'm Katka.'

'Your English is amazing,' said Grace. 'You lived in . . .'

'New York, actually. For seven years, in my twenties. My father trained a woman who ended up in New York, and she hired me in a marketing role for her business. She's from here in Mladá Boleslav. I'm sure you've heard of her, or at least her ex-husband. Elena Craig?'

6

PRAGUE, 1970

A man – no, two men – whispered outside Elena's door. The dim hallway light, disturbed by shadows, flickered through the cracks.

It was nothing. She was silly to worry about it. But the whisperers did not pass when she willed them to pass. Instead, her door handle gently shivered.

Her instinct: leap out of bed and to the window, smash it open and climb down and run. But run where? This was surely nothing, a couple of professors joking around, real life mixed with half a dream. Her days at the university had been long: classes from eight in the morning until five in the evening, and then physical training. Running and gymnastics, but strange things too: self-defense, with a professor from China, and shooting.

Recently, she had learned how to make a poison from castor oil seeds.

Break the window! Go! But if she was wrong and this was just a silly prank, it would be an embarrassment for her and for her mother. Her friend Sergei Sorokin would send her home.

The whispers in the hall changed.

A man was counting in Russian, down from ten. *Seeaym, shayst, pyaht.* Now it was too late to go to the window. Elena put her head under her covers and silently called to her father, her *tatínek*, to save her.

The door crashed open and two men burst into her room. Elena screamed and one of them hit her in the face, pulled a sack over her head, and bound her hands behind her. *Shut up. Shut up, bitch. Whore. Traitor.* They growled in her face, with sausage and beer breath so powerful it went through the sack. She called out for help and one of them hit her again, this time so hard she lost consciousness for a moment. Longer than a moment.

She was in a bus or a van, rattling over cobblestones. Under the sack, her face was wet with blood from her nose. A hand, no, a foot, rubbed up and down her left shin. Then she heard the voice of her friend, her best friend in the program.

'Elenka,' her friend whispered. 'It's me. Danika.'

'What's happening?' Elena sobbed. 'My nose is bleeding.'

'They're taking us somewhere. Be brave, Elenka. I'm here with you.'

'Did we do something wrong?'

The van stopped abruptly. Elena slid forward and her arms, tied to a bar behind her, felt like they would rip from their sockets. The door opened and cold air blew in under her nightgown. For an instant, as it sneaked in under the sack on her face, it was something like pleasure. Their thick boots boomed on the metal floor of the bus, the truck, the van. More words in Russian. A man put his hands on her bare thigh and she screamed at him. He shoved her body aside and fussed with the ropes on her wrists.

Now she was walking barefoot over cold, wet concrete. 'Where are you taking us?' she said, in her schoolgirl Russian.

'Shut up and it will be better for you, bitch.'

Elena guessed they were on the other side of the river, beyond the palace, where the city rose west out of the valley. The men who brought them here were not professors, not leaders. This one smelled like old meat. They entered a corridor of echoes, another one.

Keys jangled.

'Elena, say nothing to them!' There was a thump – a strike? – and a man told Danika to shut her ugly mouth.

'Tell my parents, if they kill me . . .' The man slammed Elena face-first against the cold concrete wall. Her nose hurt again. The man shoved his body into hers and breathed into her neck. She could feel the grotesque bulge of his penis. He spat into her ear that if she said another word what was coming would only hurt worse.

Then he removed the rope from her wrists, the sack from

her head, and shoved her into a small concrete room with mold-blackened walls and a drain in the middle of the floor.

She was in prison.

It was true what they said in school, what her father said. Sometimes people say the wrong thing, do the wrong thing, and they just disappear.

This is where they go.

She thought of Sergei Sorokin, who had been kind to her parents, thankful, solicitous. They were to be praised for raising a daughter so talented, so intelligent, so pretty, so tall, he told them. She was a Slavic princess, destined for greatness.

Elena went over what she had done, what she had said, what she had read, what she had *thought* in the past two months of school yet could remember nothing objectionable. What sort of school was it? None of the other girls there knew what they were being trained for either. 'Leadership,' was all Sergei ever said. Her professors repeated the same thing. Yet they were not to speak of it, even with each other.

Perhaps one of the women in the program did not like her, Elena thought now. There were one or two, sullen and mysterious, but surely no one who would hate her enough to put her here with a lie? This is what her father had warned her about. Always be kind: anyone can destroy you with a phone call.

She did not want to sit on the cold and dirty floor, in her nightdress, yet there was no choice. Sleep when you can sleep, they had been told. If your enemies interrogate you they will wear you down with fatigue.

But who? Who were her enemies?

Just as she lowered herself to the floor the speakers on the ceiling began to screech: repetitive, atonal guitar notes so jarring she had to block her ears.

Her parents had said something, done something, Elena thought. For different reasons both of them, in their hearts, wanted things to be the way they were before the communists came. Jana wanted to be the queen of the city or at least the boss of the plant. Petr wanted to be left alone with his work and his evenings and weekends in the country. Everyone listened: through the ducts and on the street and in the factory, the stores, over the telephone.

Her mother in particular found it hard to be silent, to keep a secret. She had been so happy when Elena went to university, so proud to move to the apartment at the top of the hill. There was only one rule and her mother had surely broken it.

Or maybe Sergei himself, and the whole program, was against the rules. None of her friends in the program believed it had anything to do with the university. She and her parents had thought it was one thing but it was another thing and now their lives were over.

Hours passed. One mealtime and then another. She tried to sleep through the guitar, through the rumbling in her belly, and she failed.

She peed in the drain, hoping no one was watching from a hole in the wall. The fluorescent lights were unbearably bright and the noise became a living being, a beast inside her. She stopped thinking about who might see her nakedness and she pulled her nightdress up and wrapped it around her eyes and ears, forced herself to think of anything but food.

Just as she was beginning to drift into sleep, the door opened with a clunk.

'Let's go! Let's go!'

The same two men pulled her out and into the warmer corridor.

'You disgusting pig,' one said, as he pulled her dress down over her body. 'I saw you shit on the floor.'

They led her through a door, into a room that was empty but for a few wooden chairs and a poster of a skeleton on the wall. Danika stood shivering in the corner.

'Elena!'

The men shoved her into Danika, and the two girls held one another desperately. They whispered, *Where are we? What have we done to deserve this? Are we going to die?* Not ten seconds later the men dragged them apart.

'You are stronger than them, Elena!' Danika screamed back at her.

This next room was dark and hot, lit with a single lamp. It carried the scent of dust and old fumes, like a garage, also cigarettes and something else, something burned – hair? There was a large basin of water. Elena wanted some but she knew not to ask for it. A bearded man sat in the corner, the side of his face barely lit by the orange lamp, smoking. He had an array of implements with him, including a car battery, a bucket, cords and ropes and tools.

The men turned her around and warned her with a slap in the ear to cooperate. They led her through the room and into a chair, and then – *Oh please no* – they put the sack over her head again and tied her to the chair, her legs and arms.

'Now. Quiet. If you fight it will hurt more.'

She sobbed and moaned. 'I want to go home.'

'Quiet.'

There was a buzz, an electrical hum. She knew what would happen next. The man in the orange light of the lamp was going to hurt her. She hated the word: *torture*. Her father could not save her because this man was the police. He was the government.

What had she said? What had she done? What did she know?

And then she remembered. She remembered what she knew, what Sergei had told her she was supposed to know if this were ever to happen.

Nothing.

She heard the man's hard soles on the dust. The door slammed shut. He was close enough that she could hear his breathing, smell his cigarette.

'Where are you, Elena?'

Nothing.

'You are part of a special program. Are you not?'

Nothing.

'Perhaps they told you it was run by the government. The secret police, perhaps, or the StB, even the KGB. They are liars. They are traitors. They have used you. Why would you, a nobody like you, be invited into a special program?'

He backed away from her. She could hear him take a deep drag of his cigarette and throw it on the hard floor, mush the butt. His voice turned soft now.

'Elena Klimentová. Daughter of Petr and Jana, whom you love. You love them. Yes?'

'Yes.'

'It is not your fault. I see how you are innocent. This is an illegal program. You did not know, did you?'

Nothing.

'Here you are, beautiful Elena, in your nightclothes, nearly naked before me. I could do *anything* to you. But I don't want to. I am not a bad person. I am only protecting the interests of Czechoslovakia. Do you understand?'

Nothing.

'You must tell me one simple thing: the name of the man who recruited you.'

Elena could feel the warmth of it now, hear the hum. The commander brought the electricity close enough to her cheek that it began to vibrate in her, to hurt in a way nothing else hurt.

'No,' she moaned. 'Please, no.'

'No what?' He tore her nightdress, in the front, and she struggled against the ropes because she did not want him to see her naked body. 'Tell me the name of the man who recruited you.' Now he brought the humming wand close to her breasts and zapped her just once. Every cell in her body exploded with the jolt and she screamed.

'Just tell me and I stop. I'll bring you a plate of dumplings and chicken and fried cheese. You can call your parents. One of my colleagues is with them now, to ensure you cooperate. Everything can go back to the way it was. You do not have to worry about betraying your friends. We have them all: all you girls, your phony "professors" and administrators. We have you all. All but one.'

He brought the wand close to her again and Elena finally remembered what she had read, what her instructor had said. *Just travel. Leave your body and travel out of the concrete room, up the beautiful river, to the mountains, perfect snow, a spring day with your grandparents where you take off your jacket and tie it around your waist and ski up, up, up above the bowl of cloud.*

'It's so simple, Elenka. One little name.'

But she was at the top of the mountain looking down, where no one and nothing could touch her.

7

PRAGUE, 2016

Grace made her way from the crowded central station to the doors that would lead her to old town Prague. The rain had stopped but the city was drenched and windy. She followed the crowd through a mini-park, down a busy road, and into a blandly attractive shopping boulevard. On the train, Grace had rewritten from memory everything Elena had ripped out of her notebook. She wrote down everything Katka had said about her father, the gymnastics coach, his relationship with Elena, though none of it was fascinating. The more Grace wrote, the more pointless it seemed. There would be no book without Elena's cooperation, but it took her mind off the more pressing crisis: calling Steadman Coe.

In the fairy-tale postcard quarter east of the Four Seasons

men and women in white kiosks sold sausages, mulled wine, and though December was more than a month away, Christmas decorations. Tourists took photographs from horse-drawn carriages in Old Town Square. An English-speaking woman carried a red stick and shouted history lessons at a massive, multicultural tour group in front of the astronomical clock. To Grace, the whole city smelled of seared pork and alcohol and she wanted some. There was no point pretending she was anything but a visitor now, in the market for cultural adventures. She joined the tour group for a moment, dodging selfie sticks, learning about this neighborhood in the fifteenth century, until she recognized two men from the train. They had sat two seats behind her and, when she returned from using the toilet, one of them had watched her. He wore a thick leather motorcycle jacket and he had pale blue eyes that would have been pretty on a woman. They did not go well with his veined nose and thin poof of blond hair.

It was cool and even with the rain poncho Grace had got wet on the walk from the sporting goods store in Mladá Boleslav to the train station. She wanted a steamy bath and she wanted to get away from the creepy men from the train so she joined the flow of tourists from Old Town Square to the Charles Bridge, past tourist shops and restaurants and boutiques selling Bohemian crystal. Every few minutes she casually turned around, to see if the men were following her.

The Four Seasons lobby was warm and fragrant. A woman played a song from the *Amélie* soundtrack on the piano. The concierge and the woman who had served her, in the main floor café, welcomed her back. When she reached her door, on the second level, her card did not work. Grace tried again and again, every way she could, and nothing happened.

At the lobby the woman at the front desk informed her she had already checked out. Her luggage was waiting for her in the storage area. Was Madame not aware?

'There must be a mistake,' said Grace. 'Can you check again? I'm booked here for five days.'

Two minutes later a manager, a small and delicate man whose nametag said Daniel, stood behind the computer and whispered that Madame Craig had departed early. She had canceled not only her suite but Grace's room as well.

'But all my stuff was in there.'

'I am so sorry. Madame Craig had said you wanted her to pack everything up for you. We have your bag. Was she . . . was Madame mistaken?'

'If I were to pay on my own, and stay as planned, how much would it be?'

Daniel the manager continued to whisper, as he fussed on the computer, 'I will get you the best rate possible.'

The rate was apparently so good he had to write it down and pass it over the counter to her, as though saying it out loud would cause trouble. Five thousand Czech crowns per night.

'How much is this in euros?'

Daniel took back the pad of paper, wrote something down, and furtively slid it over the counter: €180.

Ten minutes later, Grace was wheeling her suitcase over the cobblestones to a small Airbnb apartment above a spice shop for seventy-two Canadian dollars a night. She dragged her suitcase up the spiral stone stairs and said hello to a woman smoking and reading a gossip magazine outside the door. Anthony Craig was on the cover, along with Brad Pitt and Angelina Jolie. Here was the Czech version of her people.

There was no bathtub in the apartment, which smelled of paprika, so she took a hot shower. On the tiny kitchen table the landlady had laid out seven brochures for river cruises, restaurants, and museums. She flipped through one for the Museum of Communism, turned on her computer, connected to the wifi system and transferred everything she had written in her notebook into a new document on her laptop, then hunted around on the Internet for Katka Vacek, her father, Czech gymnastics, and Elena Craig.

Grace found a single newspaper article, in Czech, and copied and pasted it into Google Translate. It was from 2011. Despite the awkwardness of the translation it was obvious that Coach Vacek was regretful his talented trainee, Elena Klimentová, had quit gymnastics so early – in 1968.

'I suppose it all turned out for her,' the reporter quoted Coach Vacek as saying.

If she had quit gymnastics in 1968, how was Elena an alternate on the Czech Olympic team in 1972? Why did Anthony Craig claim she was on the team, in his book? Why did she lie?

Grace's phone buzzed with a call: Steadman Coe. No doubt

69

Elena or her assistant had called him to complain, maybe even his pal Josef Straka. Rather than answer, Grace finished getting dressed and stepped back out into the cool afternoon with the Museum of Communism brochure. She joined the river of tourists and, at the first white kiosk, she bought a mulled red wine. Her phone buzzed again, and again.

Just as she arrived in front of the Museum of Communism, set into a pretty Prague version of a strip mall, surrounded by restaurants and a sunglasses store, she received a text.

Call me back or I will have to fire you.

There was a farmers' market in front of the museum. Grace bought another mulled wine and drank it so fast she burned her throat.

He answered on the first ring. 'Gracie, what did you do to Elena?'

'Steadman, remember when you said something like, "You could write a book about her"?'

'I don't think I said that.'

'You did. Well, I was thinking the same thing.' It began to drizzle again, so Grace took shelter inside the lobby of the Museum of Communism. 'All I did was ask a few innocent questions about her childhood, what it was like to grow up under communism, and she went bananas and kicked me out of her car. She abandoned me in the middle of nowhere.'

'She says you were harassing her.'

70

'Steadman, she's been good to me. She's the most fascinating person I've ever met. But she's a liar. And not just about me.'

'I don't really care if she's a liar, Gracie. She pays us on time. She has a readership. And besides, I thought you two were friends. That's what she told me. That you betrayed her friendship.'

'Friends? She said that? Friendship?'

'She sounded legitimately hurt.'

Grace wanted to end the call and drink another mulled wine or two. She told Coe about the Olympics story and he sighed. 'No one in the seventies and eighties figured there would be an Internet when they grew up,' he said. 'I used to tell people I was in the Lemon Pipers.'

'What's that?'

'A rock band. *Green Tambourine*?'

'I don't know what that is.'

'The point is, people at parties in 1979 didn't carry computer encyclopedias in their back pockets. What are you saying anyway? You're going to write a whole book about how Elena Craig lied about being in the Olympics?'

'No.'

'Listen, I don't want to hurt your feelings but you know what you've been doing for almost twenty years? Since you were a kid? Working for me. Working for the *National Flash*. You're not an investigative journalist. You're never going to be Christiane Amanpour. You don't even know *how* to be Christiane Amanpour. You know how to go through court documents looking for embarrassing details in a divorce. You can make fun of Scott Baio for a readership with a seventh-grade education better than anyone in the business. But I'm sorry. I take back what I said. You're never going to write a book about anything, Gracie. Now get your ass back here. I need you to fix this thing with Elena.'

'You're breaking up,' Grace yelled. 'I'm losing you.'

'Don't hang up on me! You'll regret it.'

Grace hung up. Then, instead of throwing her iPhone against the wall or screaming she bit the inside of her left cheek so hard it bled.

The lobby of the Museum of Communism was long and thin, a marriage of white and gray with no rounded corners, and the only other person in it was the woman at the counter, who stared at her from behind a pair of comically large glasses.

'I'm sorry,' said Grace. 'Was that loud?'

The woman shrugged. 'Are you coming in?'

Grace paid and walked up the stairs into the first room, which featured placards on the walls with descriptions in Czech and English of what she had already seen on Wikipedia when she clicked on 'Czechoslovakia'. There were black-and-white photos of Stalin and his local bootlicker, Klement Gottwald. Further on she watched videos from the offices of propaganda and censorship, and read about the clever ways the government controlled the truth. There was a black market, and another market just for party officials. The KGB was omnipresent, through its Czech underlings in the StB. There was an alcove furnished and decorated to look like the bedroom of a Czech teenager. Grace imagined Elena Klimentová in the single bed. She made notes and took photographs of the most interesting placards. Steadman Coe's voice echoed: *you're not an investigative journalist.*

No, this was not investigative journalism.

She read that the hardest time to escape to the West from Czechoslovakia was between 1969 and 1979. So how had Elena managed it? Grace knew she was briefly married to a Frenchman, and this had allowed a route farther west to Montreal and eventually New York. Yet everything in the Museum of Communism suggested this was impossible, unless she had defected during the Olympics in Munich. Does an alternate actually go to the Olympics? But what if she had quit gymnastics four years earlier?

How does a poor Czech girl meet a Frenchman?

In the gift shop at the end of the exhibits Grace showed the woman at the cash register some of the quotations she had written down, about the StB and the possibility of defection.

'Is there a library or something, an archives, where I could find more information about this?'

The woman called her manager, who spoke better English. He gave her a card for a place called the Institute for the Study of Totalitarian Regimes. 'It isn't far. Just up the hill. But it will close soon.'

On her way, Grace passed the central train station. The prospect of the Institute for the Study of Totalitarian Regimes

73

was more attractive than a train, but since it was closing soon she asked herself: what would a real investigative journalist do? She already knew an express ticket to Mladá Boleslav was 280 Czech crowns, about 10 dollars.

Ten minutes into her voyage back to Mladá Boleslav, she called Manon. Manon was her next-door neighbor on Rue Saint-Christophe, and her most reliable also-divorced wine-drinking companion.

'Have you had sex with a European man yet?' Manon asked.

Grace laughed. It was soothing to hear her friend's groggy morning voice. She wanted to launch immediately into what Elena Craig and Steadman Coe had said and done, but there was something more important: the welfare of her cat. 'Not yet, Manon. I remain cautiously pessimistic. How is my Zip?'

'I was in your apartment an hour ago. I fed Zip and cleaned her disgusting litter box. It's absurd and demeaning, you know, to have a cat.'

'I'm feeling kinda low. Things aren't going so hot here. Can you do me a favor?'

'Anything.'

'Can you go next door and put the phone near her?' Grace asked.

'Near the cat. Really?' Manon sighed. Then Grace could hear her walking along the hardwood, opening and closing one door and then the other. 'This is crazy, you know?'

'I know.'

Then, despite her protests Manon cooed at the cat as she pet her. Grace could hear her purr over the line and she told Zip she loved her and missed her, that she should not scratch her furniture, that she would be home soon.

Manon was the only person who knew what Grace was really doing in Prague. While Grace had always taken non-disclosure agreements seriously, she did not see how anyone could possibly care that she ghostwrote Elena Craig's *National Flash* advice columns.

'I asked Elena if I could write a book about her.'

'Really? And?'

'It was a disaster. She shouted at me and threw me out of her car. But now I'm on my way to her hometown, to follow up on a lead.'

'A lead? I am so happy to hear you say this. A lead!'

'You know what Steadman said?'

'What?'

'After Elena flipped out he told me I'm not a real investigative journalist. He said I couldn't write a book.'

'Fuck him!' There was a bang over the line, as though Manon had just punched something. Grace worried it would startle Zip. 'I'll run down to Old Montreal right now and kick him in the neck.'

'Oh that's a lovely thought,' said Grace.

Manon, who was an archivist at the Bibliothèque et Archives nationales du Québec, gave Grace a pep talk. Then there was another call on Manon's phone. 'I should get to work but take care, okay? Zip and I need you to come home. I truly hate litter boxes.'

The train car was only half full. Once she was off the phone Grace scanned it for the two men who had seemed to follow her. They weren't following her now. When the train arrived, she walked around the corner to the house of Elena's youth. No lights were on inside, though it was nearly five o'clock. Now that Elena was not watching her, she took more photographs. She stepped into the scrubby yard and peeked into the window. There was a small kitchen with dirty plates and pots piled haphazardly. This is where Elena had washed dishes. Behind it, a carpeted floor was splattered with plastic toys and clothes.

It was warmer than it had been in the morning. Grace crossed the white bridge over the Jizera River and passed multiple Škoda buildings: a sales office and factories. The sound of grinding metal echoed through the valley. Grace tried to imagine Elena's grandmother walking through the property in a queenly fashion, the foreman here when it was still Laurin & Klement.

At a set of black stone stairs that reeked of piss she climbed to the upper city. Men in black stood in front of a barbershop and smoked. One of them played an angry Slavic death metal song on his phone and muttered something Grace did not need translated. His friends laughed.

Just as she reached the upper plaza the clouds gave up in the west and the last of the late afternoon sun shone on the clock tower. It was majestic and pretty. School was out so children shouted and chased one another around the wormy black industrial art.

There were a few customers in the sporting goods store, two parents and a pre-teen son looking at cross-country skis and an old man in a shirt and tie with a cardigan over it. He leaned on a cane and scowled at the snowboards. Katka was helping the family.

A few minutes later, the family left without buying any-thing and Katka walked them out, with a bright and hopeful tone in her voice. When the door was closed she turned to Grace. 'Don't tell me: you didn't make it to the train station. You've been wandering around all day, confused and hungry.'

Grace laughed. 'I made it to Prague and then I came back.'

'Why?'

'I didn't mention this before because it wasn't settled, but I'm working on a book about Elena Craig.'

'Oh.' Katka frowned.

'I was hoping to interview you and your father about the city, what it was like under communism, and about Elena's youth.'

Katka did not say yes or no.

'To be perfectly honest, I was with her this morning,' Grace said. 'She dropped me off in the plaza. Given how close you were, I wonder why Ms Craig didn't come by for a visit. I mean, it sounds like the two of you were quite close.'

Without a word, Katka led Grace to the old man in front of the snowboards. 'This is my father. He's known to everyone here as Coach Vacek.' She spoke some Czech to him and he turned and squinted at Grace.

There was obvious tension in the back-and-forth between Katka and her father. With a quick eye roll, Katka turned to Grace. 'He wants to know if anyone followed you.'

'I don't think so.' She thought of the two men in the train and in the Old Town Square. 'No.'

'Are you sure?'

'Well, no, I'm not sure.' Grace went to the window and scanned the plaza. 'But I can't see anyone now.'

Katka's father grumbled.

Katka went to the door, opened it, and looked out on the street and the plaza. When she was back inside, she locked it. 'We closed ten minutes ago. If we're going to talk, we can do it upstairs in my father's apartment.'

'Why is he worried I was followed?' said Grace.

'My father has become paranoid. He was young and strong under communism. My theory is he hungers for it the way he hungers for his youth.'

Katka pulled her father up the stairwell, lit by a single incandescent bulb. Grace came in behind, prepared if he tumbled back.

'How does the shop do?'

'Poorly.' Katka helped her father to the top. 'But Elena owns the building and charges us no rent.'

'Why?'

Katka translated for her father as she guided him to a chair. Up top, the low-ceilinged apartment smelled like the ghosts of five hundred years of boiled root vegetables. It was lit soft orange, from three matching lamps, the opposite of the bright fluorescent lights of the shop. The walls and beams were rosy wood. The furniture was sturdy and useful, a tidy collection of wood and artificial fabrics. Someone had crocheted a massive collection of colorful blankets, the sort Grace's mother called an afghan, and they lay on the backs of chairs and the couch, in a neat folded pile in the corner. On the wall there were photographs of gymnasts in vast halls, standing by vaults and bars and trampolines.

'Father thinks she does it to keep us quiet,' said Katka. 'But honestly, I worked for her in New York and I cannot imagine what we would say about her and to whom. To a writer of a book maybe? I will be honest, but I saw nothing in my time with her that would be interesting enough for a book. She works hard. She pretends to be less intelligent than she is, like many women. I think she doesn't charge us rent because it would be nothing to her and because she and my father were close at one time.'

Katka's father shouted at her. His eyes were wet and cloudy.

'What is he saying?' said Grace.

'Five or six years ago Elena was here. She and Father had an argument.'

'About what?'

Katka and her father spoke in Czech for a while. It was frustrating for Grace not to understand. As they spoke, Katka opened a clear bottle with herbs inside, filled three glasses neatly to the top. She shook her head and laughed, addressed

Grace. 'He has never been to New York. He does not watch television. My father believes poor Elenka has been suffering all these years because she quit gymnastics and left Mladá Boleslav. He makes it sound like they dragged her off to the Gulag.'

Her father had begun speaking again.

'Who are *they*?' Grace asked.

'The Russians, he says. My father, he is not a fan of the Russians. If you ask me, it has clouded his memory. *Na zdraví*.'

Grace smelled her drink: vodka. She had not touched vodka since an unfortunate night in her junior year at Thomas Jefferson High in Bloomington. She sipped it and sipped again. The infusion was fennel and it was delicious.

In one gulp, Katka's father's vodka was gone. He said something and Katka shook her head.

'What?' said Grace. 'What is he saying?'

'The Russians took Elena away in the beginning of 1969,' said Katka.

'Took her away from here?' Grace tried to keep up in her notebook. 'Where did they take her?'

Katka and her father spoke some more, and she did not immediately translate.

'What did he say?' said Grace.

'It's crazy,' said Katka.

'I don't care. I like crazy. Tell me.'

'Come,' said Katka's father, in English, before his daughter could divulge whatever had seemed crazy. He stood up and, supporting himself on furniture, walked to the window that opened on the square. He pointed to a building on the right of the town hall. It was carved stone, so beautiful it belonged in a photograph of Paris.

Katka translated. 'He says once she left, Mr and Mrs Kliment moved to the penthouse of the finest building in Mladá Boleslav. It was their reward.'

'For what?' said Grace. 'For something Ms Craig had done?'

Katka shrugged and finished her glass of vodka.

'Anthony Craig, and Ms Craig herself, talk about the 1972 Olympics,' said Grace. 'Either she competed in the Munich Games or she was an alternate. Then I found an article where your father says Ms Craig quit gymnastics in 1968.'

'That article is why Elena stopped speaking to us,' said Katka.

'Was she in the Olympics?'

Katka shook her head. 'Elena was nowhere near Munich in 1972.'

As he made his way back to his chair, Katka's father spoke non-stop. Grace recognized the word *Elenka*, but that was about it. When he was finished, Katka sighed and said her father was tired. 'Let me drive you back to the train station, Grace.'

They would go as soon as Katka was finished in the toilet. When they were alone, Katka's father reached out to shake Grace's hand. When she took it he pulled her close. For a moment she thought the old man was trying to feel her up. Then she realized he wanted to whisper in her ear. Grace had to press on his bony shoulder to prevent herself from falling on top of him completely.

'Sergei.' His breath was heavy with vodka. 'You look for Sergei Sorokin.'

'Who is that?' Grace said, as she stood up again. She started to write it in her notebook.

Katka's father pointed at her notebook and shook his finger *no, no, no.* Then he drew the same finger across his neck.

It was dark now and Grace was thankful for the ride in Katka's small white Renault Clio, especially as they passed the same ruffians in sweat suits. On the way, she asked Katka what her father had said that was so crazy.

'It's a myth,' said Katka. 'The KGB and the StB apparently recruited talented girls and sent them to the West to do . . . whatever.'

'To be, what?' said Grace. 'Spies? He thinks Ms Craig was a KGB spy?'

Katka laughed. 'All I know is in my time in New York I do not think I met a more American woman than Elena Craig.'

Grace knew what she meant. Elena loved to talk about how she arrived in America with nothing and achieved everything. There was not another country in the world where such a thing was possible. It was the theme of every fifth or sixth *Ask Elena* column. She was a sentimental patriot.

Katka parked half a block away from the train station and

looked around. A few people walked up the sidewalk, pulling small suitcases on wheels. 'I make fun of it, but do be careful. My father isn't entirely senile. He went through a lot in those days.'

Grace wanted to ask about Sergei Sorokin but she knew that if Katka's father had wanted his daughter to hear the man's name he would have said it with her in the room. 'I'll be honest with you, Katka. Ms Craig didn't drop me off in Mladá Boleslav this morning. She kicked me out.'

'Why?'

'I was asking questions.'

Katka nodded and looked straight ahead. 'That's why she sent me back here. She was like a mother to me, or at least a bossy aunt. I thought, in fact, that I would never leave New York. One night we were sharing a bottle of wine and I asked about the old days, about what had happened between her and my father. There were the stock answers, the ones I knew to be untrue. I thought: who cares, right? The Cold War is over. I told her she was bullshitting me. I asked for the truth. The next day I was not only fired, I was flying back to Prague with an expired visa.'

'And when you tried to speak to her about it?'

'Nothing,' said Katka. 'For Elena, I no longer exist.'

8

PRAGUE, 1970

It was a Friday, nearly dark, and snowing heavily on the cobble-stones and wind-battered shrubbery of the Square of Red Army Soldiers.

Elena stood at the window of the Great Hall of the Faculty of Arts at Charles University, exhausted from weeks of what passed for examinations in the special program: interviews in Czech, in English, in French, in Russian, scenarios abroad, and the role-playing exercises.

You are at a cocktail party in Paris. You are in the back of a car in New York and they have locked the doors. A child stands between you and the information you need, the exit. A man is holding you down, his hand on your neck. You need to kill someone and make it look like a natural death. The CIA offers you money now and a new identity, a new everything, in ten years. What do you do?

Fewer than half of the girls who had started the program with her had passed the first test: alone in a cell in a night-gown, no sleep, then alcohol and drugs, drowning in a chair. Tell us his name, they had shouted at her. Just his name and all of this ends, sweet girl.

Or maybe they had passed the test and somehow she had failed. Either way, Elena never saw them again. A few others dropped out in the summer; they just disappeared, and the rest of the girls, the ones who remained, knew not to ask about them.

There were real students of Charles University below, men and women her age, regular Czechs from towns and cities like hers, walking arm-in-arm, on their way to their small apart-ments and the train station. They would become clerks and teachers and stewardesses. In the hall behind her, her new friends celebrated the end of term with beer and bad sausage. If not for this program, her special education, she would not have known how bad it was. Elena had been ruined for bad sausage because she had tasted good sausage, good wine, champagne, truffles, caviar, American hamburgers, French confit de canard, osso buco alla Milanese. She knew how to eat them, what to say about them, how to hold a glass, which fork to use when.

'Join us.' Danika guided her back to the party: nine beautiful young women and their 'professors', a collection of genuine academics and teachers, bureaucrats, soldiers, and secret police.

Half were Russian, dispatched from the Kremlin and KGB Center, half were Czech and Slovak. They all had fine apartments and drivers in Prague, access to real food and blue jeans. Their lives were unimaginable to all but a select few in Czechoslovakia.

And their families.

This was her reward and, she now understood, their ultimate power over her: Jana was in her apartment, Petr was on his land.

A fog of cigarette smoke hung over the party, which was in a vast upper-level lecture hall of old leather and wood, a room of books and soft lamps. They listened to 'problematic' music no one else was allowed to hear: Creedence Clearwater Revival, the Doors, some genuinely strange new songs by the Beatles. They danced, they smoked, they drank, they kissed.

In every way they were different from the men and women, boys and girls Elena had watched out the window in the snow. For friends and family here in Prague and back home, wherever home might be, each of Elena's fellow students had constructed an alternative story – or stories – with the help of their professors and mentors.

The music stopped and Sergei Sorokin, the leader of the special program and Elena's lover, raised his hands until everyone stopped talking and laughing. Sergei's soft brown hair confounded her: it was perfectly parted on the left and never moved, even in bed. She had never been in his apartment but she often thought there was a closet with twenty suits tailored for him in

Italy and London, suits of every color. Her father had a single black suit for weddings and funerals and May Day.

'My gorgeous, intelligent girls,' he began, then paused.

Did everyone know about her affair with Sergei? Surely it was insignificant, next to everything else that was happening to her. Every hour of every day she thought about escaping the special program and becoming a regular, honest student like those on the Square of Red Army Soldiers. How would she do it? What would happen to her parents? What would happen to her?

The night before, Elena had gone for a walk alone. She had stopped for a glass of honey wine, which her father used to let her taste on cold December nights. When she had first entered the special program, it felt like she was going on-stage and learning to act for a small, peculiar audience. Now she understood she was going backstage to engineer a show. Everything was an illusion: her parents' lives, her neighbors in Mladá Boleslav, Czechoslovakia, the Soviet Union, America and the West, socialism, communism, capitalism, fascism.

Here was a new word for her: *nihilism*. They were slowly emptying her of everything that had made Elena Klimentová. They had shown her it was irrelevant.

And yet she loved her parents with a ferocity she could never explain in words, and not her parents in their wonderful apartment, the apartment they deserved, in the upper town of Mladá Boleslav, on their land along the Jizera. She loved them in their old house, the color of a dead carp.

Elena wanted to be twelve again. No, nine. Before the first germs of the feelings that now controlled her.

'My girls, you astonish *us all* with your talent and your determination. I think back two years, more or less, to when I met you. Today you are different people. I hardly recognize you, and I mean this in the most admiring way. We had expectations but we had no idea how strong you would be, how intelligent, how imaginative.' Sergei smiled, and looked around the room for another moment of silence. 'This will be our last Christmas together.'

'What's Christmas?' one of the teachers said.

And they laughed. She laughed! How preposterous it was that they had removed the central European ritual from European life, how absurd, how sublime. They could make anyone think anything. Elena thought of the women from the program who had disappeared.

They are dead. Their parents are dead. Their brothers and sisters are dead. No one knew, so no one could care.

'I am proud of you, each one of you,' Sergei continued. 'I know how hard you have worked. I know what you have sacrificed to be here among us and how it sometimes breaks your hearts.'

Sergei looked at Elena, just long enough.

'You know what people call this program, call you? I don't like the word. I don't use the word. I don't even like to say it.'

'You can say it,' Danika called, the strongest of them, the star of the program. She was leaving for New York City in February.

'We can't help but long for home this time of year. Love and adore your families, hold them tight. Keep them safe.'

Sergei looked around the room. *Keep them safe.* How easily he could insert the ultimate threat into an inspirational speech. No one moved or made a joke.

'Do not fret,' Sergei said. 'No matter where they go, swallows always come home.'

9

PRAGUE, 2016

Whenever she found cellular coverage on the train between Mladá Boleslav and Prague, Grace Elliott searched for the name Sergei Sorokin. There was a hockey player and a technology worker, but nothing else came up on English-language websites. Grace went through the notes she had taken, and the day's photographs. Thinking about her conversation with Katka and her father, she enlarged and reread one of the placards from the Museum of Communism.

Violence, intimidation, blackmail, and psychological terror were the basic interrogation methods of the Communist secret police, based on the model of the NKVD, the Soviet secret police . . . StB investigation methods included physical violence, brutal beatings, electrical torture methods, nighttime interrogations, extended solitary confinement, and sleep, water, and food deprivation. Physical violence was accompanied by psychological terror, humiliation, threats of the arrest of family members, and even faked executions.

Records were kept of all StB operations; an archive so enormous that, if these files had not been burned toward the end of the Communist regime, they would cover several soccer fields piled many meters high.

Grace shared Katka's cynicism about her father's paranoia, and his stories of Russian agents stealing Elena from her family. Still, Grace was an investigative reporter, or she wanted to be, and her prospects for investigative reporting did not sound terribly good: *if these files had not been burned toward the end of the Communist regime . . .*

The cold rain had returned, and Grace had forgotten to carry the transparent poncho Katka had given her. Wind blew in unpredictable gusts, so the few awnings Grace could find were useless. In a crowd rushing for shelter on the cobblestones of Old Town Square, a man in a black jacket yanked at her purse. Grace screamed, 'Thief!' and he ran off before he could wrestle it from her. In a covered arcade a British couple, who had rushed to her aid, ensured Grace was safe and asked if she could describe the man. He was . . . white and tall and thirty? They walked her to the Airbnb above the spice shop, and by the time they arrived Grace was sceptical about their motivations too.

Jamie and Claire from Leeds. Jamie and Claire sounded like the names two secret agents pretending to be British tourists would choose. When she thanked Jamie and Claire, she kept one hand on the top of her purse, to guard her phone and notebook. In a battle of politeness, she did not allow them to escort her up to the apartment.

When she opened the door, the apartment was much warmer than she had left it, and the lights were on. She was sure she had turned them off.

'Hello?'

Had the landlady come in for some reason? There was no movement inside, but she could feel a presence. She moved through the small kitchen and screamed when she entered the bedroom. Her suitcase was open on the bed. Her clothes were spread about.

Her vibrator was on the pillow.

Grace ran back into the kitchen, grabbed a paring knife from the drawer, and crouched next to the oven.

It took some effort to speak again. 'Is anyone here?'

Thirty seconds later, when she heard nothing in the apartment but her heart thumping in her head, Grace stood and crept back into the bedroom. Her computer was where she had left it, on the bedside table, but it was open. She zipped the vibrator into an inside pocket of her suitcase and explored the rest of the apartment.

In the bathroom she turned on the light and retched. The toilet seat was up and the bowl was filled with aromatic piss.

She called her landlady, Marie, who lived in the apartment above. Within five minutes Marie was walking through the apartment with Grace.

'Did they steal?' said Marie.

'I don't think so.' Grace looked through her bag again, to be sure. The only item worth any money was her MacBook, but they had not taken it. If she phoned the police, what would she tell them? 'They turned up the heat and used the bathroom.'

Marie managed three suites in the building for her father. Now, she helped Grace collect her things and moved her one floor up, to a two-bedroom apartment. 'We will change the locks in the old one. You will give us bad review, I suppose?'

When Marie was gone, Grace turned on her computer. Everything seemed fine. Next she ran the bath and opened a bottle of tall black beer a previous tenant had left in the fridge. She propped one of the heavy wooden chairs up against the door handle, like in the movies, and called her mother.

'Prague! What are you doing in Prague?' Elsie Elliott lived in a retirement complex in Florida. Complications from diabetes had rendered her nearly blind, so she was not much of a texter.

'It's for work, Mom.'

For the next while, her mother talked about how proud she was to have a daughter who took so many business trips. Five did not seem a lot, to Grace, but neither her mother nor her father had taken a business trip in their whole lives. One of Elsie's neighbors in the complex took a trip to Europe every year, on a river cruise through Germany and Budapest and who knows where, and lorded it over everyone else. Well, she can have it, said Elsie Elliott. Who needs an airplane ride, going through all that security, not knowing if the person right next to you is from ISIS?

While she could not tell her mother about the break-in, it made Grace feel better to sit in a bath with a black beer and listen to Elsie Elliott's voice.

After her bath, assuming a man had touched her clothes, she put everything into the apartment's washing machine. Then she put one knife under her pillow and two on the table next to the bed.

Grace Elliott had lived forty-three years without anyone trying to steal her purse. No one had ever followed her. No one had broken into her apartment. Yet in one day, in Prague, all of this had happened to her.

Her flight was scheduled to leave in a few days and she had not even posted a selfie on Instagram. She had not tasted goulash. She had not walked across the Charles Bridge. Maybe she was pretending to be someone she was not, just because Steadman Coe had humiliated and discouraged her. Maybe this is what a mid-life crisis felt like: the anxiety in her stomach, the confusion, the loneliness. She thought of her mother in the retirement complex in Pompano Beach, of Zip and Manon and her quiet, cheerless life in Montreal. Her mother needed her! Was it so bad, writing advice columns under the name of a rich woman? Was it so bad writing about celebrity love affairs, DUI convictions, and cellulite?

If being ordinary means no one breaks into your apartment to *leave a piss*, maybe she did not want to be extraordinary. In twenty years, if she saved carefully, she could sell the condo in Montreal and buy a little place in a warm city where everyone speaks English, with a decent farmers' market. In this imagined future Zip is still alive and Manon is still somehow her neighbor. She goes on a date from time to time with a man named Dave, Dave from Tucson, who makes dad jokes. She learns to care about sports.

Then she thought of Christiane Amanpour in her hijab, reporting from Faisalabad. She thought of Steadman Coe, telling her what she could never do.

Fuck Steadman Coe, she thought. Fuck him and the men who were trying to scare her. She would show them all.

10

STRASBOURG, 1971

Sergei Sorokin smoked at the dining-room table in Elena's little apartment and sang the chorus of 'Douce France' over and over again. The scent of the lilacs of Strasbourg blew into her modest rooms on Rue des Veaux, above a coin laundry, and competed with Sergei's cigarettes. He sat with one leg crossed over the other. His socks did not go high enough and a flash of sun warmed his bare ankles. There was a bottle of sweet Gewürztraminer and a bowl of salted pecans on the table.

Cher pays de mon enfance-uh.

Elena had asked him to stop singing it, to stop taunting her, but it only seemed to encourage him. He found it weak and silly, her feeling for this country. Everything she loved about the French, their rituals and songs, their daily commerce, their

96

vegetable and flower markets, their pretty buildings, Sergei loathed.

They had only a few nights together and she did not want to waste any time unpacking, but Sergei insisted. Though he was only twenty-six he pretended to understand the hearts of Western women. No Frenchman would believe her story if her bedroom did not look and feel correct. There had to be a place for perfume, for jewelry, for teddy bears, for her favorite hats and clothes, for pictures of her beloved parents and the city she left behind.

Sergei had explained that capitalism had its philosophies and its aesthetics. All of this had to feel natural to a gentleman caller.

In downtown boutiques they had spent nearly eight thousand francs on bracelets and necklaces, on a gold-plated watch, dresses and short skirts, loose slacks and tight blouses in pure, bright colors – polyester combinations that were unimaginable on the streets of Prague. It made Elena feel dizzy, that all of this excess was permitted. She thought of her mother with her two dresses and three sweaters: six possible outfits. Anything else of value was an inheritance from another time and Elena remembered her mother hiding those things. Now she hid nothing. Now, thanks to the program, Jana Klimentová walked through the city like a pre-communist mayor. Elena had warned both her parents about their bourgeois apartment in the central plaza of Mladá Boleslav, their new clothes, their new food, and how they all came with a new set of rules.

They did not have to worry about the neighbors anymore. Their new apartment was bugged. Secret police were always watching and always listening. When they came, they would come in the middle of the night; they would not knock on the door; they would use their own set of keys.

Like all of her classmates, Elena was to begin with a job at Kara Modeling, an international agency with offices in New York, London, Montreal, Paris, Milan, and West Berlin. In France the agency also had addresses in Lyon, Marseille, and, because of the Council of Europe, Strasbourg. Elena would have modeling jobs all over Western Europe.

Her appointment with the agency manager was the following morning, in an office on the Grand'Rue. Though it was already settled, she was nervous. What if they did not think she was pretty enough, poised enough? She was nervous about Sergei leaving her, about school ending and this new life beginning, about what came next.

There was a club of men in Strasbourg, all graduates of Sciences Po, all sons of wealthy families, all involved in business and politics who called themselves *Les Albertins*, after Albert Schweitzer, the famous Strasbourgeois. Once every six months the Albertins allowed women to join them at an event to raise money for the astronomical clock in the magnificent old cathedral. Sergei had arranged for one of his 'possessions', an Albertin, to escort her to the dinner in two weeks.

When Sergei had compromising material, *kompromat*, on a man abroad, he was a 'possession'. His possession in Strasbourg was a gay man named Chastain. Tonight, Chastain would meet them for dinner at the Maison des Tanneurs. It was busy enough with tourists on the canals of the Grande Île that no one would notice a man and a woman speaking French with Slavic accents.

'How did you come to be here, Elena?' Sergei asked.

Elena sighed. They had been over this so many times. Couldn't they just have an intimate conversation over wine like normal French lovers? She had bought a sachet of dried lavender. She brought it to her nose, closed her eyes, and smelled it.

'How did you come to be here?' There was an edge to his voice that made her tremble.

'I left when everyone else left, when it was obvious the Prague Spring had come to an end.'

'That sounds rehearsed. Details.'

'One night in August, when the rumors began—'

'What rumors?'

'That the Russians were sending in the troops and the tanks, to bring us back in line, I decided to leave.'

'How did you do that?'

'I took the train to Linz, dressed up for a hiking holiday in the *Salzkammergut*. From there I went to Salzburg, Innsbruck, Basel, and arrived here where my friends were living.'

'And what do you do now?'

'A bit of modeling. I had done this in Prague. I might also teach gymnastics. I competed back home.'

'Why did you leave Czechoslovakia?'

'Freedom and opportunity. I want adventure, to see the world. But I'm not an overly political girl, if that's what you mean.'

'Perfect.' Sergei looked at his watch. 'Sit with me.'

Elena sat across from him in a hard vinyl chair and he poured her a glass of the sweet amber wine. She wished Sergei could see her as she was: his wife, not his mistress. It was agony to be in the same room with him, to know how soon he would leave, that he could overlook the terrible, wonderful truth of what they shared. She knew he was filled with love for her yet he contained it and twisted it and he made himself cruel.

'Sergei, when this is over . . .'

'This never ends.'

'It must.'

'You *must* understand, Elena, this is our struggle, yours and mine, the struggle of exceptional people. We will meet from time to time, I promise you.'

'From time to time. When I can escape . . .' She could not say it.

'Your husband.'

She stood up straight, forced herself. 'My husband.'

Since January 1969 she had learned English and French, etiquette and music, fashion, movies, how to walk and how to eat and – this had shocked her – how to make love. She had learned surveillance and counter-surveillance, self-defense, and the basics of kitchen chemistry and clandestine photography. Deception was a muscle that needed constant exercise. How do covert meetings work? How best to pass material on a busy street? Her first objective was to marry well, which could only bring joy to a girl from the train station ghetto of Mladá Boleslav.

Lucky, lucky Elena.

Polite men, quietly confident men, good solid husbands were not their targets. The swallows were after the proudest, most ambitious, most aggressive men in the Western world, men on their way up, men who would succeed in life, in business, in politics.

'None of my other girls reacted this way,' Sergei said. 'They were excited about their adventures.'

Elena sighed. 'But none of the others were in love with you.'

11

PRAGUE, 2016

Grace woke up out of an ugly dream and into the memory of the smell of urine. The woman-of-steel thoughts that had taken her into sleep slammed into a headache inspired by mulled wine, vodka, and black beer. It was almost eleven o'clock in the morning. She lay in bed, feeling fragile, flipping imaginary coins between investigative reporter and tourist.

It would be so easy to buy a ticket for a river trip on the Vltava, to eat salty meat and potatoes in an authentic pub, to spend an hour in the Franz Kafka Museum instead of feeling like a Franz Kafka character: vulnerable and watched. If some- one was willing to steal her purse and break into her apartment, she imagined they might also hurt her.

Since Grace could not find Sergei Sorokin on the Internet,

and since Elena Craig would not speak to her, there was really only one avenue left: to hunt for any files on Elena that had not been burned by the Czech secret service. If she found nothing, Grace would take the river trip and the pork and dumplings and become a regular tourist without a hint of self-loathing.

On her way out of the apartment, she wrapped a paring knife in some paper towel and stuffed it in her purse.

A cloud had descended on Prague, so low that it met the top of the astronomical clock tower in Old Town Square. Grace had a meaty breakfast that was actually a lunch at a corner table, so she could watch everyone in the dark little restaurant. Afterward she walked through the mist with her plastic poncho over a sweater, turning every few minutes to scan the route behind her.

She was certain a man in a navy suit and beige raincoat was following her as she passed the Church of Our Lady before Týn. Then a young woman with large-framed eyeglasses talking on her phone, with a canvas Charles University bag, watched her from the Starbucks. A couple walking arm-in-arm with coffees turned right down an alley after her, and then left. As Grace passed the train station a uniformed policewoman spoke into the little black receiver on her shoulder.

If this was unwarranted paranoia, she could not imagine how to treat it. Her usual remedy, a bit of dark self-mockery, was undone by the lingering image of her dildo on a pillow. She imagined what it must have been like for Elena to grow up in a time when neighbors snitched on one another for sport and status.

The Institute for the Study of Totalitarian Regimes was a five-storey box covered in aluminum siding the color of a nicotine stain. Grace climbed its steps, beyond the train station, and looked back at the pocket park and city below wrapped in mist.

Inside the stark lobby she made for the turnstile and a bald man with clipped white hair on the sides grasped her arm. She pulled away from him and shouted back at his smoky Czech monologue in English that she would call the police.

Like the police could help her.

The man stepped back, his arms up in retreat. There was a frosty layer of dandruff on the shoulders of his security uniform. He said something else in Czech, calmer this time.

Grace apologized. Though it was clear he did not understand, she wanted him to know she was feeling jumpy for reasons that had nothing to do with him. She pulled a fold of crowns from her pocket and showed him. 'Pay? How much?'

He shook his head.

'Archives?' Grace pointed to the turnstile, mimed a book.

The guard led her back to the front door and pointed at the city below. The mist had turned into rain and the wind was up. Wet leaves and a white plastic bag blew across the square of grass and trees in front of them. 'Good day, lady. Thank you.'

His two phrases of English were better than any of the Czech Grace had picked up from Elena since the spring of 2014. She was about to step back into the rain when a thin man in thick glasses hopped into the building and shook the water from himself. The security guard pointed to him. 'English. English man.'

'Yes, Englishman.' The thin man's accent was what her father used to call *plummy*. His black hair was pasted to his head. He opened his jacket to reveal the sort of sweater that, in Montreal, straddled the line between bad taste and hipsterism. 'Can I help you with something?'

Grace extended her damp hand. 'Lovely to meet you. I'm Grace Elliott.'

'William Kovály. How do you do? American?'

'American researcher, yes. I'm trying to explain to the gentleman that I want to go upstairs and look through the archives.'

'I see.' William said something to the security guard in Czech. Then he addressed Grace. 'You can't go up.'

'Why not?'

'You aren't an approved researcher.'

'But I am.'

'How is that?'

'It just is, William. I'm a journalist at an actual newspaper, and you see where I'm from—'

'Ah yes, that's it. This isn't *where you're from*, Grace. We're in Prague.'

'But these are public documents and I'm a member of the public.'

'Perhaps you aren't who you say you are. Perhaps you've come to remove something or destroy it.' William leaned against the wall in a poorly lit alcove that carried the scent of wet leaves and soil from his shoes. 'Do you have any idea what happened to archives and records in this country in 1989? Thousands of files, millions of them, were shredded and burned. You need to be approved.'

Grace nodded. 'So how do I do that?'

William pulled his wet jacket off and draped it over his computer bag, a cheap silver thing. 'You submit paperwork to the governing authority of the Institute.'

'How long does it take?'

'Six to eight weeks.'

'What?' Grace tried to conceal her frustration. She pointed to the security guard. 'How about if he comes up with me to ensure I don't burn or steal anything?'

'What are you looking for?'

'I have some names to research.'

'Family, is it?'

She remained silent.

'None of my business, I suppose.' William gestured at the security guard and said something in Czech. The security guard crossed his arms. Then William moved past Grace and through the turnstile. 'I'm just here to drop something off.'

'Maybe I could have a quick look around, while you do it? Are you an approved researcher? Could you say I'm your assistant? Please?'

'He doesn't speak English, Grace, but he's not a fool.'

She smiled at the security guard. The security guard did not smile back.

'I tried to give him money. Maybe it wasn't enough. Would he take a bribe, do you think?'

William pressed his glasses up his long nose and squinted at her.

'What can I do? I have to look something up and I don't have six to eight weeks.'

'Submit the paperwork.' He turned and began to walk away.

'A tour! Tell him it's a tour. A cultural tour. I swear to God I'll be five minutes. And I'll give him a gift, not a bribe. Just a little something for his family.'

William talked to the security guard again. This time the man shrugged and proposed something in the form of a question.

'One thousand crowns for a tour.' William swallowed and looked away, pressed his glasses up on his nose again. 'Afterwards you buy me a beer.'

Once the transaction was completed, Grace followed William up the stairs.

'They're beginning a renovation,' he said. 'A lot of the files have already been moved downtown.'

'Is there a computer? To search?'

'It's a bit ragtag, compared to what you're accustomed to, I imagine. You tried Google?'

'Of course.'

'Not much there?'

'Not what I'm looking for.'

'It would help a lot, Grace, if you could tell me what you are after.'

They walked through a heavy door and into an over-lit library, half torn apart. Beams were exposed behind smashed drywall, covered with plastic. There were a number of cubicles, more than half of them abandoned. Three women worked behind a horseshoe desk. 'This place is lousy with asbestos. You start a simple renovation and . . . well.'

William led Grace to a long set of shelves, just above waist height. 'This is the reference desk.'

None of it was in English.

'How do I search for a name?' said Grace.

'In what context? Do you want to know if—'

'The secret police. The StB.'

'What about the StB?' said William.

Grace realized she really didn't know how to do this. If she had four or five hours on her own, with a mousy librarian, she could tease the information out of her without any humiliation. 'Say there's a person who lived here until the early 1970s. Let's say the StB and the KGB got . . . involved in his or her life.'

William nodded. With a crackle in his knees and the grunt of an older man, he crouched down and pulled out two guides from the bottom shelf, both of them the size of a big city telephone book. 'Do you know what these are?' he said, putting them on one of the tables.

'No.'

William sat and pulled out a chair for Grace to sit next to him. 'There was a band in Prague in the 1970s called the Plastic People of the Universe.'

'Okay.'

'It was an underground thing, inspired by your Frank Zappa. The voice of dissidence, at the end of the Prague Spring. Yes? But the communists were back, in a big way, and when the band was arrested a group of artists and thinkers came together and published something called Charter 77, outlining all the illegal things the regime had done. Contravening international agreements on human rights . . .'

'I read about it in the Museum of Communism.'

'Well, one of the members of Charter 77 was Václav Havel. You've heard of him?'

'Of course. The first post-communist president of Czecho-slovakia.'

'Another was this man, Cibulka.' William slapped his hands on the tops of the guides. 'He was thrown in jail loads of times, before 1989, for criticizing the regime. Probably tortured. The usual stuff. Well, *after* the fall of communism, whatever the secret police hadn't burned was supposed to be declassified over time. Czechs who'd been mistreated, they wanted revenge. Understandably, the new authorities were more interested in a calm transition. Maybe something like what happened in South Africa with truth and reconciliation after Apartheid. But Cibulka wasn't patient. He wasn't forgiving. He somehow got the list of classified names and started printing them without anyone's approval.'

'Whoa.'

'I think this edition was published in '99. It was a sensation.'

William opened one of the guides. There were hundreds of tiny names on each page. He pulled a pair of reading glasses out of his bag.

'This gives you names, birthdates, and code names. Not everyone had a code name, of course. The StB recruited about forty-thousand people between the end of the Prague Spring in 1968 and the Velvet Revolution in 1989. Some were covert collaborators and worked for the secret police in some way. Others were confidential contacts who passed on information. They named names, as Americans like to say.'

Grace moved closer. 'How do you know all this?'

William smiled. 'I've devoted my life to studying it. Rather a grim prospect, no?' He opened the second book. This one had photographs. 'We also have the names and sometimes even portraits of official StB agents. So. What names are you looking for?'

Grace stepped in to ease him out of the way. 'If you don't mind, that's private. It's alphabetical?'

Instead of answering, William stood up and retreated to the women at the horseshoe desk. When he was too far away to see what she was doing, Grace looked for Josef Straka. There were a few Strakas, but no Josefs. Grace looked back, to be sure William was far enough away, and then she went to the Ks.

She did not make it to Klimentová before William had finished his business at the horseshoe desk. On his way back to her he announced himself. 'Any luck?'

'No, actually.'

'This person you are looking for: he or she is still alive?'

'Yes.'

'Living here?'

'No.'

'But he – he? – is Czech?'

'He left in the early seventies.'

'What? When exactly?'

'Maybe '71 or '72.'

'How did he leave?'

'He escaped,' said Grace.

William puzzled over this a moment. A woman approached, from the opposite direction. She was in her late fifties or sixties and wore leather pants and a revealing top. He lifted his finger and she stopped. They spoke Czech for a while and both of them looked at Grace. They came to a determination together.

'There is every chance your friend is a regular Czech expatriate who somehow crossed razor wire fences, dodged bullets and German shepherds. That's what it was like after the so-called normalization, in the early seventies.' William paused and appeared to think some more. 'There's every chance your friend escaped but *enormously* unlikely for anyone but a superhero. You see, Grace, towards the end of the regime, in 1989, when the KGB and StB and higher-ups in the party began destroying what they could destroy there was a hierarchy of destruction. Do you understand?'

The woman, who did not seem to speak English, walked away.

'I think so,' said Grace.

'They burned and shredded files that would incriminate them personally. Revenge was coming, as I said. These men would have remembered what had happened at the end of the Second World War, to Nazis and collaborators.'

'Hangings in the village square.'

'Yes. But more importantly, these were also some very powerful men and women who were confident of one thing.'

'What?'

'They would get back inside.'

'Inside?'

'Inside the castle. These were entitled people who understood government. So they destroyed any compromising documents that could prevent their return to political power. Some documents they locked away for future use. Blackmail, usually.'

Grace turned the pages of the first Cibulka guide. 'I'm looking for someone named Sergei Sorokin.'

'That's not a Czech name.'

'He's Russian, but he worked here. Let's say he was KGB.'

'May I?' William flipped the pages to the agents section, found nothing, and then consulted the second guide, with the list. Again, nothing. 'The KGB wouldn't be in here. What does Sergei Sorokin do now? Is he still alive?'

'I don't know. Another person I was looking for, he's not in here either.'

'Like I said, maybe he was a superhero. But in 1989, the first thing people did was protect themselves. The second thing they did was to burn and shred and delete everything related to their foreign assets.'

'Assets?'

'Sorry. Human assets. Their agents and collaborators abroad. Because when they found their footing, back in power, they would need these people. No matter what the new regime looked like in Czechoslovakia or Russia.'

'So either my man was nobody or . . .'

'Or he was a somebody.' William opened and closed the giant book of names. 'I'm half Czech. My father was of the generation who made it out in 1968, before everything became ugly. He arrived in London with a suitcase. When this book was published he looked up some of his friends. It inspired some interesting conversations over dinner.'

William looked at her.

'The people he most suspected, the people he was sure about: they weren't in the book.'

Grace thought for a moment. 'Maybe they were too important?'

'Exactly.'

'Any other names? I mean, I apologize but if you're looking for powerful KGB men who are still powerful, you'll find nothing revealing in this or any archive.'

Grace stood up, taking in his awful sweater and thick glasses. 'Why are you an approved researcher, William? How have you devoted your life to this?'

'I'm an academic,' he said, a bit stiffly.

'From where?'

'I'm an associate professor of history at London South Bank University. Heard of it?' When Grace crossed her arms and dished him a suspicious look, he grinned. 'I'm currently writing a paper on recruitment methods in the Velvet Revolution and the Arab Spring. Are you looking for any other names?'

'You didn't follow me here?'

Now he laughed out loud. 'No. I did not follow you here.'

She looked at him for another moment and decided he was too gangly and awkward to be a spy. Then she sat down next to him again and looked at the Ks. William swapped his distance glasses for reading glasses.

There was one Klimentová and more than one Kliment, the masculine form, on the list.

Grace closed her eyes for a while and opened them again. There they were: Petr Kliment and Jana Klimentová. Petr's code name was the same as his real name, but Jana's was not.

'Code name Vrba,' said William. 'In Czech, that means willow.'

Grace could smell the piss in her hotel room toilet. She turned around to see if any of the librarians were looking at them, and then used her phone to take a picture of Elena's parents' names.

William put his distance glasses back on. 'Tell me about Petr and Jana.'

12

PARIS, 1971

Kara Modeling had booked a restaurant near the École Militaire in the chic 7th arrondissement of Paris for their Christmas party. The party was for agency partners and potential clients across Europe to meet the girls in a relaxed setting. Senior members of the French government were also invited, along with diplomats of other nations, heads of corporations, and journalists. A layer of wet snow covered the cobblestones of Rue Cler, and the hotel was three blocks away, so Elena wore leather boots that reached nearly to her knees, sexy but sensible. Danika chose high heels.

'I don't know why Sergei married you off so early.' Danika slipped, let out a tiny shriek, and reached out for Elena.

Elena caught her. She knew that with Danika it would never

be any other way. She held the drinks, she carried the jackets, she remained sober. She shushed Danika when she said things like this out loud, in echoey French streets, and caught her when she fell.

'I am having an absolute ball in New York,' Danika said. 'Strasbourg? Honestly, in America no one has even heard of Strasbourg. Why aren't you at least in Paris, for God's sake?'

'We have two girls in Paris already.'

At Avenue de la Motte-Picquet, where the market street opened into a slushy thoroughfare of cars and transport trucks, Danika moved Elena under the awning of a pharmacy. Her eyes and her voice turned serious. 'Are you getting anything from your Monsieur Jean-Yves?'

Elena's husband was not turning out as planned. Jean-Yves was so rich he did not have to work, though he did work – a little. The more time he spent with her, the more time they spent here in Paris, on the Riviera, in Italy, skiing in the Alps, the less time Jean-Yves spent on his original plan: to join the Council of Europe, then to be mayor, and finally, encouraged by his Gaullist grandfather: to be president of the Republic.

In Strasbourg, they lived in a stone mansion with two servants, facing a beautiful park called the Orangerie. The orange trees were the Emperor Napoleon's gift to his wife Joséphine and every fruit and flower, Jean-Yves said, carried the soul of romance. Jean-Yves bought Elena gifts. He sang to her, and he wanted to make love constantly – even now, six months after their hasty marriage.

Elena had not lied to Sergei about his waning ambition, but in their monthly debriefing sessions she had not been entirely honest either.

'He's introducing me to powerful people, Dani. He knows everyone.'

'*French* powerful. I mean, what can Monsieur Jean-Yves give you that we can't get in twenty minutes this evening? Over a glass of champagne with the prime minister's chief of staff? God damn it, I'm going to seem a street harlot tonight, soaking wet.'

'Why don't we go back? You can change.'

'I don't want to change.' They walked under awnings for what remained of Avenue de la Motte-Picquet. 'Would you like to know my theory, about why Sergei forced you to marry this bore of a Frenchman?'

'He isn't a bore.'

'So you could remain his.'

Elena stopped outside the restaurant. Through the steamy window she watched the men in suits and women in tight dresses. 'I'm not his,' she hissed. 'Why would you say that?'

In her darkest moments, Elena suspected she was just one of Sergei's many special girls, that he recruited and controlled them all with promises of a life together when this was over: there would be a vast apartment in Moscow with a view of Red Square, the dacha, a place to ski in the winter and another place to swim in the summer. Children!

'He has lots of girls.' Elena lifted her chin when she wanted to sound decisive.

'No.' Danika had begun to shiver. 'It's just you.'

It was hot inside, the restaurant moist and thick with the smells of wine and cigarettes. Danika abandoned Elena immediately and danced through the crowd, plucked two flutes of champagne from the nearest tray, both for herself. Sergei stood in the corner, speaking to two men. His French was heavily accented but he knew everything a man needed to know about wine, cheese, *nos ancêtres les Gaulois*. She knew the rules. No speaking to Sergei, not here. His latest cover had something to do with real estate. She did not understand why he could not stick to one cover. Inevitably, it seemed to her, a past client from one pretend existence would recognize him from another.

What would he say? *No, monsieur, you must have me confused with someone else.* Or would he sprinkle ricin salt on the man's breakfast eggs?

Within an hour, Danika was drunk, so drunk that Monsieur Roche, the head of the French head office of Kara, had to take her aside. Elena, who had been listening to the owner of an advertising agency tell her she ought to be in movies, made her way through the crowd, dodging lit cigarettes, to intervene. The agency man followed her, loudly assuring her that he could take care of it, make the right kinds of introductions.

Though she had been modeling part-time for less than a year, Elena had been offered a career in pictures more than five times – each at a cost of a visit to the right man's hotel room. Her wedding ring never made a difference to them.

'Listen to me, madame,' the agency man was saying to her as he pulled at her dress.

Elena was about to dig her fingernails into his face when Sergei arrived and endeavored to make his way between them. As he did, he pretended to recognize her and spoke in English. 'Is that Elena? Elena Klimentová?'

'It is, sir. And you are?'

'Why it's Graham Spector. Spector Properties. We met in Colmar, if I'm not mistaken.'

'Of course. I remember, sir.'

With this, the agency man retreated and Sergei led her toward Danika, who Monsieur Roche was forcibly guiding into a red banquette. It was a place for four, and Sergei politely removed a young man in a tuxedo and a model from Poland Elena had worked with at a photo shoot for Krug champagne. As they spoke, the only one who did not follow the rule about smiling constantly was Danika.

'People are discussing her, her antics.' Monsieur Roche poured each of them a glass of white wine. 'She threatens to ruin the atmosphere. And what's to stop her from saying something?'

'She will never.' Elena stared at Monsieur Roche. 'Anyway, Dani did not get anything to eat. I'll take her to the hotel.'

Sergei stood up. 'I'll join them and then return.'

Elena helped her friend up and over to the door. On the way, Danika snatched and gulped down another flute of champagne. 'I'm not drunk, you know.'

Elena buttoned Danika's long black jacket. 'I know.'

'It's a strategy of mine, to appear vulnerable.' She slurred her words and did not quite make it all the way through *vulnerable*. 'Then a man will tell me anything.'

They began their journey back to the hotel, Elena shouldering most of Danika's weight. They were not far from the hotel when Sergei arrived with apologies. He did not move as quickly as he once did. Life as a real estate executive had begun to thicken him around the middle.

Danika stumbled and righted herself. 'Empty leisure. That's what you gave our Elena, Sergei. Look at me. Adventure!' Her voice filled the narrow street, deserted in the cold. 'Adventure! She's wasting her talents and you, comrade . . . you know it.'

'But she lives in a beautiful house, Danika. Her husband is spending many thousands of francs, renovating it to make it even more beautiful. A beautiful life. He is, my sources tell me, a kind and loving man, very intelligent, entirely devoted to Elenka. He has given up everything to be a perfect beau. When once he worked to better himself, now he simply vacations in Saint-Tropez with his perfect wife.'

'Do you love him, your handsome Frenchman?' Danika said.

Sergei answered for her. 'Even if she does love him, love is not enough. Is it, Elena?'

13

PRAGUE, 2016

In the Institute for the Study of Totalitarian Regimes, William Kovály was silent. He had removed his glasses and now he was staring into space, thoughtfully. Grace had finished telling him about Petr and Jana and their famous daughter, the ex-wife and confidante of the man who could very easily be the next president of the United States.

When he burst into action, it was to make a list. In Grace's notebook, they wrote down a number of files to seek. They found registry numbers for Elena and her parents, and for Josef Straka. Then the women sitting at the horseshoe desk disappointed them. The files, if there were any files, had already been moved to the old town address of the Institute for the Study of Totalitarian Regimes.

Grace had the route on her iPhone but she did not want to follow it or take William's preferred streets and alleys. She couldn't see anyone behind them, in the rain, but just as before she felt a presence. 'Someone is following us. You know how you just know?'

'No.' William kept up with her, looking around constantly. 'How can you be sure someone just didn't break into your room looking for something to steal?'

Grace told him about the toilet but she did not mention the vibrator. 'Then why didn't they take my computer?'

William did not answer. It was now so windy his umbrella kept turning inside out.

They passed a hip Argentinian hamburger restaurant, and William led them down a dark, cobblestoned street. This was the final block before they reached the Institute so on the way she checked every door and alcove, looked up at the balconies. Cars were parked along the side in both directions but each of them was empty.

'I did a paper once, on conspiracy theories. Can I speculate, Grace?'

'Go ahead.'

'You trained as a journalist, you worked most of your career in supermarket tabloids, and now—'

'I'm not making this up, William.'

'It comes when we enter middle age, doesn't it, a sense of desperation? Last year I very nearly bought an old Aston Martin convertible. It was more than I could afford, and entirely impractical. Needed loads of work. But it was yellow and I remembered, in my youth . . .'

There was a gorgeous old building along the quay. Set back from it was a charcoal box of industrial stone, aggressively plain, with bars along the main floor windows.

Grace reached the door of the old building and tried it. She knocked.

'It's not really a public building,' William told her.

She knocked some more. Then she kicked the door. Ten minutes later, after William made a number of unsuccessful phone calls to people who presumably worked inside, it slowly opened.

A pudgy stump of a man with Einstein hair opened his arms and hugged William. They reacquainted themselves in Czech and he introduced Grace as *'Ameri-chan.'*

They passed something in between a mailroom and a garbage stand and turned right, up some stairs. A man behind a security desk waved at William, and then the three men discussed the time and why this was the right or wrong time, with the building about to close. William pointed at Grace and made a plea. She shrugged and smiled.

'Ameri-chan.'

Inside they passed women and men of all ages, in jeans and sweaters and security lanyards. Grace gathered, from people saying hello to him, that Einstein's name was actually Milan. In his cramped corner office there were newspapers piled on the floor and files everywhere, ironic communist propaganda posters on the wall.

As Milan slumped into his cracked leather chair and entered passwords into his desktop, William reached for Grace's notebook. She was reluctant to give it up.

'He's going to search a few names for us,' William said.

'For me, you mean.' Grace opened the notebook to the page with names and reference numbers.

As Milan looked at the notebook, William said, 'He has the master files.'

'What are the master files?'

William ran a hand through his still-wet hair as he considered how to answer this. 'If a file exists, he will be able to see it. Or at least find it.'

Milan entered names and registry numbers into his desktop and reported the results to William, who translated. He found what Grace had already found in the Cibulka books, that Petr and Jana were on the list of StB contacts, that Jana had a code name. But the Jana file had either been erased or destroyed. There were some documents on Petr and on Elena and Anthony Craig, so Milan printed them out. Josef Straka's reference number led nowhere.

'Almost everything he has on Elena and her husband has been blacked out,' said William. 'And there is very little.'

'That's strange, no?'

'The ex-wife of one of America's most famous industrialists? An icon of capitalism? A man who could end up president?' William paused as Milan typed and shook his head. 'Even in the seventies and eighties Elena would have been Czechoslovakia's most prominent expatriate. Her file should be extensive. At one time there must have been truckloads.'

Milan printed some documents.

'It's funny,' William said. 'Until this morning, I never thought of Elena Craig as having any importance whatsoever. She is famous here. But everything she does is about spa treatments and shopping and gaudy clothes.'

'It's just a role she plays.' Despite the way Elena had treated her, Grace hated it when people said this about her. 'And gaudy isn't fair.'

Milan looked at William like he was about to say something. Instead he turned to the computer and worked some more. He pressed some buttons and his printer clicked back to life. He pulled out two more sheets and handed them all to Grace. Almost every page was heavily blacked out. This was the full file on Elena Klimentová, nearly all of it connected to interviews with her father.

The page on top had a photo of Elena and her address in Manhattan. Anthony Craig's name was on it too, with a number. It was the number that had led to seven mostly redacted pages. There was a similar, older version, clearly typed, with an address in Strasbourg, France. In this one she was called Elena de Moulin. Again, most was blacked out but in the place of Anthony Craig, Jean-Yves de Moulin had been typed.

'Is there information on Jean-Yves de Moulin?' said Grace.

'Another empty file.' Milan turned back to the computer and brought up some documents, read through them, chuckled.

'Can you ask him to share it?'

William did, and translated Milan's response. 'The StB interviewed Petr – a lot. But there's nothing of real interest in the material. It was about Elena and her husband but it's banal and pointless, almost—'

'Boring on purpose?'

Milan pointed at Grace and William translated again. 'That's it. Like they removed the good stuff and left this as a decoy. So we will think it is nothing.'

'Like shopping and gaudy clothes. Right?'

Just after 4:00 p.m. they exited the old building into the street. The rainy day had turned dark and chilly. A fog from the river snaked up into the old town.

'You think Anthony Craig will be elected?' said William.

'I don't know. Elena thinks he will.'

'But the polls . . .'

This conversation bored Grace in all languages. She looked around again. Again, there was no one that she could see but she felt them. William led her to a beer hall called U Fleků ten minutes away from the old town address of the Institute for the Study of Totalitarian Regimes, so he could collect the drink she owed him. There were almost no women in the austere yet jolly room, which was decorated in carved wood. A table full of men in their thirties, dressed for white-collar work, shouted a fearsome song along with a wandering accordion player. Grace and William sat across from one another at a long table, next to strangers. Without asking what anyone wanted, a server plopped down two mugs of black beer with a mountain of foam on top and another man delivered two shot glasses full of an amber liquid.

Grace flipped through the printouts again. The two with the photographs of Elena were similarly structured, similarly blacked out. Whoever was in charge of the Czech version of a Sharpie had left one word, or nearly a whole word. William raised his mug of beer and encouraged her to do the same. They drank and looked at one another, their smiles transforming into something more awkward. Grace pulled the top sheet from the pile of paper Milan had printed off, with the partial word. She held it up to the light, and the hidden word was just about visible: *dňáček*.

'What does this mean?'

William switched glasses and held it up to the light. 'It looks like it could be *Ledňáček*.'

'In English?'

'Kingfisher, in English. The bird.'

Grace drained the shot. Mead. It was too sweet so she chased it with beer. When she looked up, it felt like at least half of the room filled with Slavic men was staring at her. She wiped her top lip, to be sure there wasn't a white moustache.

The printouts suddenly seemed exposed. Grace folded them and closed them inside her notebook. She had also taken photographs with her phone. Now she put everything in her purse and pulled it close.

'People keep looking at me.'

William's laugh powered down. 'What?'

'I don't feel safe.'

'You're a beautiful woman in a room full of drunk men.' William reached over and put his hand on hers for a moment. 'Of course people are looking at you. They can't help it.'

She didn't trust anything anymore: his compliment or his help. What was this place he had taken her to? Grace did not understand a word anyone said, and if she drank any more her judgment wouldn't be worth much either.

'Thank you, William. That's very kind.' She stood up and, at the cash station near the door, asked about the bill. She left double the amount, to buy William another round.

By then, William was with her. 'Where are you going?'

'I didn't sleep well, after everything last night, and I'm feeling . . . weird.'

'Let's have dinner at least.'

'Another time, maybe.'

'Where is this apartment? You mentioned it's above a spice shop? It's nearby? Let me walk you home.'

'No. I'm fine.'

William laughed. 'Come on. I'm a friend. Just an associate professor of history at the 979th best university in the world. Get some sleep and we can make *another time* tomorrow then. I'll come by and take you for a proper dinner.'

'Sure.'

'Let me walk you home.'

She wanted William to walk her home. While there was a clumsy aspect about him, he was more handsome the more she looked at him. He was clearly smart. Maybe it was the lingering effects of her hangover but she was suspicious of him, of his friend Milan, of this beer hall, and she wanted to go through everything in her purse without him. Grace pointed to the place where they had been sitting. There was already another beer waiting for him.

The streets of old town Prague at night, with its pale yellow lanterns and cobblestones, narrow streets, and a steamy café on every corner, seemed to Grace designed for romantic thoughts. She imagined herself in one of them, William across from her, his hand on hers again, and regretted blowing him off. It was the echoing footsteps that pulled her out of her reverie, two sets of them. When she stopped, they stopped. She looked back and two men were on the sidewalk behind her. Grace pretended to check for texts, and they lit cigarettes. It was the two men from the train, the ones who had followed her into the square. The man in the leather motorcycle jacket, with the unsettlingly pretty eyes, was now wearing a black beanie. Continuing on, she used her phone camera as a mirror. The other man wore a long black coat and was slightly bow-legged. When she sped up, they sped up, but they did not get too close. In her left hand, hidden under her sleeve, she carried the paring knife.

Nearer the Charles Bridge there were more people out

strolling in their puffy down jackets, walking their dogs, buying sausages and mulled wine from street vendors. It was at first reassuring to be among them. Then she accidentally entered a crowded mall of tourist knick-knacks at the bridge and lost sight of the men following her. She ensured her purse was zipped tight and wrapped the straps around her wrist so no one could take it from her, preparing to scream and stab if they suddenly appeared too close. Trying to look in every direction at once she bumped into people, apologized breathlessly in what had become her language of pedestrian error: French.

As she passed the entrance to the Charles Bridge the crowds thinned. Two African men in old-fashioned sailor outfits tried to sell her a trip on their boat for the following morning. She listened to their pitch, waiting for her pursuers. She could not see them.

The apartment was only two blocks away. She ran and opened the heavy door that led into the courtyard next to the spice shop, and pulled it closed. For a few minutes she remained on the other side, in the cool corridor, listening for the footsteps.

They came just as she was preparing to walk up to her apartment. At the door they stopped. Grace gently placed her purse on the stone ground. She held the knife in her right hand. In her left she held the apartment keys so the strongest of them protruded from her knuckles, like her self-defense instructor at the Avenue du Parc YMCA had taught her.

It was silent on the other side of the door. The men did not speak to one another or even move.

We are here. We know where you live.

Perhaps five minutes later she heard one of the shoes slide along the cobblestones, then they walked away. Grace was so tense she leaned against the wall of the corridor, to keep herself from sitting down.

Upstairs, she bolted her door and propped a chair against it again. She went through all of her notes and printouts. *Kingfisher*, she thought. There should be truckloads of information about you. Why is there nothing? What are they trying to hide?

Who are *they*?

Grace looked at the page with Elena's address in Strasbourg. Jean-Yves de Moulin. Elena de Moulin.

On her computer she booked a flight for the next morning at six-thirty, from Prague to Strasbourg.

14

STRASBOURG, 1972

Every morning at 9:15, after her breakfast and morning coffee, having made her way through *Le Monde* and *Le Figaro*, Elena ran through the Orangerie Park in Strasbourg.

The storks had arrived, symbols of Alsace, massive beasts that hardly seemed real. Yet here they were, long and white, across the street from her home, making giant nests out of lamp-posts and clicking their beaks at one another. They were both elegant and ungainly at once, which was not terribly far from the way Elena perceived herself.

Like nearly every man she knew in France, Jean-Yves refused to run. For him, the daily morning jog was a harkening back to his origins when men had to stalk and chase their food. While he was convinced that it was good for the muscles and restorative for the mind, he preferred the sophistication of an afternoon swim.

Elena watched the storks calling out to one another, *click click click*, building and repairing their nests. Now and then she caught a sheen of sunshine on the top of an egg. She ran, she stretched, she smelled the blooming lilac. There were ostriches, monkeys, and peacocks at the small zoo on the border of the Orangerie. Kids sprinted from swings to a mini-mountain of ropes in the small playground. At the end of her exercise, to cool down, she walked past the caged animals and felt a special kinship. They weren't so different from her.

That very morning she had watched Jean-Yves sleep. His family had been so successful for so long, through kings and queens and Germans and French, through war and through plague. He carried it in his face, even as he slept. There was not a problem a de Moulin could not solve. To enter the world this way, with this quiet, genteel confidence, she imagined the sort of children they would have. They would be good and polite and handsome, poised for leadership, gifted with modesty and curiosity.

When he opened his eyes, in the morning sunshine, Jean-Yves smiled to see her looking at him.

'What a thoughtful look on your beautiful face.'

Instead of responding, she had simply kissed him. Now, having passed the monkeys and the peacocks, she stopped. Sergei was there, blocking her way, blocking everything, at the park gates, smoking a cigarette. Again he had grown, not only rounder but around the shoulders too. When she first knew him, Sergei had seemed a dangerous youth. Here was a man. His experiences, violent and secret, had nourished and expanded him.

She was shocked by her immediate instinct: to run away.

'It smells like heaven here.' Sergei approached her. 'How lucky you are, Elenka, to have spent a year in such a lovely place.'

They kissed, on both cheeks, like regular French friends. They spoke Czech, but this was a capital of Europe. Foreigners were hardly foreign in the Orangerie.

'Why are you here, Sergei?'

Sergei, in a dark suit with pinstripes, led the way back into the park. 'I came to see you.'

'Only to see me?'

'To extract you.'

'I don't understand.'

'We thought Monsieur de Moulin would amount to more – be more – especially with your encouragement. In fact, he is less. We're going to transfer you to a more fruitful location. Our woman in Montreal didn't work out as we had hoped.'

'You haven't given me the time to—'

'You want to stay? Stay with him? I can't say I blame you. You have fallen into a life of absolute pleasure. Though I cannot see how I can justify your training, or all we've done for you and your family.'

'All you've done? I . . .' Elena thought of her mother in a

fancy new housedress, serving drinks in crystal glasses, her father out in his galoshes with a rifle and a hound.

'It's a courtesy visit, this stroll in the park. Your husband will be surprised, no doubt, by your departure, but I wanted to give you time to pack.'

'When?'

'Tomorrow, Elenka. Tomorrow evening.'

Elena took a deep breath, looked away from him. It took all of her effort to make it seem like this pleased her. 'You will come with me to Montreal?'

'I'll help you get settled. Do you remember that favor you asked of me? For your boyfriend?'

Elena knew he was talking about Josef Straka. 'He is not my boyfriend and you know it.'

'I recruited him. He's there already.'

'In Montreal?' Elena was shocked they had made all of these preparations for her.

'You will have a friend.'

'Thank you, Sergei.'

'And I am in New York now, very close.'

'Why can't I be with you?'

'You know why. We already have three girls in New York. Danika alone . . .'

The way Sergei said her name bothered Elena. Of course he had been with her. He had been with them all. Neither of them would tell her the truth. None of them told the truth. She could not be jealous.

Was she jealous?

Maybe she *could* stay here in Strasbourg. If she revealed everything to Jean-Yves he could protect her. The French secret service, or maybe the English or Americans could make a trade, get her parents out of Prague if she told them what she knew.

She sighed. There was no escape for her any more than the monkeys. Revealing who she was would mean the end of her, of them. The KGB could find anyone anywhere.

'It's a French city.' She smiled at Sergei.

'And New York is so close, Elenka. We will find work for you, reasons to visit.'

'You won't hurt Jean-Yves, or threaten him, will you? This will be hard on him. He loves me.'

'Leave all that to us.' Sergei put his hands on her upper arms and kissed her again, this time on the lips. His mouth was sour with cigarettes. '*À demain*,' he called as he walked back into the park. '*À demain*.'

15

STRASBOURG, 2016

To Grace's relief, Strasbourg was almost ten degrees warmer than Prague. Young people wandered through the compact city in jeans and stylish sweaters, dresses and Ray-Bans, nearly all of them with scarves. There were more bicycles than cars, most of them clunky on purpose. This was a flat city with a sense of humor, Grace thought.

From her hotel in a gorgeous little neighborhood of half-timbered homes surrounded by canals it was only a thirty-minute walk through the busy yet somehow calm center to the Boulevard de l'Orangerie. Though Prague's architecture was brighter, the air in Strasbourg – essentially another Central European city – was more alive, more hopeful.

In her fatigue Grace wondered if the weight of communism

had done something slow and dull to the people of Prague that Strasbourgeois had never experienced, could scarcely imagine.

She looked about her. On the way to the airport at five in the morning there had been no sign of the two men who had followed her the previous day. On two walks up and down the little airplane from Prague to Strasbourg she had made eye contact with everyone. None of them had the face of a murderous thug.

Grace took pictures of Strasbourg and imagined all of it in 1971 and 1972, which was not terribly difficult. Despite Starbucks in Place Kléber and the tram system, little seemed to have changed since the end of the Second World War.

The address of Jean-Yves de Moulin, confirmed online, was a three-storey stone mansion surrounded by foreign consulates. Up top was a fourth-floor tower or loft. The park was across the street. In the front garden, the fruit trees and shrubbery were trimmed and the leaves were raked, the flowerbeds turned and ready for winter. It was an elegant and obviously well-loved place.

The de Moulin mansion was surrounded by a sculpted iron fence with a metal gate. Grace pressed the call button.

'Oui?'

'Monsieur de Moulin?'

The man on the line explained he was Monsieur de Moulin's major-domo. In French Grace explained who she was, that she was working on a biography of Elena Craig. There was at first a long silence. She could hear him breathing through the speaker system.

'Do you have permission from Elena Craig for this book?'

'Of course. I can tell you more about that if you and Monsieur de Moulin permit me.'

The gate buzzed open. An elderly man in a pair of slacks that seemed cut for him, a perfectly white shirt, and a black unbuttoned cardigan sweater opened the door.

'Madame Elliott?'

'Yes, monsieur.'

'I only pretended to be my major-domo. It's his day off. I am alone.' He had made no move to invite her in. 'Did Elena speak of me?'

When Grace shook her head, he smiled with disappointment and looked away.

'How did you find out about me?'

'Through the archives, in Prague.'

'Ah, at the Institute?'

'Yes, monsieur.'

'I would have thought they'd removed it, along with everything else.'

'They?'

Jean-Yves de Moulin looked at her for some time, with his hands behind his back. 'Your accent. Québécoise?'

'I guess so, monsieur. I'm American but I've lived a long while in Montreal.'

'Do you have a document, some proof, that Elena wants me to speak to you?'

Grace shook her head. 'I'm afraid not.'

More time passed in silence. The sun disappeared behind a cloud and reappeared. It smelled good in his magnificent garden.

'My instinct is to send you away, madame.'

'Please don't.'

After a moment, de Moulin spread his hands, allowing her in. He led her around a grand staircase and along a corridor. The architects and builders of the house had done brilliant things with wood, creating loops and swirls and lattices on the staircase banister and along the ceiling. There was a fleur de lys pattern on the parquet floor. The French impressionists had either inspired the paintings on his walls or they had created them.

'Is the art authentic, monsieur?'

Instantly Grace understood it was a question somewhere between naïve and insulting. She was in the house of a wealthy aristocrat. They passed the kitchen: stylish and modern, a hint of Scandinavia in all of this Franco-Prussian adornment.

'Did you grow up here, Monsieur de Moulin?'

He ignored the question and ushered her into his library and office, a festival of leather and dark wood. The moment she stepped inside, and thanked him, there were other footsteps in the hall. Slow and creeping, and then quite fast. Another man stood in the doorway now, younger than Monsieur de Moulin, in black pants, a black vest, and a black tie.

It took a moment for Grace to register that the metal object the man held in an awkward but sure angle and pointed in her direction was a handgun.

'Jesus.' Grace backed into the books.

'This is Nicolas, my bodyguard.'

'Tell Nicolas to put his gun down.'

'Who are you really?' De Moulin spoke a sort of French she rarely heard in Montreal. 'Whom do you work for?'

Grace took deep breaths. She scanned the room for objects she could use as a weapon. 'Monsieur, in my day job I work for Steadman Coe, the publisher of the *National Flash*. Search my name online, if you like. Search his.'

Nicolas came into the library. Grace ducked, to put the desk between herself and Nicolas's gun.

'And who are you to Elena Craig?' said de Moulin.

'I am her ghostwriter.'

'This makes no sense. If you were a ghostwriter, you would simply write what she tells you to write. And she would certainly omit her time in Strasbourg. Another journalist called, back when Elena and her buffoon of a husband were divorcing. He *called*. He certainly did not arrive without an appointment. Would you like to know what happened to him, this British journalist? He jumped off the Clifton Suspension Bridge, in Bristol. I would say he had help.'

Monsieur de Moulin nodded at Nicolas, who moved around the desk. Grace raised her hands.

'Easy, Nicolas.'

'He is simply going to search you for weapons.'

She picked up a stone stork. 'If you search me in the wrong spot, Nicolas, I'll smash your head in.'

'Noted.' Nicolas was a dainty and respectful searcher. He touched her pockets and squeezed her ankles. When he was finished, he shrugged and Grace put the stork back on the desk.

Monsieur de Moulin motioned toward a leather chair and sat across from Grace. His socks were the current socks of young men, with a whimsical blue and yellow pattern. Nicolas stood at attention just inside the door.

'Why are you nervous about me, monsieur?'

Jean-Yves de Moulin looked up at his patterned ceiling. 'Because of the past,' he said. 'Much of it will have been burned and shredded and hidden away in the vaults of extraordinarily powerful people for the purposes of blackmail. But still: there may be something, some errant file, sitting in the wrong drawer. I can imagine one of Elena's former colleagues looking for one of those files in my home.'

'Former colleagues?'

'Current colleagues. Perhaps, madame, I am one of their *errant files*. A truth-teller. These colleagues are men without the capacity for empathy. And I am an old man: ripe for a stroke, a cerebral hemorrhage, a jump off a bridge.'

'Elena married you to escape Czechoslovakia, to get a Western passport. Once she—'

'Madame, when are you publishing this book?'

'Books take years to write and publish.'

'So this conversation is pointless, really.'

'Pointless?'

He leaned forward. 'Nicolas, can you bring Madame Elliott

142

and me a bottle of Gewürztraminer, with some tapenade and Muenster-géromé and crackers?'

Nicolas left the room.

'Madame, if Anthony Craig wins this election, your visit and your book project are worthless. They win. You see? It will be too late.'

Grace laughed. 'The election is in a little more than a week, monsieur.'

'Yes, it is both the most and the least comical thing at once, is it not? This notion that she married me for a passport . . .' He pointed at Grace's notebook. 'When Elena began showing up in the press, in the late 1970s, one of her lawyers or a man posing as one of her lawyers paid me five hundred thousand American dollars to go along with this story.'

'It's not true?'

'I did not need the money. But I do not want to go to sleep at night worried if I will wake up or not.'

Nicolas arrived with a tray. On it there was a tall bottle, open and sweating, two crystal glasses, and a platter with black tapenade, cheese, and some rice crackers. He poured the wine.

'Elena did not need me to escape from *l'Empire soviétique*. She had already escaped, if that is the word one can use. She never did get a French passport. She never needed one.'

'I don't understand.'

It did not seem right to propose a toast or even to touch the rims of their glasses, so they just drank. The wine was bright and sweet.

'She makes it appear we had a sham marriage, an uncon-summated business arrangement of some sort. I was to be a friend of a friend, a sports acquaintance. There is some truth in this. We met and began dating, grew close to one another through a shared interest in physical activity. I had been a ser-ious swimmer, she a gymnast.'

'What I don't understand is how she got here.'

De Moulin shook his head. 'She made it sound like a great escape, in the middle of the night, over the Austrian border. Sneaking past gunmen in towers, dodging the searchlights, tip-toeing over minefields. We all loved this story. We were young and it was very romantic. She was a gorgeous, funny, intelligent woman from an exotic place. We believed every word. It was only later, long after she left me, that I suspected the truth: no regular small-town girl was getting across that border in 1971 without help. I suspect she flew over it in a government plane.'

'You met in 1971?'

'Shortly after she arrived. Elena had a modeling contract with an outfit from Paris, and she came to a big fundraising dinner my friends and I organized twice a year. She sat at my table. I was not terribly keen on my date and she was not ter-ribly keen on hers. For good reason. He was gay as an antelope. We had sport in common, as I said, and she seemed to under-stand my financial position.'

'Which was?'

'Family wealth. Back then I was rather involved in the com-munity, as a young lawyer and as a philanthropist I suppose. I managed my grandparents' trust fund. And I was planning to get involved in the Council of Europe, politics.'

'And what happened?'

'Very little. I worked . . . less. We traveled a lot, to Paris and London and Edinburgh. The Côte d'Azur. I have friends with rather lovely properties in various places. We stayed with them. I thought it would impress her, a peasant Slavic girl.'

'It sounds great.'

'Doesn't it? But it wasn't nearly enough for our Elena. I wasn't her idea of ambitious. She had not risked her life, crossing an uncrossable border, to drink champagne and play charades in Saint-Tropez. I had promised her politics. I had promised her power. Though I don't think I actually promised her any of that.'

'How long were you together?'

'Less than one year, but it was glorious. The best months of my life. It truly was. And I know she thought so too. She left in 1972, for Montreal.'

'Why?'

'I don't know. Two cars arrived. One of the cars had a driver and a man in the back. The driver put her luggage in the boot while the man in the back watched me in the window. We did not speak but I understood what he was saying.'

'What's that?'

'The men in the second car came in without an invitation and they made it quite clear indeed. They stayed four hours. It was, I suppose, an interrogation. They had photographs of me with a prostitute. These photographs were the grounds for divorce. They had the divorce papers already prepared. My only job was to sign them. I owed her nothing, they told me. No money, none of the things we had purchased together. I did not know the woman was a prostitute, and the photographs were taken three nights after I met Elena *before we had even gone on a date.* They said the photos were taken during our marriage, that the prostitute had attested to it, and were therefore grounds for a no-contest divorce. It was so obviously a lie. When I disputed it one of the men slapped me in the face with the back of his hand. I remember one of them said, "From now on if you live, you live at our discretion. Do you understand?"' Monsieur de Moulin looked up again, took a deep breath. 'I think about them every day, these men, how they diminished me in my own home. I did not seek another wife or a family, despite all my dreams and desires, to spare them the . . . danger and darkness, I suppose, that has hung over me since that night in 1972.'

He paused and removed his glasses, wiped them with a little red cloth. His eyes had gone glassy.

'Do you have any proof of this?' said Grace.

'These men were professionals. Are professionals.'

'You said it was an interrogation. What did they want to know?'

'They wanted what I knew about Elena's past. What had she revealed? She was a model, a gymnast, a lovely and clever girl who had a degree from Charles University. For some reason she had chosen me, though I was not nearly her equal in energy or ambition. When her modeling career was over she planned to work with athletes, with sport in some way. She was, as I said, deeply interested in politics and power. I was, increasingly, not. My inheritance provided everything I needed. My career did not interest me as much as Elena did. I was interested in our friends, the family we might build together. We talked about it, the children we would have.'

'Who were they, these professionals?'

'Years later I came to have a friend in the DGSE.'

'What's that?'

'La Direction générale de la Sécurité extérieure. You're American? The DGSE is the French equivalent of your CIA. This friend, my friend in the French secret service, I told him, in confidence, after the fall of the Berlin Wall, what had happened on the night Elena left me. He said they were KGB, most likely, or the Czech equivalent under orders of the KGB.'

'The StB.'

De Moulin nodded.

'The man in the back seat of the car, who drove away with her, what did he look like?'

'About my age, back then, in his late twenties but somehow going on sixty. You know what I mean? High cheekbones, pale skin, eyes without expression. I don't know. It was rather an upsetting night and I'd had a few drinks by then.'

'Who do you think he was?'

'Her handler. Her boyfriend. Her secret service pimp. How am I supposed to know? You must publish this book. Soon or never.'

'But like you said, monsieur, the Berlin Wall came down. All of those men are irrelevant now, aren't they?'

He looked at his watch. 'Don't taunt me. You're here because those men are more relevant than ever. Elena found what she was looking for, not in Montreal but in New York City. I suppose it didn't turn out exactly the way she wanted. The divorce was certainly off-script. But I hear she and Anthony remain quite close.'

Jean-Yves de Moulin stood up with some effort, a hand on his lower back. 'It seems to me, Madame Elliott, that you won't be safe and I won't be safe until this – whatever *it* is – becomes public. Do you agree?'

De Moulin walked her to the door. Grace did not know how to shoot a gun but for the first time in her life she understood why so many of her fellow Americans insisted on carrying one.

Before they said goodbye, he put a hand on her arm. 'Perhaps, as you write, I'll take this opportunity to visit one of our overseas territories.'

'In school, back in Minnesota, I had a pen pal from Martinique,' said Grace. 'That's still a French territory, isn't it?'

Nicolas opened the door and the sun shone in on the parquet floor. Monsieur de Moulin smiled and looked outside.

'Martinique.' The birds called from the Orangerie. Slowly his smile crumbled and he walked back into his home.

When his door closed, and Grace stepped down into de Moulin's garden, she looked around and felt small and fragile and alone.

16

MONTREAL, 1975

It was the fifth day of a damp, windless heatwave in Montreal. Elena Klimentová filled a bowl with ice and rigged it so the fan would blow cool air at their naked bodies. Every twenty minutes, she would empty the meltwater and refill it with ice. Their neighbor at 2311 Boulevard de Maisonneuve Ouest was so in love with the Bee Gees she played their latest album over and over again, and now 'Jive Talkin' was playing so loudly the floor thumped.

In the middle of the song, at almost two in the morning, there was a knock on the door. Neither Elena nor Josef Straka, who lay beside her, had slept.

'Maybe she's come to apologize for the party.' Elena sat up.

'That woman does not apologize.' Josef refused to move. It

was Elena's job to cook dinner on their faulty stove, to wash the dishes in their tiny sink, to take out the garbage, to answer the door. Josef worked long hours at an American consulting firm while he finished the courses and examinations that would make him a chartered accountant. This was all Josef could manage, along with camping trips and nights of *mariáš* with his Czech and Slovak buddies, a card game from back home that she considered an utter waste of time.

She tied a terry robe around herself and walked barefoot to the door. The floorboards were the coolest things in the apartment.

For a moment she did not recognize the man in a suit, standing in the hall, when she opened the door. The fluorescent light had burned out. Behind him, the thumps of feet and the voices of the Bee Gees were punctuated by the occasional whoop from their neighbor and her friends.

'May I come in?'

Sergei Sorokin's crooked smile had not changed, and neither had the darkness in his small eyes, though his hair had thinned to a wisp. This was the look Elena imagined on his face when he sentenced a man to death.

On the first of every month Elena received a check for $3,000 from Kara Modeling Canada, no matter how many modeling jobs she had done. With Josef's salary and the extra money she earned from teaching gymnastics in the winter months they had nearly saved enough for a down payment on an attached house in Westmount, where the wealthy English-speakers lived.

She and Josef were a normal couple, on the way to Canada's upper middle class. In the special program at Charles University they were always told the same story: once you are out in the world, we may never call on you. You may never hear from us.

But you probably will.

Elena took a breath, to calm herself. 'Of course, Sergei. It's lovely to see you. Please.'

His black shoes were, as always, perfectly shined. The only accommodation he made for the punishing heat was a cotton suit.

Elena turned on the lamp in what served as their living room and dining room. There was a television in the corner, next to the fireplace.

Josef stood at the entrance to the bedroom, a towel around his waist. His voice quivered slightly. 'What are you thinking, coming here at this hour? How dare you?'

Though he looked larger, Sergei was not nearly as tall as Josef. Slowly he walked toward the bedroom. Josef backed up as Sergei approached. They whispered at one another, rather grimly, and then with his right hand on his arm Sergei led Josef through the apartment and to the door, opened it, shoved him into the hall with only the towel around his waist.

The door closed. 'But she is my wife,' Josef shouted, feebly.

Josef was her gift from Sergei after her time in Strasbourg: her old friend and gymnastics companion could help her find her mark in Montreal. The marriage itself had been Josef's idea. He had assured her Sergei was not coming back. Who knows if he was even alive? These Soviets, these spies, they disappear without a word, they eat one another for dinner.

The dining-room table was a mess of newspapers and dirty dishes Elena had not cleaned up. And what was dinner, in this heat, but tuna sandwiches with onion and cheese, a six-pack of Molson Export? She was suddenly embarrassed by the state of the apartment, the smallness of it and the disorder. Sergei sat at the table and considered it all, smiled up at her.

'Lovely.'

'Let me just . . .' Elena gathered up the plates and took them into the kitchen, dropped them into the sink. Back in the living room that was also a dining room she folded the newspapers and wiped the crumbs onto the floor. 'I'm sorry.'

'Sit, please, Elenka.'

She sat and he stared at her.

'Sergei, I didn't know what else to do. I was lonely. I met men, but they were men like Jean-Yves. Nice men, regular men, wealthy but . . . I don't know, satisfied. Maybe it's a Canadian thing. They lack a certain—'

'You're not even twenty-five. You've hardly begun.' Sergei gestured toward the door. 'Josef is not your equal. You will divorce him and we will reward him. He will have a good life, a fine career. We will remove all trace of this error. When I saw the article in the newspaper—'

'That was so stupid.'

'It was below you, Elenka. Boasting about your quiet

married life, the life of a model and sportswoman. Did you think I would not see it?'

'I suppose I thought you had forgotten me.'

'Maybe you wanted me to see it.'

Elena put her head in her hands. 'Maybe.'

Sergei took her hand and leaned over the table and kissed her. He reached into her robe and it disgusted her but she could not stop him. 'You will receive a call tomorrow, from the agency in New York. If you cannot find a suitable man in Montreal, perhaps you will have to fly farther.'

'But Danika's in New York.'

'It's a big city. And there are no other girls like you.'

'Josef stays here?'

'The divorce papers will be here by Monday. He has mistreated you.'

'No. He is a buffoon, sometimes, but—'

Sergei leaned forward. There was no malice in his eyes. There was nothing, which was worse. 'He has mistreated you. There are irreconcilable differences.'

She tightened the belt on her robe. 'How long are you in Montreal?'

'Tonight and tomorrow night. I have air conditioning in my room. Will you come?'

'I'll get dressed.' She stood up.

'The car is out front, waiting for us.'

Elena put on her finest summer dress and packed another.

She filled a bag with makeup and toiletries and stared at herself for a while when she passed the bathroom mirror.

It had given her no pleasure to leave Czechoslovakia, to leave Jean-Yves and the friends she had made in Strasbourg. She did not want to leave now, but Josef was her brother first and lover second. There was not really a word for how she felt about Sergei.

Sergei led the way, down the stairs.

'Now listen here.' Josef slammed his open palm into the wall when he saw them together. 'Where do you think you're going?'

In the next apartment they were now doing the hustle. 'Do the hustle!' they shouted, these regular men and women of Montreal.

'I'm sorry, darling,' Elena said, tears in her eyes.

'You can't do this.' Josef hit the wall again. 'I'll kill you.'

Sergei, who had passed Josef without looking at him, turned and quickly climbed back up the stairs. Elena noticed a feline quality about him, as he chased Josef, even with his new weight. She followed them. Josef backed into a brick wall inside the apartment, next to the potted cactus.

'You,' Sergei said, with an eerie calm in his voice. 'Your family, your friends, everyone and everything you love and care about, Straka, I own them all. You're here because I want you here. If you try to fight me, you will lose. And I will enjoy your destruction.'

'Fuck you.'

Part of Elena did not want to watch but she did. She saw the dark, hot, miserable little place for what it was. Behind her, they all shouted, 'Do the hustle!'

'On your knees, Straka.'

'You bastard.'

'Calm your mind. Think. On your knees.'

It took him nearly thirty seconds but finally Josef lowered himself to his knees on the hard wooden floor. The towel came off but it did not matter, not now. For a while Sergei watched him there, far longer than Elena could allow herself. She went downstairs with her bag and opened the door into the hot night, then turned and looked back at 2311 Boulevard de Maison-neuve Ouest, the yellow brick and the maple as thirsty as she was in the ridiculous heat.

A black town car waited for her with its back door open. She stepped inside.

17

STRASBOURG, 2016

On her walk through the lively old center of Strasbourg, Grace could not stop thinking about Jean-Yves de Moulin and the haunted, hunted life he had been forced to lead. They would find him in Martinique. His pursuers would find him in Polynesia, Réunion, or New Caledonia, they both knew it.

It remained so bright and warm she took off her jacket and carried it on her arm. She bought five perfect carrots and a little box of blueberries at an outdoor market and wandered in the direction of the steeple of Notre-Dame de Strasbourg. At Pont Royal, a tidy old bridge, she stopped to take a picture of other bridges, the canal sparkling in the sun. And then she saw the two men from Prague, leaning on the handrail. The bow-legged one was watching her while the other, who had swapped his leather jacket for a red tourist hoodie, typed something into his phone.

They would do to her what they had done to Jean-Yves de Moulin in his mansion, if she gave them the chance: hurt and belittle and haunt her. Grace dug her white earbuds from her purse and spent three long minutes separating them from used tissues and untangling the little wires. When they were plugged in, she dialed her ex-husband, Jason.

Though it was early in the morning he sounded like he had already climbed a mountain. 'Babe. Oh my God. How are you?'

In the background Grace could hear clangs and clanks, the adorable voices of his little girls. She waited a moment. Her instinct in calling him was to ask for help, for advice. Should she walk away from this? Run toward it? 'Really good, yeah. I'm in France.'

'What? Fabulous! Hey, Caitlyn. Grace's in France.'

'Fabulous!' Jason's second wife, Caitlyn, seemed to be incapable of anger or sadness, let alone small emotions like jealousy. She owned three yoga studios in Fort Lauderdale and volunteered as a counseling psychologist in the public school system.

Grace walked down Rue des Pontonniers, toward the center of the city. The two men followed her at their usual distance, made no effort to conceal it.

'Is it just a holiday?'

'No, no. It's work.'

'The *Flash* sent you to France? Or did you finally get another job? Oh my God, Grace, did you get another job? Worthy of that fine mind of yours? No, wait, let me guess: the *Washington Post*. Caitlyn, guess what—'

'Nope, Jason. Same old job.' She passed a white stone building with baby-blue ironwork. As she spoke her phone buzzed with two new texts, from numbers she did not recognize.

Go home
Its not too late

'Grace?'

She realized Jason had been talking. 'Yeah. Sorry.'

'No, no, I'm sorry. Um, did you just call to chat? I really want to catch up but we're trying to figure out Halloween here. Do they trick-or-treat in France?'

'I don't think so.'

'You sound weird. Everything okay? Why would the *Flash* need you in France?'

Grace stopped again and turned. The men stopped behind her. 'I was wondering if you could pick me up at the airport. I'm flying into Miami to see my mom and—'

'You know what: I will cancel whatever I have to cancel. Just shoot me the details. Okay?'

'Are you sure? Is it cool with Caitlyn?'

'Beyond cool. She would hate for us to lose touch.'

Grace tried hard to bury her small emotions. 'Thanks, Jason.'

'Bye, Grace!' Caitlyn shouted and encouraged their daughters, Kellie and Claire, to say goodbye too.

In Place de la Cathédrale there were hundreds of tall senior citizens speaking a Nordic language Grace could not trace and taking photographs of themselves. She confirmed the men were still following her and approached an armed policeman observing the crowd from the steps of the cathedral. It felt so good to be in his presence she said nothing for a moment.

'These men are harassing me.' Grace pointed to them. They were now posing for pictures themselves.

'What are they doing?'

'Following me. They sent these texts.' Grace translated for the policeman. She noted the grammatical error in *Its*, which was difficult to explain in French and only confused the man. 'I'm a journalist and they're threatening me.'

The policeman, who did not yet seem thirty, looked across the plaza. 'How did they threaten you?'

'They broke into my hotel room.'

'Here in Strasbourg?'

'In Prague.'

'You called the authorities?'

'No, because they didn't steal anything. They're professionals. They work for an undercover organization.' As she said it, Grace realized how she sounded.

'Madame, do you have evidence they are threatening you?'

'Just these texts.'

The young policeman sighed and adjusted his hat. 'Wait here.'

When he approached them, the two men made no effort to flee. They smiled as they spoke, and when the policeman turned their attention back to Grace both of them appeared genuinely confused. Less than a minute later the policeman returned. 'There was a misunderstanding. They were walking back from the Orangerie Park. You were too?'

'I was, but—'

'They say they have never been to Prague and that they've never seen you before, madame.' The policeman spoke as though he were bored. He pulled a card from his pocket and showed her the address of the *gendarmerie*. 'If you remain concerned, I encourage you to go to this address and make a formal complaint.'

'Did you get their names?'

'Of course not, madame. This is France. Good afternoon.'

Grace watched the men as she passed through the square. Neither of them looked at her. At the hotel she had booked the previous evening she entered her room, locked it, and went straight into the toilet. The seat was down and when she lifted it she was delighted to see clear water.

For the first time in her life she made the bad financial choice of choosing something from the mini-bar. She cracked open a small bottle of Riesling, sipped it like a beer, and looked out over the River Ill and the olde worlde houses across the way. But the silence was too much. She turned on the television and Anthony Craig was speaking on BFM, the French version of CNN. It was the replay of a rally in a hangar. The crowd was massive, and the cameras tracked thousands of latecomers waiting outside on a sun-baked rectangle of tarmac.

Grace was midway through her Riesling when she noticed something on the computer desk: five Russian nesting dolls, placed in order of size.

There was a small but sturdy electric kettle on the desk. Grace picked it up and wielded it like a bat as she sneaked through the room. There was no one and nothing was out of place.

Grace put the kettle down and inspected the dolls. They were painted wooden shells, light as tissue. Beginning with the smallest, she opened and shook them until she reached the second-largest doll. Grace twisted it open to find a page of newsprint crumpled and tied with elastics into a tight ball. She unfurled it and flattened it on the desk.

The article was in Czech and the only words she recognized were Mladá Boleslav and Vacek and Katka. The photograph was of a burning building. She flattened the article further and realized it was the sporting goods store, with the apartment up top. With the translation app on her phone she discovered the phrase *zemřeli při požáru* meant *deceased in the blaze.*

She felt sick and wanted to scream, but no one was there to hear her. She picked up her purse, opened the door, and sprinted to the stairway. Down the stairs, in the lobby, her heart pounding in her ears, it took a moment to remember what language to speak at the desk.

The woman greeted her with a typically flat, professional French smile. 'Madame?'

'I have to check out early.'

'May I ask why?'

'A family emergency.' There was no mirror behind the desk, but in the reflection of a giant gold plaque with a logo in the middle she saw two men sitting on a couch reading a newspaper together. One of them wore a cheap beret and a tourist kiosk hoodie that said *Strasbourg*. The bow-legged one wore a navy suit and sat with one leg crossed over the other. A picture of harmlessness.

'I hope everything goes well. Though I do apologize, madame. To receive a refund one needs to give twenty-four hours' notice. In this case—'

Grace leaned over the desk. 'Do you want to know the real reason I am leaving?'

'Yes, please.'

'The two men behind me are following me. They have just broken into my room and left a threatening note. They murdered my friends in the Czech Republic, made it look like an accident, and—'

'What?' The receptionist looked past Grace, her eyes wide. Then she asked, discreetly, 'Can you please repeat that?'

Grace repeated herself and the receptionist picked up the

phone, whispered something, and another woman came out from the back. This was the manager, who introduced herself and made her way around the desk.

'These guests?'

'They aren't guests. Well, maybe they are. But they're criminals first. Murderers and stalkers.'

The manager approached them and Grace followed, though she did not like to be this close to them. They were older than they appeared from afar but these were definitely the men from the train, from the square in Prague. Surely at least one of them had pissed in her toilet. Both of them stood up and listened attentively to what the manager said.

The man in the Strasbourg hoodie placed his hand over his heart and turned to Grace. 'You poor woman. I am so sorry this happened to you.' His French had a faint accent about it, but it was obvious he had learned and practiced it in France. 'You have mistaken us for someone else.'

'I just spoke to a police officer in Place de la Cathédrale and these two scoundrels played the same game: *there must be some mistake.* You know what? There isn't a mistake. I'm calling the police.'

The second man, the bow-legged one in the suit, nodded at the hotel manager. 'This is for the best.'

Grace did not know how to call the police in France, as the card for the gendarmerie only contained an address. She asked the manager. The number was 112, the manager said, flatly. Grace dialed it and waited. The woman who answered seemed

to have trouble understanding her accent and Grace's grammatical errors compounded as her heart rate increased and her
voice rose. She could feel the hotel manager and the men looking at her, with a kind of pity.

The dispatch operator asked if she might speak to the
manager.

'This is just terrible.' The man in the hoodie raised his hands
to his mouth in a forced, effeminate gesture. 'Don't you feel for
her, Eric?'

Grace handed the phone over and the manager took a few
steps back and turned away. The bow-legged one, whose nose
was crooked too, winked at Grace.

'Will you two gentlemen please wait here?' The manager
held the phone some distance from her ear. 'Madame, please
accompany me to your room.'

'Of course.'

Grace followed the manager up the stairs and down the hall.
With a master key the woman entered the room and waited
for Grace to pass her and enter. 'Please show me the threatening material.'

'With pleasure.' Grace went straight to the desk, only to see
that the article and the Russian dolls were gone.

The hotel manager stood in front of the bed, whispering
into the phone.

'Well, it's obvious what they did here.' Grace looked at
the manager for a hint of understanding. 'They came in and
removed them.'

'You heard that?' The manager spoke softly into Grace's phone.

'They're trying to make me seem crazy. This is what they do to us, every time.'

'Us?'

'Women.'

The manager ended her call and handed Grace's phone back to her. 'I cannot say what has happened here, but—'

'I'm a journalist, working on a story those men don't want me to tell. They broke into my hotel room in Prague and they broke into this one. They're sending me texts. Do you want to see them?'

The manager sighed. 'I would be happy to give you a full refund.'

Grace followed her down the stairs and, at the desk, waited as they put 112 euros back on her card. The men were reading their newspaper again. 'You watch. They won't stay at your hotel.'

The clerk looked at her manager.

'They will come after me, I am telling you.'

When she was finished and the sliding doors opened for her, the man in the Strasbourg hoodie called out: 'Good luck, madame. Remember: you're not alone.'

18

NEW YORK, 1976

'This is not where we wanted to have this party, okay? Let's be honest: this is an old and ugly room and New York deserves better. This is a night to celebrate American luxury, and no one, *no one* wants to do it in a drafty barn. But we couldn't find any ballrooms in this bankrupt city – hey, are we bankrupt yet? Mayor, Mayor Beame, are we bankrupt yet? – any ball-rooms with doors big enough to bring in my beautiful cars. I had good people on it, the best. Still: nothing. New York, the greatest city in the world, bankrupt or not, deserves so much better.'

Elena had never heard a more bizarre opening to a speech. The speaker had papers in front of him on the podium but he was not reading from them. Surely, the owner or manager of the New York Coliseum was in the room somewhere, feeling miserable. Why would he say those things about the mayor right in front of him?

The brochures on each table had a photograph of Anthony Craig on the front, standing with cars and women. Inside, there was a brief story about how Craig Bearings, a family company, had become Craig International under the leadership of its new CEO.

Bizarre or not, the man could draw a crowd. Then again, Elena and her friends from Montreal were only here, at tables in the back, because the organizers had given Kara Modeling a bit of money, a pile of tickets, and promises of free champagne and gourmet food as long as the women wore gowns. Looking around the room, at other young women in gowns, Elena decided the organizers had probably given free tickets and a check to every agency in New York.

'America invented cars.' Craig looked down briefly at his notes, but again he seemed to abandon them. He wore a pin-striped three-piece red suit with an enormous tie, and he kept struggling to keep his mop of hair in place. 'We invented luxury. We did that. It never existed before us.'

Elena looked around, to see if anyone else knew about Europe.

'But we're losing in luxury cars. We've become lazy, lazy and stupid. When I was a kid a Cadillac meant something. Today, what does it mean next to a fake luxury car, the Monte Carlo, an absolute phony? Lincoln once felt like luxury. Now it's a joke, lipstick on a pig, an absolute pig. My father, he's here tonight, my father had a Continental Mark II in 1956. Remember that, Dad? Now that was a luxury car. You sat in it and you felt like all that hard work had come to something. That was *American luxury*. And you know what, my friends? We've given up. What's a Continental today? A jalopy. We're not building American luxury anymore and you know who's figured it out? The Germans. The Germans are back, my friends, and they are *cleaning our clocks*. Cleaning our clocks.'

Ever since her first month in the special program in Prague, Elena had known what she was looking for. Yet he was an abstraction, this ideal man. Nearly everyone she met, with money and power, with wild ambition, was *healthy* in a way that made him irrelevant to her and to her mission. Jean-Yves was her first mistake. He was not egotistical. He was not a liar. His friends were not closeted homosexuals or secret gamblers.

This man on the podium was something else. This man burned with spirit. Yet he also, very clearly, felt he was not good enough. Elena tried to imagine how many times he looked at himself in the mirror in the course of a day. She knew how to speak to a man like this.

You flatter him.

His speech went on for nearly an hour. He complained about the building some more, about New York's roads and sewers, about the poor state of first-class airline travel, about Germany and its cheating ways, about the Japanese who were also figuring us out and cleaning our clocks, all our former enemies making fools of us, and then – finally – six exceptionally tall women in white satin dresses lifted the sheets off three cars.

Craig led the applause. 'Yes!' he said, about his own creations. 'America has luxury again.'

He invited his audience to touch the cars, to sit in them, while another group of women in matching white dresses distributed new brochures, each with a photo of Anthony Craig on the front.

Dinner was served and a band started to play.

Danika refilled her own flute of champagne, her fourth or fifth already. She was dating the senior assistant to John J. Marchi, a New York State senator. His name was Carlos. His family had practically been royalty in Cuba until Fidel Castro had stolen everything and kicked them out. Now Carlos was angry but in a different way than Anthony Craig appeared to be, and Elena suspected he mistreated Danika.

'What did you think of that speech?'

Danika looked down at the program. 'It was only supposed to last ten minutes. I'm starving.' She looked around to be sure none of the other models could hear. 'What a dingdong. No wonder he had to pay us to come.'

They were seated far from the front, far from Anthony Craig, and it would be a long time before they were served their first course. Elena excused herself from the table, to go to the restroom, and she took the long way – past his table.

Anthony Craig was standing up and speaking to Mayor Beame, a tiny man with gray hair and dark eyebrows. When people talked about the mayor, they always said the same thing: *he has the hardest job in the world.*

She eased close enough to hear their conversation, pretending she was looking for someone at the adjacent table.

'It was theater, Abe. You of all people understand theater.'

'But I'm sitting at your table. Everyone can see that. We've been exceptionally good to you . . .'

'And my business spends an exceptional amount in this fucked-up city of thieves and murderers. You need to clean it up, Mayor Beame.'

The mayor shook his head and laughed. His wife, clearly uncomfortable, pulled gently at his arm. She was carrying her jacket and her purse.

'You might spend a lot, Anthony, but you sure do ask for a pretty penny from city hall. I mean, for a free enterprise guy . . .'

Elena chose this moment to walk slowly past the table, close enough to brush Anthony Craig's arm. He was already looking away from the mayor, as though he had lost interest. The mayor was not going to get the apology he wanted, and Mrs Beame knew it.

As their arms touched, Anthony Craig reached for her. She pretended not to notice at first, even when his hand was on her shoulder.

'Thank you for coming,' he said. 'What do you think of the cars?'

'Lovely. Congratulations.'

'Oh my God, I love that accent. Don't you think you'd look good in one?'

'I suppose so, Mr Craig.' Elena didn't stop walking or turn around.

He called after her, something else about her accent and 'that eastern look'. Elena pretended not to hear, and made her way back to her table as the salad course was being served. She was about to sit when a young man in a black suit stopped in front of her.

'Mr Craig wants to know what you're drinking,' he said, a little breathlessly.

Elena gestured at the bottle of champagne on their table.

'He'll send you another one.'

She smiled and looked down. 'If he insists.'

The young man pulled a small notebook out of his pocket, and a pen. 'What's your name?'

Danika and the others at the table were listening.

'Why would he want to know that?' said Elena.

'Mr Craig likes to keep track of his guests, that's all.' The man lowered his voice. 'VIPs like yourself.'

Elena told the young man her name, guiding him through the spelling of it. When he asked if she was a New Yorker or a tourist, she told him the truth: she was here to promote American tourism to Montreal as the 1976 Olympics approached. There was an event at the Plaza the next day.

'You're staying at the Plaza?' said the young man.

172

Elena nodded.

'Sorry, it's my job to do stuff like this. Thanks, Miss . . . Klimentová.'

Elena and Danika stayed for the salad and soup courses. When the new bottle of champagne arrived, Elena poured it for her tablemates. Danika drank three glasses, then accompanied her back to the Plaza.

In her room they ordered a pot of mint tea. Danika poured vodka in her cup, from a flask she kept in her purse, and finally told Elena about Carlos, how he fell into rages.

'Let's contact Sergei, tell him.'

'Sergei was here last month. I told him.'

'And . . . ?'

'And nothing, Elenka. Carlos is going to run for the Third Congressional District in the next election. The crazier he is, the better. You know that. If it comes with a bit of violence, all the better.' She sat up straight, feigned perfect sobriety, and impersonated Sergei. 'We want him and we need him.'

'I'll visit your Carlos tonight with a baton. Then he'll think twice about hurting you. Where is the bastard?'

'Washington.' Danika poured a bit more vodka into her mug.

'I'm sorry.'

Danika blew into her tea and vodka. 'I suspect we will spend our lives apologizing to one another.'

There was a knock on the door. Elena looked through the peephole to see a porter carrying something enormous. She

opened the door and he entered with a basket of fruit and chocolate and nuts. Both women laughed at the size of it. Danika
gave him a dollar while Elena opened the card.

Dear Elena,

   Tonight was a great night. The cars were a hit. They are
going to sell like crazy. My only regret was that I couldn't
get to know you better. I hope to rectafy that.

                                             Yours, Anthony

She showed the card to Danika.

'Sergei will love this one,' said Elena. 'He even misspelled
"rectify".'

'You're a very lucky girl.'

Danika laughed, but Elena thought for the first time since
entering the program that she might be.

19

Grace begged her taxi driver to pull over in a village called Lingolsheim, on the way to the Strasbourg airport. Her face was hot and she was faint and dizzy. If she did not get out of the car, immediately, she would either pass out or throw up. In a mess of ferns and evergreens between two tidy whitewashed houses, she suspected the men following her had found a way to poison her.

'Madame?' the driver called through his open window. 'Should I take you to the hospital?'

It felt somewhat better to be bent over, her hands on her knees, with the scent of wet fern. No, they hadn't poisoned her. She was feeling exactly the way they wanted her to feel.

A lovely woman and her father had burned to death and it was her fault. She retched.

'Maybe I will go.' The driver stepped out of the car, opened the back door, and began to lift her bag out.

'No, wait,' said Grace. 'I'm fine.' While she was not fine, seeing a strange man hold her bag with her phone and note-book inside inspired a jolt of adrenaline. She ran toward him and shouted at him to put the bag down. The driver dropped it and backed into his Citroën with his hands up.

At the airport she paid the driver and looked at herself in his rear-view mirror. Her hair was wild, and there was a sheen of sweat on her forehead. She wiped it away with a tissue and, from the back seat, scanned the area behind her for her pursu-ers. What had Jean-Yves de Moulin said about men like these? They lived *without the capacity for empathy.*

In the security lineup she looked in every direction. Even now, knowing what she knew, there was no way to report the men to the police. There were no immediate flights back to Prague so she settled into a ninety-minute wait in the airport bar with her back to the wall. She had abandoned her carrots and blueberries in the hotel room, and while she was not hungry she knew she had to eat. She ordered an oniony tarte flambée and a water instead of another glass of white wine.

She thought of William. Would he also die in an accident? How about her mother, or Jason and his family, Manon, Stead-man Coe? She had spoken to them too. Grace was staring at the tarte flambée when a woman she recognized – from where? – walked through the bar with a giant smile.

'Oh my God. Grace?' The woman wore plenty of makeup and seemed dressed for a cocktail party instead of a flight, with a red tight-fitting dress. She carried a glass of white wine in one hand and a little red Yves Saint Laurent handbag in the other. 'Grace Elliott?'

The moment she heard the woman say her name she remembered. 'Tanya?'

'What are the *chances*?' Tanya gestured at the chair across from Grace. 'Are you . . .?'

'Alone, yes. Please, join me. Wow, it's great to see you.'

While great wasn't honest, Grace did welcome the comfort of distraction. Tanya Bischoff had been one of the top students in their graduate program, a master's degree in journalism, where the grades didn't matter. Success was networking: building a national or global team of people who could potentially hire you. When last she saw Tanya it was at the fifteenth anniversary of their graduating class at the Hilton in Galveston, Texas. Fewer than twenty of them showed up and only nine people were still in journalism. Grace had gone because she had been such a bad networker when she was in her twenties. Now that she had confidence and lacked shame, she could ask anyone for just about anything. The only problem was that no one could possibly help her do what she really wanted, which was to leave the *Flash*.

Had she even spoken to Tanya in Galveston?

177

'What are you doing in Strasbourg?' said Tanya. 'Holiday?'

'Just a bit of work.'

'Does the *Flash* have overseas bureaus?' Tanya did not do a great job of hiding that she found this comical. 'What are you working on?'

'It's too boring to tell.' Grace looked over Tanya's shoulder, to be sure her pursuers had not arrived. 'What about you?'

'I had to cover the signing of a trade agreement today.' Tanya yawned. 'But I'm off to Paris, and then to New York and Washington to cover the election. Hey.' Tanya pointed. 'We're growing. You're not looking for a more typical reporting job are you, a senior correspondent job somewhere?'

'Who do you work for, Tanya?'

'RT.'

Grace did her best job of hiding her reaction by stabbing her tarte flambée with a plastic fork. 'That's Russia Today, right?'

'That's the old name. It's like the BBC, only from a different country. We broadcast in English, French, Spanish. Even Arabic, if that's your thing.' Tanya leaned over the table. She had freckles on her nose and under her eyes, and a hint of them peeked through her makeup. Grace felt the panic from the back seat of the taxi creeping back into her chest and she beat it back, faking a smile, as Tanya talked about her employer. While she had never seen a broadcast or clicked a link, she had first heard about RT from taxi drivers in Montreal, who tended to blame every bit of woe and suffering in the world, including their own, on American malevolence and aggression.

'I don't understand,' Grace said. 'Every news organization in the world is shrinking. Except yours?'

'Our only shareholder is an enterprising government, and they understand our value.'

'And what is it?'

'The truth, of course.'

'And you have hiring authority at RT? You can make me a job offer at a bar in a tiny airport in eastern France?'

Tanya shrugged. 'They like me. They want more of me.'

'I'm forty-three years old. Isn't that too old to be on-air?'

'And I'm forty-four. They're very ambitious. Very aggressive.'

Grace looked around the airport bar again, this time without any worry about seeming impolite. '*Very aggressive.* So what did they tell you about me?'

'Pardon?'

Grace watched her classmate's face.

'If you're going to bribe someone, it has to be slightly better than this.'

'I have no idea what you're talking about. We're expanding. You're a good journalist.'

'How do you know?'

Tanya placed her hands on the zinc table and pushed her chair back. She stood up and finished her glass of wine in one gulp. 'If I knew you were going to be hostile . . .'

'They're murderers, Tanya.'

'I don't know what you're talking about.' She would not look at Grace. 'I was just trying to help an old friend.'

'We were never friends.'

Tanya smiled again. Her teeth were even whiter than Violet Rain's. 'You're no better than me, Grace. Don't even pretend to be.'

'I guess I should be thankful you didn't just walk up and stab me.'

Tanya placed a hand on her purse. 'I don't know what you're caught up in, Grace, but . . .' And she left, weaving through the tables and down the corridor in her red cocktail dress.

Grace only managed a few bites of her tarte flambée. She wanted to call her mother, Manon, or even Jason again. Instead she pulled out her computer, connected to airport wifi, and searched for anything to do with spies, sex, the StB, the KGB, kingfisher, and defection. She found a *Washington Post* article by Michael Dobbs from 1987 with the word *Sexpionage* in the headline.

The list of known KGB entrapment victims since World War II is long, distinguished and remarkably varied. It includes men and women, bachelors and married couples, young and old, homosexuals and heterosexuals, military attaches and journalists, security guards and ambassadors. No category of Western resident in Moscow, it seems, has been immune from the charms of Soviet 'swallows' and 'ravens', KGB jargon for professional seductresses and their male counterparts.

Grace wrote 'professional seductresses' and 'swallows' in her notebook, and read about a number of prominent men who had been lured into compromising relationships with beautiful and intelligent women. She wrote down a quotation from an author who had studied the KGB and had published standard books on the subject, John Barron.

What people fail to realize is that operations like these involve much more than simply a boy-girl relationship. It's not a situation in which the lone westerner is confronted by the lone Russian temptress. In reality, it's one isolated individual against a massive, very experienced apparatus. All the circumstances are controlled by the KGB to maneuver the victim to a desired end. Sexual enticement, and the lure of a fulfilling relationship, is just a first step across the threshold. But once it is taken, retreat can be very difficult.

20

PRAGUE, 2016

Her pursuers were not on the flight to Prague. Now that Grace knew who they were and what they were capable of, she doubted they bothered to fly commercial.

When she landed she looked up the address of the FBI's office in Prague, which was housed in the American embassy in Malá Strana. It was late evening, but she could not imagine it had opening hours. Her Uber driver spoke no English. Grace was alone in the back seat of a Volkswagen, bombed with air freshener, and her fears. If they could break into her hotel rooms, and find her at a restaurant at a little airport in Strasbourg, these men without empathy could find her mother in Florida.

The American embassy was a beige stone building in a well-lit cobblestone plaza. Soft lamps shone in upper-floor windows and three luxury cars were parked opposite: a silver BMW and two large black Craig sedans. No one stood in front of the building keeping guard, though two men in black watched from the shadows across the street. She was pleased to see them.

Grace pressed the call button outside the door.

'I'm a journalist,' she said, when a man's voice asked if he could help her. 'I've been threatened.'

'American?'

'Yes. Threatened by killers.'

Ten seconds later the door opened. A handsome black man in an armed forces uniform stood in an enclosed chamber. She repeated she was a journalist, working on a politically sensitive story, and that she had been harassed and violated by foreign agents who had murdered two Czech citizens.

'Slow down. Agents?' He opened a small notebook and prepared to write. 'How do you know they're agents?'

Grace drew a breath, aware that her voice was becoming shaky. 'Sorry. Men.'

'So not agents. Men are harassing you. Have you spoken to the police? And what's this about a murder?'

'I spoke to police both here in Prague and in Strasbourg, where these men followed me. Also, there was a fire yesterday in Mladá Boleslav. In the press they're calling it an accident but believe me it was no accident.'

'Why do you believe this is the case?'

Grace explained, without naming names, about a powerful

American who had been seduced by a woman who might be a spy, a swallow. Had he heard of swallows? This woman, this swallow, had a KGB code name and so did her parents, and while Grace knew the KGB wasn't a thing anymore it didn't matter: it might have been the StB, not the KGB. One answered to the other.

The soldier stared at her in an appraising way. She had rambled a bit, and wished she could start over. He had not written anything in his notebook.

'The integrity of the American election is at stake!'

After a while, with a faint sigh, he stepped into a small office. Then he emerged with a clipboard and a three-page form to fill out. 'Please describe your situation.'

'Wait.' Grace knew what the young soldier thought of her. 'Once I'm finished describing it, what happens then?'

'Tomorrow morning, when the staff come in, they will evaluate it and contact you.'

'I want to speak to someone now about this, rather than write it down.'

'Why?'

'Because of the nature of the story I'm pursuing.'

'Can you tell me the nature?'

'I just did!' Grace handed the clipboard back to him. 'It's very sensitive. I'm in danger.'

He readied his notebook again. 'What publication do you work for?'

'It isn't for my publication.'

'You're a freelance journalist, then?' Now there was genuine fatigue in his voice. 'Unemployed?'

'I work for the *National Flash*.'

The soldier frowned. He had still not written a word in his
notebook. He gave her the clipboard again. 'Fill out the form,
ma'am. Let me know when you're ready.'

Grace looked through the three pages. 'Can you let me into
the embassy, so I can speak to an FBI agent?'

'No, ma'am.'

'You don't have a tipline?'

He pointed to the form on the clipboard. 'You can do it here
or you can do it online.' He went into his office and re-emerged
with a card. 'You can also phone this number and leave a message, if you prefer. Someone will call you back for more
information as needed, in one to five business days.'

'As needed?'

'Yes, ma'am.'

Through the blastproof glass the main floor of the embassy
was dotted with soft lamps, the same ones she had seen from
outside. Grace imagined sitting next to one of the lamps in a
brown leather chair, on the other side of safety, a glass of whiskey in her hand. Then she imagined the number of people who
came by the American embassies of the world with stories.
There was a word for what these murderers, what this *massive,
very experienced apparatus* had done to her: gaslighting.

Grace saw herself the way the young soldier saw her: crazy.
She handed the clipboard back to him.

'You have a great evening, ma'am.' There was a trace of triumph in his voice as she stepped out into the street.

She decided to walk back to her apartment. It wasn't far. With one turn she would reach the pedestrian street that led to the Charles Bridge. Before she reached it, just as she passed from the light of a streetlamp into a pond of shadow, she heard, 'Stop.' It was not the way an English speaker would say stop.

She turned and the two men in black from the embassy plaza jogged through the shadows. Heavy items on their belts rattled as they made their way over the cobblestones. For an instant, while they remained in darkness, she thought these men were here to help her, to call what had happened in the foyer a travesty and to escort her into leather chairs, soft lamps, whiskey, whispers.

But only for an instant.

When they entered the yellow streetlight, she recognized them. She turned and ran, but they were faster than her. She had removed the knife from her bag, for airport security, and as she ran she could not find her keys.

They reached her and shouted in her face, shoved her onto her knees and then onto her chest. One of the men yanked her bag away. The other pulled her hands behind her back and it hurt so much she thought her arms would snap. Her head fell forward and she scraped her chin on the stone.

She tried to scream, 'Help,' but it was too hard to take in a deep enough breath.

In the distance she saw some people walking past. She tried to scream for help again and they turned to look but did not come to her aid.

'Please!' she sobbed. 'Help me!'

There was a knee on her back now. She was certain she would die, that she would never speak to her mother or her friends again. They would kill her like they had killed Katka and Coach Vacek.

She thought of Jason – lovely, kind Jason. Why had she not wanted to have kids with him? Now she was going to die alone, with gravel in her mouth and a knee on her back, in the shadows of a street in Prague.

'Let me go. I'll do whatever you say. Please.'

Rough hands reached around and under her, into all of her pockets. Breath mints, tissues, a dogshit bag from walking Manon's Yorkshire terrier.

Then they were off her, allowing her to turn so she could see them again. The bow-legged one was lighting a cigarette. His partner with the pretty eyes and the bulbous nose pulled the printouts from her notebook and stuffed them into his pants pocket. Then he played with her iPhone.

'What is the password, Grace?' He was a bit breathless, from running and fighting her. 'Your password, and we go. Otherwise . . .' He mimed a kick with his big black boot.

'I'm calling the police!'

The bow-legged man laughed.

'Password, Grace.'

They liked saying her name. 'Fuck you,' she spat.

A moment later the one with her phone and the notebook stepped forward and kicked her to the ground again, with his heavy boot. He placed it on her chest and she tried, with all of her strength, to move it off or to wriggle away but he was too strong. She could hardly breathe. 'Grace. You can stop speaking to the FBI now.'

'Or anyone else,' said the bow-legged one.

Grace tried to create a gap between her chest and the man's boot so she could breathe.

'We know who you are. We know who your loved ones are. We know where you are going.' He held up her iPhone and the notebook. 'Soon we will know everything, and we'll have no need for you. Unless we work together. Yes? Now who have you spoken to about this?'

The man took his boot off her chest for a moment and she gasped.

'I've already written the story. The people who have it, if they don't hear from me—'

He stepped on her again. 'What people?'

Light shone from behind the two men, headlights, and a car approached. The murderer slid his boot from her chest to her face and pressed hard enough that her nose exploded with pain. With a final push the back of her head cracked into the cobble-stones. Then as the car came closer the men walked past her and turned left away from the Charles Bridge.

Grace struggled to her feet and shouted at them, too furious to cry. Her nose was bleeding. The car, one of the Craigs from the embassy, slowly passed her. She could not see inside.

The men had stolen nothing else from her purse. Her wallet and passport were still there, with panties and socks, deodorant, a brush, tampons, Four Seasons shampoo and conditioner, lipstick, and an eyebrow pencil. There were no tissues so she used the panties to stop her nose from bleeding.

Rather than go back, pointlessly, to the embassy and fill out a form, she walked towards the Charles Bridge, wondering why the men had not killed her. When they discovered whom she had spoken to, that no one had the story, that there *was no story*, would they be as gentle with her?

Among the tourists, there was a bright store selling phones, phone cases, SIM cards, and accessories. Grace bought a cheap Samsung with a minimal data package.

It was late afternoon Montreal time when Steadman Coe answered.

'You in your office?' she asked.

'I am. Where are you calling from? This number—'

'I'm still in Prague and I've just been attacked. These men have been following me. They stole my notes and my phone. I realize now they've hacked into my computer and they knew what I'm working on. I'm so stupid.'

'What men, Grace? *What* are you working on? What do you mean *attacked*?'

'Steadman, listen. I'm working on a story. It's big.'

'Is this about Violet Rain? That's not a story. I should know because I own it. And if this is about that book idea, I already said no. She doesn't want it. Josef Straka told me—'

'I was with Elena, in her hometown, and then I went back. I met these people who told me about her childhood, about a man, a Russian man. I think he was KGB. And her own parents—'

'What does this have to do with getting mugged?'

'I didn't get mugged!' Grace paused, took a breath. 'Elena isn't who we think she is, Steadman, and I think it's important for next week, for the election. If we hurry . . .'

'If we hurry, what?'

'This could change everything. The people who told me about her, from her hometown, they died yesterday in a fire.'

'An accident?'

'No, definitely not.'

'Wait, wait, wait. Is this Russian shit?'

'Yes. I'll write it up, what I have now, from memory, and I'll send it to you.'

'Grace: no. We can discuss this when you're home but don't you write a goddamn word about this. First of all, Anthony and Elena divorced a million years ago. Second, no one fucking cares about Elena despite our best efforts to keep her in the starry firmament. Third, this Russian shit: no goddamn way. It's fake. We haven't worked this hard to let it all go, based on a bunch of garbage rumors. Listen to me: come home.'

'I'm flying to Miami to see my mom tomorrow, then I'm

coming straight to you. And you'd better cancel my phone and report it stolen.'

'Do not write a *word* about this.'

Grace ended the call and looked down into the darkness of the Vltava River. She thought of the British journalist who had been helped off the Clifton Suspension Bridge. She realized she had been out of breath the whole time, like she had just climbed three sets of stairs.

Then she crossed the bridge with dozens of ordinary late-night tourists who were – like her – on their way back to their beds for the night. But unlike her, they did not have blood on their faces or boot marks on their chests or the taste of cobble-stone in their mouths.

21

The day before her wedding, Elena Klimentová told her fiancé she needed to do a bit of last-minute shopping. She had forgotten to buy gifts for her bridesmaids: Danika and two other Kara girls, one Russian and one Slovenian. Anthony did not seem to care about her absence. The new Craig sedans were not selling well, and he was having trouble managing the expectations of 'whiny, impatient, weak' dealers in Podunk, America.

Happily, the bearings side of the business, the part that interested him the least, was doing well enough that losing money on cars was not yet calamitous.

Elena had helped him see that marrying a glamorous woman with an exotic accent would help the Craig brand. It was a good story and he was already telling it: *an Olympic gymnast who*

192

comes from European car manufacturing royalty is squished by communism. Her parents, who can't even get out of the country for their only daughter's wedding, languish in Czechoslovakia. Lining up for hours, for bread and toilet paper! Yet here she is, one of the chief designers at Craig International.

Anthony was not yet famous enough to draw press photographers and no one in the city knew who she was, so it did not matter where Elena went after the driver dropped her at Bloomingdale's. It was a ten-minute walk south on Lexington Avenue to the Hotel Beverly.

The Beverly was a lovely Beaux Arts hotel but it would be on no one's top ten list. Elena did not think Anthony would allow a client or partner to stay in a place like this. If it were her hotel, she would rip down all of the old curtains, replace the carpet, and shine a light on the carved stone. Elena went straight to the elevator and hit the button for the third floor. Sergei had taught her a way to identify herself at his door. It went *knock [pause] [pause] [pause] knock-knock-knock.*

By the time she reached his room Elena had worked herself into an emotional wreck. For over a year she had been pretending, but never more than in the past weeks. Whenever she broke down in tears, Anthony assumed it was because her father and mother could not be here for the most important day of her life. She did not know many happy women but there were a few, and what they had in common was choosing the life they led. Nothing made a woman more unhappy than feeling trapped – by the wrong man, by poverty, by religion, by tradition.

Danika was now married to Carlos, who still worked for the senator, who still planned to run for the House of Representatives, who still called her a whore and blamed her for his failures and hurt her when he was drinking. Danika drank as much as Carlos did now, and needed cocaine for fun and Valium for sleep. She had become a genuine New Yorker.

It felt queer to choose Danika as her maid of honor, and other swallows as bridesmaids. There was no *honor* in anything they did, but they were her only real friends, the only ones who understood.

Of course Sergei would claim the opposite: their work, their sacrifice, was all about honor.

Knock [pause] [pause] [pause] knock-knock-knock.

When Sergei was visiting New York under his pseudonym, pretending to be a violin dealer who had defected to Paris, he dressed like other Western men in bright, garish polyester jackets. But today, in the lamplit quiet of his hotel room, he wore a muted blue wool suit.

She had hoped it would make her feel better to see Sergei, but now she felt worse. The room smelled of whiskey. His shirt was untucked and what remained of his hair was greasy and combed haphazardly.

Once she was inside they kissed and embraced and he whispered Czech into her ear. 'Speak no louder than this.'

'But they don't know who you are.'

'They could, Elenka.' He went to the desk beside the bed, where he had set up a portable typewriter. There was a bottle of Jameson off to its right and two glasses. One was half full and there were drips and little puddles all about it. Sergei filled up the second glass, nearly to the top, and handed it to her.

'To love.'

She lifted her glass. 'To love.'

Neither of them spoke. The sounds of the city below, honking, sirens and random shouting, leaked in through the thin windows. She had wanted to tell Sergei everything, to shout it at him the moment the door closed behind her. But here he was: clammy with perspiration and heavy on his heels, like a fighter at the end of a losing night. He put his left hand on her face. She thought he was going to kiss her again but instead he whispered in her ear that none of the other professors in the program had seen what he had seen in her. There were a hundred swallows around the world but not one of them had achieved what she had achieved. His success was assured.

Elena wanted to leave. She had imagined all of this differently. Sergei was turning into someone else, no better than Anthony. Now he took off his jacket and began unbuttoning his shirt. There was not a drop of blood in her body that wanted what he wanted.

'Sergei,' she said, 'I don't have enough time.'

This was not true and he knew it wasn't. He held her roughly and she dropped the glass full of whiskey and he laughed. 'You're in luck. I don't need much time.'

Under him, in the soft light, willing him to hurry, she began to cry. For a moment she was afraid of what he might do but he only licked the tears from her cheek like it was something he had done before, with another woman on the day before her wedding.

She had brought her diary with her, with the list of weak and failing men, the bankrupt, the men who propositioned her, the secretly gay. Elena had never considered herself to be an agent or a spy. She did not do the work of turning or compromising anyone. There were no fistfights or gun battles. She had formulated no poisons. Compared to the other women in her social circle in Manhattan, her life was boring.

When Sergei finished he sat naked and moist on the bed, Humpty Dumpty with hair, she thought.

'Good girl.' He read through her diary and sipped his whiskey. 'This is more perfect than perfect.'

The more she achieved, the more her parents would receive. There were advantages. In September, she and Anthony would move to a four-bedroom penthouse apartment with a view of the park, a two-million-dollar wedding present from Anthony's parents, which she had already begun renovating. Anthony trusted her completely to do it, and to plan the children's bedrooms as well. He wanted a big family: five kids, maybe six.

'We want to make as many babies as we can,' Anthony had said aloud, at a dinner in Aspen with his most successful dealer and his wife. 'Look at this woman. Hell, look at me! It's our duty.'

Elena knew what Sergei would ask of her when she heard Anthony speak this way: praise him, laugh at his wit. The goal of the program was achingly simple: to encourage and create agents of disorder and chaos in America, to use democracy as a weapon against itself.

Sergei mumbled into his glass of whiskey and waved at Elena, who was nearly finished getting dressed. 'Go on. Marry your industrialist before you get too old. Let's divide. Let's conquer.'

22

PRAGUE, 2016

William stood up from the stone steps in front of the spice shop where he was waiting and took a tentative step toward Grace. 'My God. What happened to you?'

She reached into her purse and pulled out the keys, fashioned them into a weapon. 'What are you doing here?'

'We had dinner plans.' He retreated. 'Well, sort of. This is the only real spice shop in the old town, so I made an assumption. When you weren't here, I—'

'You what?' said Grace.

'Well, I worried something happened to you. After what we learned yesterday, at the Institute, I was a bit spooked. You were too.' William approached her again. 'For good reason? You're bleeding.'

Grace was too exhausted to interrogate William, to assure herself he wasn't a different sort of spy, or agent, or thug. For the first time all day she was hungry, and there was no food upstairs. There was no point sneaking around, as the pursuers now knew everything there was to know about her: where she was staying, what she was discovering, what she had written.

'I'm hungry. Can we eat?'

'Of course. You mean, now? No offense, Grace, but you might want to wash up just a bit.'

Reluctantly, she allowed William into her building and up the stairs. She asked him to wait in the small kitchen of the Airbnb while she tended to herself in the bathroom. The blood from her nose had somehow smeared all over her face. Her hair was a mess. There was a visible footprint on the front of her jacket and on her forehead. The warm water on her face felt so good that something between a sob, a laugh, and a hysterical scream escaped from her.

'You okay, Grace?'

'Yes. Thank you.'

She put on a pair of jeans and a sweater, and on the way out with William she put the knife back in her purse.

They ate at a Czech-Indian fusion restaurant that was open late, with dark tables, plush gold chairs, and romantic lighting. Once they were seated in the corner, with water in their glasses and menus in their hands, Grace scanned the room for anyone who might be watching. No one was close enough to hear them.

On the walk over, Grace had recounted the day's exploits

and she had watched his face for reactions. William had seemed authentically horrified, though perhaps he had been well trained at spy school.

'You have to stop. You have to go back to the embassy.'

'No point. They think I'm a nutcase.' She stared at him, his dirty glasses. 'Who do you work for, William?'

He slid his glass of water over to make room, as he liked to talk with his hands. 'You think I followed you to the Institute, reluctantly brought you upstairs and then across town in the pouring rain, introduced you to Milan, pretended to be excited by your revelations to . . . what, exactly? What's my sinister motive here?'

She shrugged. 'Maybe you work for them.'

'For whom?'

'I don't know. I don't know! Are we ordering wine? Three days ago I was a supermarket tabloid hack. No one cared what I wrote. No one believed a word of it.'

'Now that these men have attacked you, perhaps the embassy officials will take you more seriously.' William spoke softly. 'I'll vouch for you. Nothing is worth getting hurt, or worse.'

'I have no proof they attacked me.'

'Your face! And the police could—'

'I threatened the killers with that, with calling the police,' said Grace. 'They laughed at me. They're so far beyond all of that.'

'So far beyond?' said William.

'They are the police, somehow.' She finished her glass of

water. 'Ever since I stood up from the smelly cobblestones where I thought I was going to die I've been wondering: *why didn't I die?* It would have been easy for them, even preferable. The only answer is they – *you, William?* – need to know exactly what I know and who I might have spoken to about it. I've spoken to you and Milan, to Steadman, to Elena herself . . .'

'Last night after that second beer I called Milan and I went back to his office. I was a little drunk and feeling conspiratorial. If you go through Elena Craig's biography online, point by point . . .'

The server, a mop-haired man in his late twenties, arrived at the table and bowed. William ordered a bottle of Moravian Muscat – *Mopr* – and asked that the chef do his best to mix Czech tradition and tandoori delights.

When the server was gone, William leaned forward and lowered his voice. 'The first problem is her degree from Charles University. There is no record of it whatsoever. So what was she doing here in Prague, after she left Mladá Boleslav? Let's say she was studying. What exactly was she studying? Next: the man in Strasbourg. We are to believe he was an athlete, that they met at a competition of some sort. Guess what? Despite all the talk of her gymnastics prowess, her name falls off the list of competitors in 1968. When she was eighteen. From 1969 to 1972, when we are supposed to believe she somehow met this Frenchman . . .'

'Jean-Yves de Moulin. I just met him.'

'Well, she wasn't competing at all, according to the records, and there were no Czech-French competitions whatsoever. So either someone removed these records, which makes no sense because they are part of her official story. Or . . . none of this actually happened. She didn't do a master's degree at Charles University. Or gymnastics.'

'Which makes it hard to join the Czech Olympic team.'

'Indeed! So how did she get to Strasbourg? And of all places, why there? I wish you had asked me to join you in Strasbourg.'

The server returned with the wine, opened it, and invited William to smell the cork. Then he poured a bit of the Muscat and William swirled it and stuck his big nose into the glass, tasted it, and said the Czech word for *delicious*.

After cheers and eye contact and their first proper drink, ten seconds of silence hung over the table. Grace interrupted it. 'What should I do?'

'The only reasonable option is to give this up,' said William. 'It's dangerous and impossible. *People are dead.* They'll kill you the moment they feel like it. Your own boss has forbidden it.'

Appetizers arrived: a salmon and crab dish that smelled of curry, a bit of quail marinated in honey wine, and a pâté of deer. Grace found it absurd. You think you are going to die and an hour later you're eating a quail.

'But you're not going to stop, are you?' said William.

'No. I fly out tomorrow, to Miami, to see my mother. Then I go back to Montreal.'

'Where Elena Klimentová lived before she moved to New York.'

'Yes.'

'You'll go through the archives.'

'Of course.'

'Can I join you?'

Grace paused before answering. The wine had begun to work on her, but she was not sure about him. He had waited two hours in front of a spice shop, in late October. 'What do you mean?'

'I mean, can I please come with you to Montreal?' William refilled their glasses. 'I'm a historian. I study totalitarian regimes, popular movements, politics. Elena's ex-husband could soon be president. I'm on sabbatical until January, to work on a research project. Until yesterday, I thought I knew what it was, the kind of thing nine of my colleagues would read and immediately forget. But this? *This* is a research project. I could . . . help you? Protect you?'

She stared at him.

'There is nothing at all wrong with London South Bank University.' He removed his glasses, cleaned them with his serviette, and put them back on. 'I always suspected I'd be there until retirement and that would be fine. Fine! But I'll be honest with you, Grace. I'd much prefer to be teaching at Cambridge and this is surely the only chance in my life to make it happen.'

23

Petr Kliment held Kristína, his six-month-old granddaughter, on a patch of grass on the shore of the Jizera River. When Elena reached for Kristína, to take her away, her father kissed the baby's chubby cheeks and bald head and spoke into her tiny ear. Elena worried he would squeeze her too hard.

'I cannot let her go, Elenka. She is the most beautiful, best-smelling creature on the planet.'

Elena had never before seen tears in her father's eyes.

But the car was waiting and the men inside were impatient because their bosses in Prague were impatient.

Petr Kliment was spending more and more of his time at their country home along the river south of Mladá Boleslav. At first it was only summers but now that he no longer had to work so much he preferred to fish earlier in the spring and later in the fall. Jana, his wife, joined him from time to time. But she preferred life in Mladá Boleslav and in Prague, now that she could live the life she was always meant to lead.

It was more pleasant and more beautiful in their apartment in the upper town. Neighbors looked up at them instead of down. They could stay in hotels in Prague, even spend ten days at the Hotel Croatia in Duga Uvala. None of their friends understood what had happened with Elena, not precisely, but Mladá Boleslav was a city of gossips. Their daughter had not *defected* because Petr and Jana were not sent away to work camps or thrown in prison. On the contrary, Petr and Jana had entered the quiet elite of Bohemia. They shopped at the Tuzex stores and bought blue jeans and sweets with the special currency reserved for party officials.

If others envied them, it did not bother Jana one bit. She had been born into a special class and now she had returned to it. As for the advantages they sought and received: this was no different than buying and selling wares on the black market, which everyone did. There were many versions of the proverb: *if we are not stealing from the state, we are stealing from our children.*

If they offer it, take it; this was what Jana had always believed.

Now, Elena took the baby from her father. He wiped the tears from his eyes and shook his head. 'I am so sad, Elenka. The feeling will not go away. It gets worse and worse.'

'Sad to see us go, *tati*? Kristína and I will be back soon.'

'I want you back for good. I want them to release you from all of this.' Her father reached out and squeezed her arm. 'Now that you have a baby with one of them . . .'

'With one of them?' She smiled. 'He is my husband. I love him. I have a very important job, designing cars, and—'

Her father walked slowly back toward the house, a new slouch in his shoulders, as though he could tell his daughter was lying.

'Don't worry about him,' said Jana. 'This work you are doing, it is very important. You are so lucky to have these opportunities. And it has made us so happy.'

Elena hugged her mother and the driver opened the back door of the Škoda 120 GLS. She had gone from knowing nothing about cars to knowing everything about them, just as her mother had transformed from a jealous nobody into the Czech version of a society matron.

'Will you come back soon?' her father called.

Jana rolled her eyes. 'When you can, Elenka. Though we would love to meet your mysterious Anthony.'

Kristína was a good baby and fell asleep almost immediately as the car climbed out of the valley. It was a bumpy road, and despite being a 1978 model the suspension on the Škoda was so stiff the child bounced in her arms. Anthony would want all of the details. She could hear him telling guests at their table: 'Russia might be a huge military force. They might be. I don't know. Do you know? All I know for sure is this: if you can't make a car that isn't an utter piece of shit, how tough can you be? How tough can you really be? Based on what Elena tells me about communist cars, we should attack *yesterday*.'

The men in the front of the Škoda did not speak to her, which was preferable as it didn't disturb Kristína. Besides, Elena had learned enough in the past years to see these men had no power. They knew they had no power. If they felt obliged, out of personal weakness, to fill the silence with talk of the weather or the car or the population of New York City, that was fine. But these men in the Škoda were not permitted to discuss anything of consequence.

What she had come to understand in the program was that communism as a political system was as irrelevant as capitalism. The revolution had traded tsars for party leaders. In New York almost no one moved from the bottom of the pyramid to the top. It was not entirely impossible: she had met Holocaust survivors at gala dinners, haunted people who had arrived with nothing but suitcases and had amassed great fortunes. But these survivors were rarer than wolves in Central Park. Statistically, they were insignificant. Yet this was the noblest achievement in American mythology. All of the rich people Elena now knew preferred to boast about launching themselves out of poverty than tell the truth about their fortunes. Even Anthony liked to pretend he was a 'self-made man', because it seemed cleverer than inheriting a profitable family business. This way, he was more American.

In Moscow, in Prague, she thought, at least they were honest.

There was only one way to reach the top of the pyramid. You had to be born there and you had to follow the party rules.

Or you did what she had done.

They parked in front of the Inter-Continental Hotel in the spot reserved for taxis and official hotel vehicles.

With Kristína in her arms, Elena walked through the busy but almost silent lobby and into the elevator. A short, plump, middle-aged woman with rosy cheeks greeted them with a curtsy as the elevator door opened into the rooftop restaurant.

'Mrs Craig? I am the nurse assigned to you for your upcoming meeting. I am honored to take care of baby Kristína so you can focus on the discussion.'

'But . . .'

The nurse reached for the baby. 'Do not worry, Mrs Craig. I will remain on this floor, within sight. If Kristína awakens, I will feed her.'

While the lights were on and a small team of waiters and waitresses stood at attention in the middle of the restaurant, there seemed to be no customers. The maître d'hôtel silently led Elena to the corner table overlooking the Vltava River and the palace.

No, there were two customers.

Sergei stood first. Then, more cautiously, the man next to him stood up. In the special program at the university, not far from here, some of her 'professors' had cultivated this look over the course of their careers. The man next to Sergei was blank. He revealed nothing. She could not tell if he was happy or sad, impressed or disappointed, thrilled or bored.

Yet his eyes were on her and it made her feel like she often felt: that her inner secrets had been revealed. They knew. They knew she hated what all of this had done to her father, who would never be impressed by her clothes or the photographs of her apartment in New York, of her houses on the water, her vacations, her famous friends. She could not fool her father and she could not fool this man.

'I am Aleksandr Mironov.' The man's hand was white and faintly moist.

'Elena Craig.'

'Sergei has told me quite a story about you and your impressive husband. Please sit.'

She did, and a waiter arrived with a bottle of champagne. He popped it and poured it in their flutes. At the same time, a waitress arrived with crackers and a black paste – tapenade.

Mironov did not take his eyes off her.

If they were going to execute her for a transgression, Elena assured herself, they would have met her on the shore of the river where no one could see them, not in a brand-new restaurant full of waiters and waitresses. They would not waste champagne on a woman they planned to murder. They were giving her champagne and tapenade because they knew it had hurt her to leave Strasbourg and Montreal. Perhaps a hot tray of escargots was on its way, with some baguette and some Alsatian choucroute. For another woman in the program, another swallow, it might have been a bottle of Brunello di Montalcino and bruschetta, or bangers and mash with an English stout.

The hot afternoon was transforming into a long, warm evening. Some of the windows were open and a breeze blew through the restaurant. With it came the voices of families, of children walking along the river or on the distant bridge. Elena looked back to ensure the nurse and Kristína were still there.

Sergei lifted his flute. 'To Elena Craig.'

'Thank you.' She lifted her flute.

'To Anthony Craig,' said Mironov.

They drank. No music was playing in the restaurant, one of the reasons why Elena felt so strange. It was not just the quiet and the formality, the distant nurse and her baby. Invisible ants crawled over her body whenever Mironov looked at her, and it seemed he could not look away.

'Tell me about Craig,' said Mironov.

'But Sergei already told you about him.'

'Sergei has never met the man. I want to hear it from you.'

It was not the first time Elena had reported to the KGB, but this was different. This was not official. Sergei and this man Mironov were not leaders, not yet. They were plotters. Neither of them took notes or made her feel like she would be punished if she made an error.

Still, she tried to be as precise as possible, and to focus on what Sergei and Mironov wanted to hear: that she had never met a man more confident yet so lacking in confidence. He was the most ambitious, least disciplined man in New York. There were no secrets with him. He said aloud every thought that arrived in his brain, to anyone, and a good number of these thoughts were lies. He was vengeful yet he forgave easily. All you had to do was praise and flatter him.

'What do his peers think of him?' said Mironov.

It hurt Elena to say what she was about to say. 'They find him inferior, a crass and boastful *arriviste*. He received money from his father, who was also an *arriviste*. He married a dumb blonde from Czechoslovakia who can't even speak decent English. Anthony thinks his audience, the market for his products, is a cadre of wealthy and powerful men, aristocrats. But he is wrong. The men who buy his cars are hopeless strivers.'

'Does he know this?'

'I think so, in his secret heart. Yes.'

'And it hurts him?'

'His pride is everything.'

Mironov dipped a cracker in tapenade and noisily ate it. 'Remember always that a wise man walks with his head bowed, humble like the dust.'

'I don't understand.'

Sergei laughed. 'Elena, you *must* understand. Aleksandr is no fan of America. But there is a television show, *Kung Fu*.'

'It's on reruns.'

'Aleksandr likes it very much. He quotes liberally from it.'

'I study ancient fighting systems.' Mironov's face was an odd color in the light of dusk. 'I'm an actual kung fu master.'

Elena did not know what to say to that, so she took some tapenade. The waiter returned to fill their flutes, his hand trembling.

Sergei coughed to announce his intention to speak. 'Tell Aleksandr more about the quality of your Anthony's ambitions.'

'If the right person tells him he ought to do something, ought to make something, he will do it.'

Mironov dabbed at his mouth with a napkin. 'Who is "the right person"?'

'Someone he admires,' said Elena. 'A successful capitalist, someone with "old money". The CEO or the chair of a media enterprise: for a man like this he would do anything. Give up the bearings and automobile businesses and go wholeheartedly into the manufacture of toilets. If the owner of the *New York Times* were to befriend him and call him a titan of business, a genius, and tell him to make toilets, I believe Anthony would do it.'

'Is he unfaithful?' said Mironov.

'He is the most unfaithful man in America.'

'Is there a risk he will leave you?'

'No.'

Sergei interjected. 'Elena can handle him. She will not divorce him. This is a partnership, a business partnership, more than a marriage.'

Elena was now on the design team for the line of Craig cars that would launch in 1980. She had chosen the exterior colors and crafts for all the interiors. The Craig Swift, the upcoming 'woman's car', was based eighty percent on her designs, inside and out.

But it was not entirely true, what Sergei had said. Anthony

had romanced her in the beginning. He had taken cross-country ski lessons and had traded a vacation in the Caribbean for a cold week in Colorado. Despite his infidelities he was loyal, in his way, and proud of Kristína, though he rarely saw her.

Anthony and Elena had found excuses not to make love.

'Nothing suggests the CIA or FBI have any idea about you. Not from our end. At least the files we can access.' Mironov looked at Sergei and back at her. 'Have they ever approached you, Mrs Craig?'

'Never.'

'I know you are an intelligent and capable woman,' said Mironov, continuing to study her. 'But you have to play dumber than you have, as things progress.'

'Why?'

'You are Czech. Craig married you because you are beautiful, not because you are smart. You are a "trophy wife", an aesthetic consideration, the status symbol of a rich man.'

'It does not have to be so. In America, women—'

'If you are too smart, Mrs Craig, and everyone knows him to be stupid . . .'

'I don't think they do.'

'Never interrupt me.' Still there was no anger in his eyes. 'Never.'

Elena did not understand what was happening.

'I am sorry, Mrs Craig. This is probably difficult for a woman of your age and intelligence, living in New York City, to hear: but we are only interested in your husband. And we are patient.

He has enormous potential for us and we will not jeopardize it for any reason. Do you understand?'

Elena looked at her champagne, at the bubbles. What did he mean by 'we'? This man was a non-entity in the KGB, like Sergei. Young and mean and, so far, powerless. This was not even a real meeting. A champagne bubble popped out of the flute and fizzed on her hand. She wanted to be away from this place. She wanted to tell Anthony, so he could . . . no, there was nothing he could do. Besides, if she confessed, Anthony would see only the risks to himself, to his reputation.

There was no running from Moscow Center, no running from Sergei and this new man, Mironov. There was not a village in the jungles of South America where they could not find her and destroy her, let alone on the Upper West Side of Manhattan. She would die of a drug overdose, a heart attack, a car accident.

Her parents would be eliminated. *Kristína*.

'Tell us, Mrs Craig, about our plans as you understand them.' Mironov filled her flute and his, and he did not fill Sergei's. 'Be frank with us. Tell us why you are in New York, married to this buffoon, where you intend to take him.'

Despite the champagne her mouth was dry.

'Kingfisher,' Mironov said, sternly. 'We are waiting.'

24

MIAMI, 2016

At Miami International Airport, sleep-deprived and exhausted from worry, Grace bought an American SIM card and more data for her phone. She texted Jason with her new number, and coordinated a pick-up location. Waiting near the doors, she Googled William Kovály and found his staff photo on the website for London South Bank University School of Law and Social Sciences. His hair was tidy in the picture and his big, open smile obliterated any mystery or intrigue. He was an associate professor of history, and his two-paragraph bio listed his degrees and papers published and his area of specialization: totalitarianism and revolution.

Of course, this did not prove or disprove anything. It would take ten minutes to invent a name and a personality profile for a skilled agent, a morning to create a web page for a university. Everything that had seemed natural, up until this moment, could have been manufactured: their meeting, his friend Milan with the Einstein hair, the beer hall, dinner at a Czech-Indian fusion restaurant, the uncomfortable moment next to the spice shop when she decided not to invite him back upstairs after dinner. His gallant response: 'Perhaps, in Montreal, we will come to know one another better.'

Goodnight, goodnight, sleep well, you too, bon voyage. It felt like he prolonged this exchange on the medieval street to hide his true message inside a series of banal words of departure. She did not trust her instinct in this matter because no one had tried to pick her up in any obvious way since the summer of 2012.

Her suitcase arrived with new scrapes and wounds, and she rolled it out into the hot sandwich between wet and dry season. After the slate gloom of Prague the impossibly sunny, cloudless joy of late afternoon in Miami was almost too much. When had she last slept a full and proper night? Latin pop bounced from the open windows of clean, new cars. No one, not one person, wore a down jacket. She understood why her mother and ex-husband and twenty-one million other people loved it in Florida, although for Grace the brightness and clarity of the place now hid something sinister.

She texted Jason and five minutes later he pulled up in his frosty-white Buick SUV. He hopped out of it in a pair of tan shorts and a purposely faded yellow beach shirt. He jogged around the front and hugged her and kissed her ear. 'You look fabulous.'

'I look old. My nose is swollen and puffy. And I stink. But thanks.'

'What happened to your chin?'

'Scraped it.'

'What? How?'

'On cobblestones.'

Jason took care of her bag. Inside the Buick, a shiny black universe of elegant dials that smelled of leather and freshly opened plastic, it was ten degrees cooler. Before she could ask her ex-husband to ease up on the air conditioning, there was a harmonic mini-chorus of, 'Hello, Aunt Grace.'

The two little girls, eight and ten, were in princess costumes.

'Hi, Claire. Hi, Kellie,' Grace said, a little uneasily. This had not been part of her plan. 'Was there a Halloween party at school today?'

'Yes, there was.' Kellie, the ten-year-old, made a stern face. 'Guess who I am.'

'A princess?'

'Yeah, but which one?'

'Oh sweetie, I can't keep track of them all.'

'Elsa from *Frozen*?'

'Of course. You look just like her.'

The girls began singing 'Let It Go', and as they pulled into the mad airport traffic, Jason asked them gently to sing a different song. 'This is only the fiftieth time they sang that one today.'

'Can we turn down the air conditioning, Jay?'

'And I'm Ariel.' Claire sang a few bars. 'Remember that one? *The Little Mermaid*? I'm when she isn't a mermaid for a little while.'

'Because she made bad choices.' Kellie leaned forward and her polyester dress swooshed. 'Can you turn up the music, Papa?'

Jason turned up 'Shake It Off' by Taylor Swift.

In the back seat, the girls grooved and sang along. They merged onto the interstate. Jason and Caitlyn and the girls lived in a lakefront mansion in Coral Springs, thirty minutes from her mother's retirement community in Pompano Beach. Her ex-husband visited the formidable Elsie Elliott far more often than Grace, which was noted in phone calls and in selfies Jason helped Elsie to send.

With his daughters consumed by Taylor Swift, Jason gently elbowed Grace. 'How do you scrape your face on cobblestones? And what work were you doing in Prague of all places?'

Their breakup involved no betrayals or secrets or sneaking about. Three years into their marriage, Jason wanted children and Grace did not. Not yet, anyway. They had entered their thirties and he was becoming nervous about it. He had imagined his life a certain way: coaching soccer, joining parent council, crying at animated movies, tucking someone in every night, singing Taylor Swift in a white, American-made, late-model SUV. He was more than ready to move away from Montreal: the language, the fashion, the politics. For their fifth anniversary, he joined Grace on a trip to Vermont, where she spent one day working on an article and three with him. In a sushi restaurant in Burlington, where the snow was melting, he said he needed something more than *maybe*, about children, about Montreal, and maybe was all she could give him.

Over a carafe of warm sake Grace had surprised herself by suggesting they break up and remain friends. Jason cried. She didn't. Less than a year later he had met Caitlyn in New York. She worked in the property development industry with her father. A short while later they moved to Coral Springs for Caitlyn's career, the climate, and North Broward Preparatory School.

Before Grace answered his questions about the chin scab and Prague, she checked the side mirror. There was a black SUV behind them.

'Can you take a weird turn-off in a bit, and then get back on the interstate?'

'Why?'

'This story I'm working on, it will upset some people. They're trying to intimidate me.'

'Who is?'

'The people I'm writing about.'

'Writing about for the *National Flash*? Nobody even believes it. And you can't threaten an American citizen for exercising free speech. The Constitution is pretty clear on that. Have you gone to the cops?'

She pulled down her sun visor and inspected her chin. The

wound looked like a large spider. 'I think it might have been the cops who did this, Czech cops.'

'So? Tell our cops.'

'I tried. They wanted me to fill out forms.'

'You should fill out those forms, Grace. Look, surely you can tell me what you're working on.'

She looked behind her again. The black SUV was still following them. Of course, half of Florida's population drove enormous black SUVs. 'Turn off soon.'

The girls knew all the words to 'Bad Blood' too. Grace sat back, determined to remain calm. 'Kellie, you don't wear uniforms to school?'

'Yes, Aunt Grace. That is why today is special. We get to stay in our costumes all day.'

'We're trick-or-treating.' Claire had trouble making the -ing sound. *Treat-en*.

'But you're only keeping three choices of candy each, right girls?' Jason winked at Grace. 'They put the rest in a bag and hang it outside on the branch of our eucalyptus. Then in the night the switch witch comes.'

'The switch witch trades our candy for books.' Kellie folded her arms. 'I don't know why.'

At a suburb called Ives Estates Jason turned off the interstate. The black SUV followed them.

'Go slow, Jason, please.'

The strip malls offered manicures, fast food, computer repair services, and loans. As a girl growing up in wintry

220

Bloomington, Grace had always imagined Florida as an endless beach with white and perfect towers, palm trees, swimming pools, and glistening boys of many colors. When her mother decided to move here, Grace was shocked to discover a bland grid of unloved homes and palm trees.

'Turn right.'

'Grace?'

'Please, Jason, now.'

Jason raised his arms in defeat and pulled into a loop of trailers and trailer-like houses where men and women drank beer on white plastic chairs. Several front yards had more than one vehicle parked on them, right on the grass amid the tropical vegetation. They did not look like vehicles that moved anymore. A hot wind blew a hint of dust over everything. Even with the windows closed and Taylor Swift going full blast, Grace could hear a couple shouting at one another on a stoop. Kellie and Claire watched them as they passed. Jason sighed. Grace thought of their final two months together, when he was already in New York but insisted on meeting once every two weeks in an upstate hotel room *to make sure* this divorce was right for them.

'What's happening to you, whatever it is, it's in your control to alter it, Grace. It's no one else. It's just you. And you're powerful.'

The SUV turned in behind them.

'Okay.' Grace tried not to sound terrified, or even agitated. 'Now back to the interstate.'

Jason turned back onto Ives Dairy Road. 'You're scaring me.'

'It's fine. I'm fine.'

'How long are you in town? Can we have you for dinner? Not tonight, with the Halloween madness, but maybe tomorrow?'

The SUV had fallen three and then four cars behind them. 'I'm just here for a few hours.'

'Why don't you change it up? Have a bit of a holiday? Caitlyn's really plugged into the wellness community in Coral Springs. A couple of spa days couldn't hurt. I would be delighted to take care of it for you, an early Christmas present.'

The SUV was right behind them again.

'It was happening to me, in the year after we broke up, in crazy New York, before I met Caitlyn. I was working too hard. I had fallen deep into my own head, if that makes sense. My world, the way I saw and felt it, had so little to do with the *real world*. With actual energy, if you get my meaning, all we feel but cannot see, and I know this will sound like hocus-pocus, Grace, especially to you, but . . .'

In the rear-view mirror Grace realized the two men in the SUV were her pursuers from Prague and Strasbourg. Her stomach curdled. They were not being coy or sneaky. They *wanted* her to see them. The passenger, with the pretty eyes, mimed writing something down. Or maybe he *was* writing something down: their license plate.

Grace imagined reading it online, or receiving a balled-up copy in a set of Russian nesting dolls. A tragedy on Halloween night, carbon monoxide poisoning in a mansion in Coral Springs, Florida: Jason, Caitlyn, Kellie and Claire Kroeker.

'Can you drop me off here?'

'What? On the interstate?'

'It was crazy to involve you in this, beyond selfish. I was so tired and scared when I called you. I wanted to feel safe, I guess, like something normal could happen. These men were following me in Prague and Strasbourg, and they're following me again.'

'Are they the reason your chin is scabbed?'

The girls were no longer singing along to the music. 'Papa?' said Kellie. 'What's happening?'

'I'm taking you straight to the police station in Coral Springs.'

'Pull off the interstate.'

'Grace, no.'

'Jason, the girls are not safe.'

This was too loud. Kellie leaned forward as far as her seat-belt would allow. 'What girls aren't safe? Us?'

Jason shook his head and clenched his jaw, looked straight ahead at the I-95 traffic. The next exit was for Hollywood, Florida, and he clicked his indicator on decisively. Grace had never been to Hollywood, Florida.

'Why aren't we safe? Daddy?' Kellie slapped his arm. 'Daddy?'

'Sit back and be quiet, princess. We'll talk about this later.'

She did. Claire, in her booster seat, began to cry.

'I didn't mean it, girls.' Grace felt monstrously ill prepared for this moment. When she was around children, she tended to speak to them like adults. 'I'm just a funny person to have around. I don't mean you girls aren't *safe* with me. I just mean it's weird to be in a car with me, and that weirdness can feel unsafe.'

'Can you say that again, Aunt Grace?' said Kellie. 'I don't understand.'

Jason turned off the interstate and they rounded into another secondary route of strip malls and schools, randomly dotted with palm trees.

'Just take a right.'

'*Just take a right.*' Jason repeated her phrase with incredulity. 'Grace, can I say something without you getting mad at me?'

'How am I supposed to respond to that?' Grace watched the SUV creep closer.

'You haven't changed. You haven't grown. It takes courage, yes, but we've reached middle age and we have to realize that nothing is going to go our way unless we take action. Montreal isn't right for you. It wasn't right for me. It isn't right for any Americans. I'm just going to say it because I've said it before and it's based entirely in love for you: you're too good for the *National Flash.*'

'Can you turn left and then speed up?'

'All I have ever wanted to do is help.'

'Turn left slowly, keeping it cool, and then speed up. When

I say stop, stop. I'll call you in a while, to get my bag. I'm really sorry I put you through this.'

In the back seat, both girls were now quietly crying.

'Sweeties? I'll make it up to you two somehow, okay?'

'Okay, Aunt Grace,' said Kellie, through her tears.

Jason turned left.

'Now floor it!'

He did, down a slightly more prosperous suburban street.

'Stop!'

Jason put his foot on the brake so abruptly that the Buick skidded on the dusty road.

'I love you all. So sorry. Thank you!' Grace opened the passenger door and Jason began pulling away before she closed it. She sprinted into a private yard, into the back, and scaled a chain-link fence. Then she climbed down the other side into another yard, where a man and a woman were drinking bottles of beer with their feet in a wading pool. She could hear the roar of an engine and squealing tires behind her.

'Hey,' said the man. 'Who are you?'

Grace had not run like this in years. It was blisteringly hot and already her chest and head hurt, but it was better than nausea. On the next street some men were gathered in front of a white house with dirty siding next to a car with its hood open.

'Guys, can I run through your yard?'

'No goddamn way,' said an obese man with a Harley-Davidson shirt and a Dolphins cap.

She did it anyway, and the man cussed at her as she ran up a gravel driveway and over another fence, through a blessedly empty yard and into a quiet cul-de-sac. There was a liquor store at the end of the block with two taxis parked out front. With a final burst she ran into the parking lot and waved her arms in front of the taxis.

The taxi drivers' doors were open. The drivers had been talking to each other but now they both stared at her. The man on her right, with black hair and a salt-and-pepper beard, leaned out. 'You need taxi? Where you going?'

'Away from here.' Grace bent over and put her hand on her heart.

When she looked up, neither of the two men seemed keen to take her away from there.

'Russian killers.' She pointed in front of her and behind, unsure of where they were. 'They're after me, in an SUV, and—'

The man with the beard clapped his hands once, stepped out of his car, and opened his back door. 'Get in, lady.'

25

NEW YORK, 1984

At an awkward ceremony in 1982, Elena had been named senior vice-president of design for the automotive division of Craig International. The New York press had made fun of it for weeks. How was a ditzy foreign housewife remotely prepared for the impossible job of selling Americans something they did not want?

Anthony hired a public relations firm to tell her story: Olympic athlete, communist defector, born of a long line of female automotive executives. Soon it was rare for a month to pass without a photo or an article about the scrappy yet glamorous young Craigs in one of the newspapers.

Then it was almost every week: Elena in a cocktail dress;

227

Elena performing a perfect cartwheel in Central Park; indefatigable Elena in the design lab; Elena with her daughter, little Kristína.

She led the team in Manhattan three days a week, sometimes more often, and she worked in the design lab on Long Island. You can't just *draw* the most luxurious car in the world: you have to sit in it.

Where she really wanted to be though was in her apartment, playing with Kristína. Anthony had never changed a diaper or given voice to a Cabbage Patch Kid, he had never attended one of Kristína's pretend tea parties, yet it was not possible to make him feel a whiff of guilt about it. Most aspects of parenting were inefficient drains on his time. He was worth thousands of dollars an hour. A nanny could take care of it all for a hundred bucks a day.

And that's for a good nanny, the best.

He began work early in the mornings and usually finished late. He traveled across the country and back to New York in the course of a day – once or twice a week. Tonight was the first night in twelve they were not going to a business dinner, a gala, or a fundraiser.

That Tuesday night, when Anthony's assistant arrived with two boxes from Pizza Hut, Kristína cheered and danced. It was the closest thing to family time they could manage: a pepperoni and a three-cheese. Sancerre for Mommy and Diet Coke for Daddy.

The television news was on.

Walter Mondale, the former vice-president, had won the Iowa caucuses and carried a massive lead over the other Democrats keen to take on Reagan.

'Look at those eyes.' Anthony ate standing up, his hands shiny with grease because he picked the cheese off his pizza and left most of the dough. He pointed a crust at the television. 'There's something wrong with Mondale's eyes. He's a boring guy, I've met him, fucker never stops talking, lips don't move, weird whistling thing when he hits an S, but those eyes. Smart guy, smart and boring. But those eyes make him look stupid. Stupid Eyes Mondale. Reagan's as stupid as Mondale's eyes look, but here's the difference: *he understands show business*. He's a movie guy. What does Mondale think this is? Debate class? Who told that boring stick he should run for anything? If Jesse wasn't black he'd take this. But you know what? He's black. You hear what Jesse called the Jews? Elena, hey, hello? It was in the *Times* today. You hear it?'

Kristína climbed up on her lap. The sweetie wanted to pick a slice of pepperoni from mommy's pizza. Of course Elena had seen the article. 'No.'

'No what? No to the kid or no to the Jesse thing?'

'To Jesse.'

'Hymies he calls them! And it was on tape or something, the dumb fuck.'

'*Language*, Tony.'

'You know what? Jesse's dead. He might as well roll over for Stupid Eyes Mondale right now. I should run.'

'You have to run, darling. It's your destiny.'

'And there's Reagan. Podunk would vote for his corpse. It doesn't matter what he says. He could recite *Hop on Pop*. And Mondale thinks Joe Lunchbox is gonna vote for him? Dream on, Stupid Eyes.'

'When you run for president, you will be like Reagan.'

Anthony threw his crust into one of the boxes, and chose another piece of pepperoni. He pulled the cheese and meat off and rolled it up and ate it.

'This is why Mr Joe Lunchbox will love you, Tony. You are a secret savage.'

Elena was the only human being permitted to call him Tony. He thought it made him sound Italian and insignificant, a bit of a midget, like an olive oil sales rep in 1962. 'Say that again.'

While she had experienced none of the depression some women experience after childbirth, for months there had been a shroud of sadness over Elena. It wasn't just her marriage, the prospect of being with a man like Anthony the rest of her life. She had lost touch with Danika, who had fallen into a life of drugs and mayhem when Sergei did not allow her to divorce Carlos. She disappeared one night in November, after calling Elena from a payphone. Her husband was not successful enough to be happy yet he was not enough of a disaster to abandon – not yet. Carlos's family connections were worth a lot to Sergei.

Elena had wanted to tell her friend to quit, to run away. But they both knew there was no quitting. There was nowhere to run.

Danika's body had been discovered in the East River. Carlos spoke through his tears at a press conference, using Danika's struggle with pills and her death as an opportunity to cast himself as a soldier in the war on drugs even though Elena knew he had introduced every pill and powder to her.

The morning after the pizza night, in Anthony's Challenger, Elena flew with three of her closest friends – two swallows from Ukraine and one from Bulgaria – to Bozeman, Montana.

Lone Mountain Ranch was the best place to cross-country ski in America. Elena was never a great skier but she had done it with her father and grandparents from the age of four. The four women were a bit buzzed from champagne on the tidy little jet, but the cold, dry mountain air woke them out of it.

They arrived at a six-bedroom cabin in the snow, full of blond wooden beams. A fire was burning and the women spoke of it reminding them of a much cleaner, much more beautiful and better-smelling version of home. After dinner the rest of the girls changed into their pajamas to watch a movie together: *Risky Business.* They made popcorn in the microwave.

'I think I'll go for a walk,' Elena announced, when the others were already cozy on the couch.

Are you sure? I'll go with you! You shouldn't be alone out there!

Of course, Elena could not allow company and none of the women really wanted to join her. They had been through almost three bottles of wine together and out in the shadows of the mountains it was well below freezing. None of them was quite sure whether or not the bears were still hibernating.

His cabin was a ten-minute walk through the snow. The curtains were closed and she looked in her purse one last time to be sure she had everything. Not bothering with their secret knock, she opened the front door and went into the bedroom. Blue and orange lights flashed on the body on the bed, naked but for white underwear and a pair of socks. A fire burned. *Cheers* was on TV.

Without a word of greeting Elena took off her parka and sat next to him on the bed.

Sergei had called this reunion a month earlier. He had just returned from Moscow. At the Center, the leader of the First Chief Directorate had presented the heads of stations' own work back to them. He had been angry. There were plenty of re-cycled news stories and unsubstantiated rumors, but Sergei and his peers had produced almost no actionable intelligence. They were still trying to find assets based on 1960s thinking. No one in America or Great Britain was enamored with com-munism anymore, and those who were – divorced professors, mostly – had no access to power. They were social dunces. Entirely useless.

From now on it did not matter if their assets had any affinity whatsoever with the founding principles of the Soviet Union.

Sergei imitated the man in charge of the First Chief Direct-orate. 'This is a new world and we need new strategies. We will be bold. We will be creative. We will win because we are willing to try anything, do anything. They will not see us coming.'

'He sounds like Tony. With an accent.'

'You know them, Elenka, what they could do to my parents. To my wife. I'll end up in a salt mine in Surgut, if I am lucky.'

'I hear Surgut is very beautiful in August.'

'It isn't.'

'I was joking.'

'You've become such an American. I don't know when you are joking.'

For the past week, and on the plane, she had tried to remember what it had felt like to be in love with Sergei. Her ultimate goal back then had been: a place in Prague or Moscow and a country home, a dacha on the Black Sea. The children in her dreams had always been their children.

'I brought drinks,' she said now.

'I have drinks.' Sergei reached for a glass beside the bed and gulped the last of his whiskey. Elena took the empty glass from him and carried it into the kitchen. In her purse were six airplane vodkas and a bottle of tomato juice.

'Have you ever had a Bloody Mary?'

Elena's hands were shaking. Sergei looked across the room at her.

The light in his small kitchen came from above the stove. She poured two ounces of vodka into a tall water glass and filled it with the tomato juice. In a sandwich bag she had packed Tabasco and Worcestershire sauce, celery powder, two sticks of celery – and a tiny container of ricin salt. Danika had made it based on a chromatography technique they learned in Prague, from a slurry of castor beans and a few chemicals her drug dealer had found for her. Elena had kept it safe for the day her friend found the courage to mix it into her husband's cocaine.

Now she opened the vial. For hours he would suffer. She wanted him to suffer.

'Come, Elenka,' Sergei called.

'What do you need me to do? I mean, to help? Is it something with Anthony?' She dropped it in and stirred. More vodka. 'Do you want a stick of celery?'

'I already had dinner.' Sergei turned off the television. 'We don't need fancy drinks.'

She carried the Bloody Marys on a tray. He was sitting up in bed, and looked better in the flickering orange of the fire, his posture straight, his eyes on her.

'They think Reagan is planning a pre-emptive strike,' he said. 'Moscow and Leningrad, military installations.'

'Is it . . . is that something you want me to find out?'

'Put down the tray.'

She slid it onto his desk, next to a novel by Gabriel García Márquez translated into Russian and a pile of newspapers: the *Times*, the *Post*, *The Guardian*.

'Is he, Sergei?'

'You think the man who played Papa in *Bedtime for Bonzo*

wants to be known, for the rest of time, as the man who destroyed the world?'

She was having trouble focusing. 'Anthony's been talking about Jesse Jackson. We had dinner with Mario Cuomo. Ed Koch—'

'Soon there will be a new general secretary, Elenka. It will be someone who cares more about the economy than ideology.'

'So . . .'

'So your Anthony is no communist. There is no turning him. If he were to design a political system it would be an absolute monarchy. As long as he is monarch.'

When Anthony spoke to his daughter, it was to tell her she was the prettiest and the smartest in America. No one could ever be prettier or smarter than Kristína. Because she was a Craig. *You'll be the toughest negotiator in New York. You'll kill them. Destroy them. You'll be on the news every night. The queen. The queen!*

Six years old: the queen.

Sergei took the Bloody Mary without the celery and brought it to his mouth. Just as he was about to drink it he placed the glass on the bedside table.

'Take off your clothes.'

'What?'

'You heard me.'

Elena laughed. 'You're acting strange.'

'Take off your clothes.'

She started with her shirt.

'Slowly.'

Elena slipped one side of her jumper off her shoulder.

'Don't act like a whore. Just undress.'

In the airplane she had tried not to think about his death. Now she wanted to watch it.

Sergei sat up tall, reached for his Bloody Mary. 'Would he come to Moscow?'

'Who? Anthony?'

'The coming change means opportunities for foreign investment.'

She waited for him to drink. Just a sip.

'Our license with Fiat could end anytime. I'm not talking about luxury cars. Just . . . *manufacturing cars*. We can make sure it is profitable for him.'

Elena was in her bra and panties now. Though she had worked hard to rid herself of the extra pounds since giving birth, in the light of the fire she wanted to cover herself.

Drink.

'Well?' The Bloody Mary was still in his hand.

'It doesn't fit the brand, Sergei. Communist cars. Maybe Volkswagen . . .'

'We wouldn't use "Craig". It would be something else. You can come up with the name.'

'The car business isn't doing well. The bearings keep Craig International alive.'

'We could do a bearings deal.'

'He hates the bearings business.'

'Okay, cars.'

Drink, God damn it.

'You remember Aleksandr Mironov, in Prague?'

'Of course.'

'He is obsessed with your Anthony.'

'But Aleksandr is not important.'

'He will be. Take off the bra.'

She did.

'And the panties.'

Elena was feeling bashful so she lifted the covers on the bed.

'Don't move.'

'What? Why?'

Sergei took his time slipping off the bed in his underwear and brown socks. With the drink in his hand he walked around to her. Again she tried to get into the bed, and this time he shouted. 'Don't fucking move!'

Whatever happened, no one would hear. For a while he stood behind her but she did not turn around. Then he reached around, with the glass, and held her tight with his free hand.

'All I have to do is splash this on your face. It could go up your nose, just a few grains, and that would be enough.'

'What are you talking about, Sergei?' Elena's voice was shaking.

'Bend over.'

'Please. No.'

'You know I can do it anytime to you, to your daughter, to your parents.'

'Sergei, I didn't—'

'Shut up. I don't even want you to tell the truth. We didn't train you to be a truth-teller. You're angry about Danika? Vengeful? You think you're next?'

He had taken off his underwear. Not the socks. Now he released her and put the poisoned drink beside hers on the bedside table. She could tell, by his breathing and by the sound of it, what he was doing. Then without warning he began to shove himself into her.

She pulled the sheets off the bed to her face, to stifle a sob.

'You think you're next, Elenka? You're right. Remember your place, what you are here to do, or you are definitely next.'

26

The taxi driver was from Azerbaijan. He loved to drive fast and he hated Russians. Grace watched through the back window, for the SUV, as her driver told her about Black January, when the Russians came into Baku and killed his father in the street. And for what? For nothing! It was 1990 and the communists had already lost.

'And, lady,' he said. 'Have you heard of Khojaly Massacre?'

There was still no sign of the SUV. Grace had asked the driver to head in the direction of Pompano Beach and her mother's retirement home. She did not want to lead her pursuers there, but they already knew where to find her. They knew everything.

'No,' said Grace. 'I haven't.'

'Everyone in the world should know!' They were on the South Federal Highway, Highway 1, not the interstate, and her driver was going seventy miles per hour, weaving in and out of traffic. The highway was lined with skinny palm trees, warehouses, and cheap apartments. 'Over 160 Azerbaijanis killed by Russians and Armenians. You Americans don't know anything. You think after fall of Berlin Wall everything was sunshine and dancing? This was 1992, my friend.'

They stopped at a set of lights next to a school in Dania Beach. Thirty or forty children, dressed in costumes, crossed the highway. The black SUV, glinting in the sunlight, sped up the road.

The terror gripped her again. 'Oh God, no. How did they find us?'

The driver looked in the rear-view mirror. 'This is the fuckers?'

'Maybe I should get out and run again.'

'The Russians follow with drones, lady. There is no running.'

'I don't want to put you in danger.' The last of the children ran across the highway as the light changed.

'Put me in danger?' Her driver floored it the instant the light turned green. The newer and more powerful SUV had no trouble keeping up. 'Let's give them danger for a change.'

Grace had never gone so fast in a car. She wanted to hide her eyes, to jump in the nearby ocean, to check into a passing Best Western and sleep for three days. She longed for her old worries: to feel like a failure, to lose her job, to hurt Johnny

Depp's feelings. Instead, they roared past an IHOP and a busy little kiosk called a Dairy Belle so fast that people turned and lined up in the parking lot to watch them go.

Suddenly, the SUV was only a few feet behind them, and the man with the pretty eyes and the awful nose was pointing a gun through the windshield, at her. Grace ducked.

While he drove, at blistering speed, her driver spoke calmly of his father, whom the Russians had shot in a crowd, unarmed, like an animal. 'My father they killed for nothing, worse than an animal. An animal, at least, we kill for sausage. All he wanted was freedom.'

Grace dialed 911.

'What is your emergency?' said the operator.

'I am in a taxi, driving north on Highway 1,' said Grace. 'And men with guns in an SUV are chasing us.'

'Stay calm, ma'am. Can you describe the SUV?'

Grace began to describe it as the man with the pretty eyes aimed his gun at her again. It seemed a game to him. He smiled as he did it. She ducked a second time.

'Lady,' said the driver. 'Hang up.'

'What? Why?'

'Maybe they listen.'

Grace hung up. Calmly, as his speedometer reached eighty, the driver reached forward and opened his glove box and pulled out a handgun.

'When I tell you, open your window and point it.'

'Point it?'

241

'Point it at the driver. When I tell.'

They were approaching a construction area with barricades and fences. Grace opened her window. Only two of the lanes were open on the left side of the four-lane highway, and each side was marked with heavy concrete barriers. On the right side of the barrier there was a deep hole. Cars were coming in the opposite direction toward them.

Grace wanted to scream. At this speed, how would her taxi driver make it through an unusually thin lane with cars on the left and heavy concrete on the right?

'Now.'

'Now what?'

'Point the gun!'

Grace pointed her gun at the driver of the SUV, and screamed as she did it. The sun shone into the SUV from the west and she could see the shock on his face and then, for an instant, his fear.

Grace's taxi made it past the construction site as the driver of the SUV swerved. His partner reached for the wheel but it was too late. The SUV ripped into the concrete and flipped high into the air. It rotated and landed on its roof, on an empty patch of Highway 1.

Grace's taxi driver slowed down, then stopped. He opened his door and Grace opened hers. They got out and looked back at the wreck. It had made a terrible crunch when it landed. Glass had shattered. Now it hissed. There was no sign of the man with the pretty eyes or his companion.

'Are you okay, lady?'

She hugged him. He was about her age and smelled of his cherry air freshener. 'Thank you. I'm so sorry.'

'If those fuckers are not dead they will want to be dead.' The taxi driver had gone stiff from the hug. It seemed to make him more nervous than driving eighty miles an hour on a secondary highway.

In only a few days, Grace thought, she had been responsible for the deaths of four people.

A small crowd had gathered around the black SUV. A man shouted not to get too close. 'We better go, lady. Pompano Beach?'

'Yes, sir. Thank you.'

Looking at the handgun on the seat next to her, Grace thought maybe her pursuers would be severely injured – not killed. Maybe they had wives and children who were dependent on them. They had been children once themselves.

But as they started north toward the interstate, the SUV exploded behind them.

Jason stood next to his white Buick, waiting for her, when she arrived. Her bag was on the sidewalk. She insisted on giving the driver from Azerbaijan another hug, after paying her bill and giving him a fifty-dollar tip.

'I should give you tip, lady,' he said, shaking off the hug. 'My father is proud of me now.'

He drove off and Grace pointed at the Buick. 'The girls are still inside?'

'They are,' said Jason. 'I'll take them to crisis counseling shortly.'

'Oh God.'

'Don't worry about it. I told them Aunt Grace is mentally ill, that we should pity you. They learned a new word today. *Delusional.*'

'Nice one.' Now she hugged Jason. 'You really are a good man. And I'm so glad things have worked out the way they have, for you and Caitlyn. Those girls of yours. They're lovely, and it really seems like . . . I mean, I never could have.'

'Sure you could have,' he said. 'You could do anything.'

Grace hugged him harder, and held him a moment too long. 'Okay. Are you sure you can do this for me?'

'Of course. Just make it kind of snappy. The moment it starts getting dark, the girls will want to be getting free candy they're not allowed to eat.'

She jogged toward the front doors of the complex, Vaucluse by the Sea.

'Grace?'

'Yeah?' She stopped and turned.

'Should I be worried?'

'No, absolutely not.' Grace dished a fake smile at her ex-husband. 'I'll be right back.'

There were a few palm trees and some cacti in the dusty inner courtyard of Vaucluse by the Sea but almost no vegetation that required actual gardening. The pump on the central fountain had been broken for eight months.

Her mother had fled the Minnesota winter and could not abide living somewhere colder, in a foreign country, just to be close to Grace. So it was a monthly commute, and not a terribly uncomfortable one. With half of Quebec retirees escaping to Florida for the winter months, there were daily flights between Montreal and Miami.

Pompano Beach had been walloped by the subprime mortgage crisis, with unemployment figures still over thirteen percent and plenty of surplus real estate, which is how Grace could afford Vaucluse by the Sea. But the adjacent waterfront was now a massive construction site after years of seeming the saddest place in Broward County, and Grace was sure her monthly bills would soon go up. Even now, it came with the shame of knowing this place, with its grumpy nurses and ninth-tier visiting doctors, its 1980s furniture and its smell of chlorine, medicine, and feces was the best she could do for her mother. Soon her mother would be blind after some years of mismanaging her diabetes. In July Grace had toured assisted living facilities north of Miami and she thought afterwards that it might have been the most melancholy afternoon of her life.

'Honey.' Elsie Elliott stepped out of her apartment with her arms out. When Grace took her hand, at the circle of cacti, her mother finally looked in the right direction for eye contact.

The small consolation of her mother's worsening sight was she could see neither the chin scab nor how sweaty and disheveled Grace looked.

After a hug and a kiss, her mother took her arm. 'You have to tell me all about Europe. Can we have dinner? There's a Mexican place in the strip mall called Dos Amigos. It was started by two friends.'

Grace led her back into the one-bedroom apartment that carried the scent of smokers long departed. 'Mom, we have to pack you a bag.'

'Why?'

'You're staying with Jason and his family for a few days.'

'No, I am goddamn well not.'

Grace told her just enough as she packed her mother's bag: that she was working on a story that will make some powerful people very angry, that she had already been threatened. 'Once it's published, I'll get you right back here.'

'If they know about me, sweetheart, surely they know about Jason.'

'It's just better. I'd put you in a hotel but they'd find you by your name anyway. It's the best possible solution.'

'Does Jason have a gun?'

Grace sighed. 'He's a man in Florida. Of course he has a gun.'

27

MONTREAL, 2016

Back at the airport, waiting for her 11:55 p.m. flight, Grace scanned the crowd of retirees, families, and deeply tanned young Québécois. She could find no one who looked like obvious replacements for the Russians, who had surely burned up on Highway 1. Three or four of her fellow passengers wore Halloween costumes, but they were too young and too happy to be pursuers.

She texted Steadman Coe, Manon, and William with the number from her new SIM card. On the airplane, before she dozed, she opened the Elena file on her computer and added everything she remembered from her stolen notebook and from the printouts. When she landed in Montreal, more exhausted than at any time in her life, she turned on her phone to see a text from Coe, sent at 4:22 in the morning:

The office at 8, non-negotiable thanks

After sitting on the tarmac inexplicably for almost an hour, and waiting in customs, there was no time to go home first so Grace took a taxi straight to the office in Old Montreal. It was not yet seven in the morning and still dark in the warehouse. She opened her laptop in her cubicle and imagined she had to file a front-page story for the *Times*, on a deadline.

How would she write the lede? For ten minutes she stared at the white screen, at her airplane notes. All she knew for sure was that Elena's parents were in the Cibulka book, along with other Russian informants and spies, that her mother's code name was Vrba, and that other files had been removed or destroyed. William had said Elena never graduated from Charles University. Yet Grace could not link anything she had learned about Elena to the fire that had killed Katka and her father, Coach Vacek. Officials in Prague and Moscow were unlikely to take her calls for confirmation. She could write nothing about the men stalking, threatening, attacking, and stealing from her because she had no idea who they were let alone who they represented.

Then there was Sergei Sorokin. Who the hell was he?

Records uncovered in the former Czechoslovakia show connections between Elena Craig, ex-wife of presidential candidate Anthony Craig, and the country's Cold War secret police organization, the StB.

Grace knew what her professors at Austin would say about this: it was not enough to *show connections*. Rather than changing it to a more precise, more dangerous verb phrase or reconstructing the opening sentence altogether – with the word *spy* or even *swallow* – she continued writing.

The sun rose over the St Lawrence. French hip hop growled to life from the northwest corner of the building, where the video game developers liked to start early. It was loud enough that she didn't hear Steadman Coe sneak up behind her. By the time she spotted his bald head in the reflection of her screen he had already read too much.

'What the fuck is that?'

She slammed the laptop shut. 'Nothing.'

'The eternal plea of the innocent. Let's go.'

Grace followed him to his office, her computer under her arm.

They were almost two months past Labor Day, in the northern bit of the northern hemisphere, yet Coe wore a suit in between white and tan. His cologne was musky fresh and his shoes were new. It only added to her fatigue, that she knew all of her boss's shoes.

At his door he stopped and turned. Grace stopped too. His freshly shaved chin shone in the fluorescent light. 'Have you looked in the mirror recently?'

'I haven't, actually.'

'Didn't think so.'

His office was vast and faced southeast, into the rising sun. Instead of sitting, as he usually would when they discussed a dumb feature or a bit of gossip, his sex life, or the whims of the owners of the company, Coe turned away from her and into the sun.

'Close the door.'

She did.

'Grace: I'm firing you.'

'What?' She looked at him for signs it was a joke. No, he was serious. 'Why?'

'Insubordination.'

'What are you talking about, Steadman? I'm stupidly loyal to you.'

'You work for the *National Flash*. You traveled to Prague on my dime.'

'I traveled to Prague on Elena's dime.'

'On assignment for my magazine. And instead of doing the work you were assigned to do, you harass Elena about a book project that is entirely outside the scope of your contract.'

'What contract?'

'Outside of your . . . purview.'

'That's made up, and it's entirely relevant to what I do. The better I know her, the better I can mimic her voice. And I won't miss any deadlines.'

'You're fired. Three months' severance is already in your account, as of 7:45 this morning.'

'Steadman.' She slapped the top of his desk. 'Turn around and look at me!'

'No.'

'What is this?'

He shook his head.

'Please tell me what's going on. Is the *Flash* in trouble? Is—'

He whispered something she could not quite hear.

'Pardon? Steadman, what?'

'Please go. I'm sorry.'

'Is this for real?'

Coe put his hands on the window and removed them. They left a moist print.

'There's nothing I can say to change your mind?'

'No.'

'Because this isn't your decision. Is it?'

Finally he turned. Grace had known Steadman Coe a long time but she had never seen him afraid.

'Steadman, the more of us who know, the safer we are, and –'

'Grace, you don't understand. This isn't journalism anymore.'

'What is it?'

He shook his head and pointed at the door.

All she packed from her desk were framed photographs of her mother and of Jason, of her cat Zip, and the cat before Zip. When she was nearly finished, Coe showed up to carry her box downstairs.

He didn't say anything and she didn't either, not on the third floor and not in the elevator. They did not pass any of their co-workers in the lobby. No one started until ten on non-production days.

Out on the street Coe waited with her while she hailed a cab. It was a cold and drizzly morning with a discouraging wind howling up off the river.

A red Prius pulled up.

They had never hugged and they never would. Coe put the box in the back seat and spoke softly. 'Let this go, Grace.'

'I'm not letting it go and you shouldn't either.' As she spoke, she did not have to remember to stand up straight. 'What did they say they'd do to you?'

Coe looked like he might answer the question for a moment. Then it passed and he walked toward the lobby of the old ware-house without looking back. Grace was tempted to call out to him that he was a coward and a scoundrel, but she loved Stead-man Coe in her way and knew this would not accomplish anything. She changed her mind and opened the passenger door of the taxi.

'You coward!' she yelled. 'You scoundrel!'

He seemed to shrink a little bit as he opened the door.

She checked her phone as the Prius pulled away, and there was a text from William.

Just arrived, knackered. You ready to start? Where should I go?

252

Grace was too knackered herself to come up with a better solution so she wrote, 'My place,' and her address.

She added her personal email account to the phone. The latest email to arrive was from Jean-Yves de Moulin, with an attachment. He wrote in fancy French that out of a morbid obsession in the days after their 'divorce' he had kept track of Elena. The attachment was a black-and-white page from the Montreal *Herald*, February 7, 1975. Grace opened and enlarged it. There was a photograph of the gymnast and glamor girl Elena Straka.

'I no longer compete. I model and I work, these are different things for me, and I have my life at home with my husband.'

William had already sent her several entirely British texts about staying with her.

My intentions are entirely professional and I certainly have no unction about booking into a hotel. If you could give me a recommendation?

I think I used unction incorrectly.

Grace of course I do appreciate it, if the invitation stands. Living in an authentic Montreal apartment. An honour! Ha ha.

That said if this makes you feel remotely awkward in
the remotest manner . . .

Grace ignored it and sent him the JPEG of the clip from the
Herald. He texted back:

Husband? My God. Elena Straka? Does the newspaper
have an archive? You think Straka'd speak to us? Do
you know where he lives?

Grace settled into her seat, unemployed for the first time
since her twenties. She did know where Josef Straka lived, and
she was looking forward to visiting him – with William.

28

HORKY NAD JIZEROU, 1986

The air in Bohemia was so clean it had a taste. Every night Elena and Kristína fell asleep in silence, in her parents' country home, and woke up to birds singing. There was no traffic, no sirens, no gunshots, no madmen shouting in the streets.

Elena had been concerned about her father for years, but the day before they were scheduled to leave he carried a haunted and distracted look she had never seen in him. While he was no madman shouting in the streets, Petr Kliment was not healthy.

'We live two separate lives, Elenka.' Her mother, Jana, crossed her legs in her reclining chair in the garden. It was a sunny late afternoon and they were sharing a pot of cold, sweet tea. 'I stay in the city and he stays here, with his fishing poles and his dirty boots.'

'Do you think he is lonely?'

Jana looked at Elena. 'He has the dog.'

Kristína, in boyish short pants and a T-shirt, was tramping along the river with Petr and his German pointer named Hektor. After three weeks in rural Czechoslovakia Kristína's arms were covered in bug bites and her knees were scraped.

'You're not worried about him, Mom?'

'Of course I am. He says things.'

'What things?'

'This is not our house, Elenka. Not really. They can hear us, you know that. Your father used to be disciplined. Now he's risking everything.'

'How? What does he say?'

'That he should have fought for you. That he thinks you're in some sort of American hell.' Jana looked around, as though someone might be listening. 'He says things about Anthony, about Sergei.'

'I'll speak to him.'

Her mother smiled, as though the problem was now solved. 'Should we switch to beer? I could have a beer.'

Elena went into the house for the beer. The sun shone in the kitchen, which was large enough for a staff to prepare meals for twelve. One of the Emperor Franz Joseph's lawyers had built it as his retirement home, and it had remained in his family until the government had seized it, and Jana had decorated it with all of the opulence a well-connected family was allowed. In the communist system the house and land made no sense, but it was far enough away from both Prague and Mladá Bole-slav that no one had denounced it as a symbol of aristocracy and greed. Besides, anyone who cared to know about the estate would understand it was granted to the Kliment Family by forces that should not be questioned – at least in public.

That evening, her last in Czechoslovakia this year, Elena strolled along the river with her father after Kristína was in bed. Petr had insisted on tucking her in and singing songs to her until she fell asleep. The two of them had a special connec-tion; she spoke Czech with him and showed a genuine interest in his outdoor passions.

'Mom says you're spending most of your time alone.'

He shrugged.

'Is everything okay, *tatínku*? You seem sad.'

The river moved gently around a corner, and an animal – maybe a muskrat – slipped into the water. Hektor sprinted after it and barked. The dog was so well trained that all Petr did was snap his fingers and he heeled, returning to his master's side.

'Sad is not quite the word.'

'Is it Kristína? That you don't see her enough?'

'It is not how I imagined life as a grandfather.'

'I'm sorry to be so far away.'

'You're sorry?' He took her hand in his and stopped her. While he was not yet sixty, there was something of the old man about him. His face was permanently tanned from being outside even in winter, and he was thin and muscular. 'Sweetheart, I am the one who is sorry. Sorry beyond reckoning. This is my fault.'

'What is?'

'I let him come for you. I let him take you.'

'There was no choice. The moment he arrived, this was inescapable.'

'A man of courage fights for his children.'

'You would be in prison, probably dead. Mom and I would still be suffering.'

'I believe in the republic. I do.'

'Dad . . .'

'But look what they've done to you.'

She laughed. 'I live in a penthouse apartment in New York City. I lead the design team for a major car manufacturer.'

Petr raised his eyebrows. 'Elenka. I know who you are.'

She took his hand and squeezed it. They continued walking.

'My only job was to protect you, and I failed. I know you have spared me the worst of what they do to you. But I imagine it. I see it in sweet Kristína, the product of all this, and they will do it to her too. They own her just as they own all of us.'

'I don't know what you imagine, *tati*, but it is wrong. I love my daughter and I am challenged in my job. They do not ask much of me.'

'What if you fail, if Anthony fails? What about your interests? The interests of Kristína? The more you love her, we love her . . .' He released Elena's hand, took a tissue out of his pocket, and touched his eyes. 'Elenka, they can take all of this away in an instant. They can make us all disappear if they think we are the faintest risk to them.' He stopped and turned to face her, his eyes a mess of tears. 'It is unbearable, what I have allowed. When I close my eyes at night, I think of hunting him and killing him.'

Elena shivered with fear. 'Never say it out loud, please, *tatínku.*'

'If we do not defeat these men, Elenka, they will defeat us. It is unbearable, unbearable.'

She took his hand again. 'Listen to me. They can't be defeated. I am happy to bear it for us all. Please, not a word of this. Do you promise? Never again.'

29

MONTREAL, 2016

Grace climbed the outdoor stairs to her second-floor apartment on Saint-Christophe and opened her door to the scent of natural gas. She could only smell the slow leak from her old stove when she returned from a few days away from the city, and for her a faint whiff of gas had come to represent Montreal, along with Québécois swear words, the cross on top of the hill they called a mountain, and the sweet dense bagels of her neighborhood.

'Zip?' She dropped the box of her accumulated career on the kitchen table. 'Kitty?'

It was unlike her but Manon might have accidentally let Zip out on one of her feeding visits. Zip was an inside girl but Saint-Christophe was an unusually safe place for wandering cats. Even if Zip were to be outside for weeks, someone would feed her. Grace opened her back fire escape door and shook the vacuum pack of all-natural salmon treats she spent too much of her salary on.

'Zip!'

She waited to hear the familiar tinkle of her bell collar before she called out again. One of her neighbors, a sculptor from Mali named Sekou, sat smoking on his fire escape next door. In French, Grace asked if Sekou had seen Zip.

'This is the fat orange one?'

'Yes.'

'I will keep watch.'

Grace closed the door, crossed the kitchen, and returned to the hall. At the front door she shook the bag of treats. 'Zip!'

Nothing. She texted Manon.

When did you last feed Zip?

Manon responded almost instantly.

Two days ago? Yesterday? When did we chat on the phone? Why, is she even fatter now?

Grace grabbed a broom from the kitchen closet and held it up like a staff. Her stomach had gone sour in Florida and it had turned worse in Steadman Coe's office. Now it felt like she had eaten razor blades. Slowly she walked into her bedroom.

Maybe Zip had gotten herself stuck somewhere? Manon had made her bed too, and had artfully arranged her pillows.

No Zip.

'Please, please, please, no,' Grace whispered.

In the bathroom she went straight to the toilet. The seat was down. She lifted it and there were no gifts of stalker piss.

Relieved, she turned to sit on the toilet and stopped herself. She never left the shower curtain closed over the bathtub. It made the room feel small. She counted the water dripping from the spout and twelve seconds elapsed between every drop. Manon had washed her dishes and she had made her bed but there was no way she had taken a bath.

There was no other sound in the apartment but Grace was not sure she had secured both the front and back doors so now she locked the bathroom door. She lifted the broom in her right hand and with her left she grabbed an end of the waxy shower curtain and opened it. Her orange cat was floating on the surface.

She climbed over the edge of the tub into the cold bath in her jeans and sweater. It was so full the water slopped over the side onto the wooden floor, but Grace did not care as she held Zip and told her what she always told her, that she was the best kitty, her best friend.

The buzzer rang. Then it rang again.

Grace stood up out of the bath and with Zip still in her arms she walked dripping to the front door, opened it, and stood shivering in the entrance. As the wind had promised, the rain had turned to wet blobs of snow.

William lowered his carry-on bag to the wooden platform at the top of the outdoor stairs, opened his arms to take her or Zip into them, and then he reconsidered and stepped around her and sprinted into the apartment. He slipped in a puddle, talked to her, talked to himself, and ran back with two towels. One he wrapped around Grace, who had not registered any of the words he had said. With the other towel he coaxed Zip out of her arms and wrapped the cat, stiff as a loaf of bread, and put her on the blue velvet footstool Grace had bought at the Saint-Michel Flea Market.

Together they looked down at Zip. Then William ran out, dragged his bag inside, and closed the door. In the bathroom he drained the tub and, talking all the while, began filling it again. He used several other towels to sop up the water from the floors and then he led Grace into the bathroom, the window and mirrors steaming now, and directed her to remove her wet clothes. She let him help her.

It wasn't until Grace was in the hot bath that the sadness and frustration bloomed in her and she finally allowed herself to cry. Zip had been with her for six years, since she was a kitten.

'It's all because of my selfishness,' she sobbed.

'What? No.'

'They warned me. I didn't listen.'

'You think they did this?'

'A cat does not drown itself, William. They already killed Katka and her father. They tried to kill me. They said it: *everyone I love.*'

She could not bring Zip back to life. She also knew that three months' severance pay would not last long. If she stopped writing the book, she would get her job back, protect her mother, protect Jason and his family, and sleep without worry. She could just send William away, save him from this, and turn it all off. Someone else would figure this out, a producer from *60 Minutes* or Seymour Hersh, and Grace would read it and watch it and feel exactly the way she had felt since graduating university: that eventually, one day, she would get her chance.

She wrapped herself in another towel and made her way into her bedroom. What would it take? She could write a note: 'You win. I give up', staple it to her front door, and crawl under the covers and sleep for a week.

'Grace. Are you okay?'

'No.'

A minute passed, though she could tell William was still standing in the hall because the old hardwood creaked under his weight. Now and then, since her fortieth birthday, on the verge of sleep, it struck Grace that she had already made all her big choices. Though she always felt young enough to start over, as a lawyer or a schoolteacher or the CEO of a technology concern, that naïve and hopeful part of her life was over. Outside the movies, there was no such thing as reinvention.

This was it! All she could do now was play in the box she had created for herself.

There was a thin pair of boxing gloves next to her bed, from the women's self-defense program at the YMCA. Grace had bought them in a glow of endorphins immediately after the final class of level one. Caught up in a wave of silly ambition, she hugged her fellow classmates, signed up for level two, and bought the gloves.

William knocked gently on her door. 'Would you like me to leave?'

In the full-length IKEA mirror hanging on the inside of her closet door Grace looked as tired and defeated as she felt. Even now her instinct was to call Zip for a cuddle. She did not often look at herself naked – really look – and she avoided it now. Her sheets were soft flannel, worn in over many years, and she had splurged on the natural rubber mattress and the goose-down duvet. In the crushing Montreal winter she was never too cold in this bed.

She could say yes, sorry, *go*, and crawl into the bed. No need for pajamas. This is what her body wanted. Instead she straightened her posture, lifted her chin. It was not as though she had lost the courage or the confidence of her youth. It had always been there, beneath the surface, waiting to be coaxed or called or forcibly dragged into the life she was actually living. It was the way some people dieted or stopped smoking: I'll start next week, they told themselves. Next week forever. She was going to start now.

William knocked again. 'Can I come in?'

'Just a minute.' She thought about the rest of their morning. 'Can you go knock on the door of the apartment below? The superintendent lives there. His English isn't terrible. Ask if you can borrow a shovel.'

30

On a beautiful autumn day there were hundreds of people in and around Parc La Fontaine. In an unwelcome snowstorm on the first of November it was deserted. Grace did not want to blemish the park in any way so she dug a hole in the sandy soil under some weeds along the pond, then lowered Zip into her grave and stood over her a while.

'Did you want to say something?' said William.

Grace shook her head. 'Zip knew how I felt about her.'

William took the shovel to bury Zip, and while he did, Grace imagined scenarios of revenge. One set of murderers had burned up in Florida but there were more men out there, more men without the capacity for empathy.

It was a fifteen-minute walk to the Grande Bibliothèque,

with a quick stop at Grace's apartment to drop off the shovel. The wet, swirling snow made it difficult to see, and William had to remove and wipe his glasses every few blocks. Grace watched for any sign of the cat killers. Her own paring knife was not as good as the one in her Airbnb in Prague but it was plenty sharp and she hoped to see them.

The Grande Bibliothèque was a striped monster of a building. Grace had been inside many times, for work and for fun, as it was on her way home from the office and a respite from both the hottest and the coldest evenings of the year. She read novels and magazines, attended lectures, and sometimes just stood in the beige of the place to stare out the window and daydream.

On one of those evenings she had met Manon, who took singing lessons. She'd handed Grace a postcard invitation to a three-song concert she and some fellow students were giving in a small bistro on Rue Saint-Denis. After the concert, they had a drink and it turned out they had books, divorce, wine, and a lively middle-point between introversion and extroversion in common.

The moment Manon spotted her, from behind her desk, her eyes opened wide and she hopped over the gate that separated the archivists from the people. She hugged Grace, and despite her headache from crying in the bath Grace cried some more.

'They killed her.' She hid her sob in Manon's turtleneck sweater.

'Who? Killed who?'

'Zip. My lovely Zip. I don't know who did it but when I find them . . .'

'Jesus, Grace, what does that mean? I don't understand.'

'Neither do I, Manon, not really. The moment I can tell you, I will.'

William handed Grace a clean white handkerchief and then he shook Manon's hand. 'William Kovály. London South Bank University. I'm working with Grace.'

'On what, Monsieur Kovály?'

'Call me William, please.'

'Do you speak French?'

'No, madame.'

Normally, Manon would now make a number of comments, in French, about William's age and height and relative handsomeness, local wisdom about what long noses can portend in the bedroom, his lack of a wedding ring. Only Zip was dead and Grace was still wiping her eyes.

They told Manon who they were looking for and she led them to her small, orderly office where Grace read her email from Jean-Yves de Moulin and the newspaper interview with Elena about her husband. The request was easy enough: they needed all the marriage records from Greater Montreal between 1972 and 1977.

Manon looked up Elena Klimentová, Elena Moulin, and both Elena and Josef Straka. 'Sorry. Nothing.'

'But if Elena and Josef got married, it would be in your system?'

'Absolutely. Unless someone took it away before we digitized it.'

'Took it away?'

Manon winked. 'Let me check.'

She picked up her phone and dialed a number. When someone answered, Manon launched into a friendly conversation in French.

As they spoke, Grace turned to William. Like his nose, his feet seemed too large for his body. She recalled his arrival at her apartment, how he had dealt with her and with Zip. William had plenty of capacity for empathy. For a moment Grace was stricken with the desire to reach for him.

Grace listened to Manon's phone conversation. While he wiped his glasses again, William asked Grace to translate. She explained Manon was checking with the head office of civil records in a suburb of Quebec City.

'There is a problem.' Manon put her hand over the receiver.

'What sort?'

'Another moment.' Then Manon said variations of *yes, I understand*, and *how strange* for a while, dished an *Oh là là là là là là*, and then thanked her colleague.

When she hung up the phone her eyebrows were up.

'What?'

'There are empty files on all of those names you gave me. You can find plenty on Monsieur Straka in more recent years.' She looked at her notepad. 'He was married in 1979 and again in 1985, divorced twice. Neither of the women was named Elena.'

'And the empty files?'

'Removed, *mon chou*.'

'By whom?'

Manon shook her head. 'Almost no one has the power to remove a file.'

'But someone did?'

'The *premier ministre* might have the authority. God? A thief? A cat murderer? My God, Grace, who are you dealing with?'

The snow continued to fall so they called an Uber to reach their next destination, the Montreal *Herald*. Out the back window of the car she tried to watch for anyone following them but there were only two car lengths of visibility.

On the walk to Parc La Fontaine Grace had told William what had happened to the murderers in Florida. Now, in the back of the Uber, he whispered new questions. 'Who are they working for, do you think?'

'I don't know. Jean-Yves de Moulin, in Strasbourg, thinks he is in danger and I am in danger – and I guess you're in danger too, William – until this comes out.' Grace read through her notes, from their visit with Manon. 'I'm already halfway through an article, if I can sell it.'

'If you can sell it? I'm not even a publisher and I'd buy it.'

The Uber stopped in front of the offices of the newspaper, they ran in, and Grace asked for her friend Lucy. Lucy had been the *Herald*'s librarian but in 2010, her hours had been cut to one day a week, and Lucy had become a part-time, casual employee and lost her benefits. Four days a week she *volunteered* for a corporation owned by a coalition of hedge funds that had transformed Canada's most esteemed journalistic institutions into a New York-based debt servicing scheme. Grace's feeling on the matter: this was criminally insane. After two glasses of wine she had told Lucy how she felt at one of their quarterly Women in Journalism meetings at the Upstairs lounge. Why, Lucy? Why would you do this for a horrible company, horrible people?

The answer was simple, and the conversation stopped for a while after Lucy said it. 'Why? This is all I have.'

Grace admired this answer, but the conversation had been so flinty afterward that Lucy had never forgiven Grace for the question. In subsequent Women in Journalism meetings they had sat at opposite ends of the table.

On any other day Grace would be nervous about seeing her, about asking this favor. She leaned on a hunk of marble. There was so much marble in downtown Montreal, in buildings like this no one cared about. If Grace had money and understood a thing about making more of it, she would buy up all the ignored marble of Montreal, mush it together, and build something fabulous in Florida. She pulled her hands away and there was a layer of moist dust on them.

The elevator door opened. Lucy was a three-hundred-pound woman with a wilted poinsettia for hair. She wore a brown muumuu.

'How are you, Lucy?'

'Criminally insane, didn't you say? Nothing much has changed in my world.'

'I was an idiot for saying that.'

'What can I do for you?'

'I need to search something in the archives.'

'Of course. We have some forms. It takes two to three weeks, and there is a standard fee.'

'Please, Lucy.'

'Please what, Grace?'

William stepped between them and introduced himself with a bow. 'Madame Lucy, Grace and I are caught up in something frankly ... unprecedented. My university has sent me here, from London, to help solve a mystery. It has a Montreal *Herald* connection, a Lucy connection.' He put his arm around her. 'You tell us what an hour of your time is worth and we'll double it.'

'Ková́ly? Of the West Island Ková́lys?'

William's arm remained around her significant shoulder. He led her past the elevators and around the corner.

A few minutes later they reappeared. Lucy pressed the up button on the elevator. She would not look at Grace. 'You have an hour.'

Upstairs, it didn't take nearly that long. There were a number of hits, in Lucy's system, for Elena Klimentová, Elena Straka, and Josef Straka between 1972 and 1977. But the clippings and photo files themselves weren't there. They could not even find a copy of the article Jean-Yves de Moulin had sent.

Lucy stood in a corridor between two metal shelves, where the material should have been, and shook her head.

'This isn't possible.'

'Why not?' Grace joined her.

'I'm the only one with access. I'm the only one who's here. I know how to find things. If someone were to take a bunch of files . . .' she turned to Grace. 'I'm the someone. It's just me.'

'When did you start working here?'

'I was nineteen. It was right after Christmas break in 1971.'

'Well.' William sighed. 'These people are certainly consistent.'

'Who? What people? You know who did this, don't you?' She looked at William.

William stepped in close, to comfort her. 'If someone were to break in, Lucy, or if someone were to pay a staff member to come in on a weekend, how might they find and steal files?'

'I have the passwords.'

'Before computers?'

She led them to a bright wooden cabinet and asked Grace and William to turn away. Then she entered a combination and pulled out the card catalog. 'This hasn't been opened in years. But even then the only other person who had the combination, ever, was the editor in chief.' She lifted out a card. 'We computerized in 1985. All we did, at that time, was enter this information into our system.'

'But the actual files could have been empty, even then.'

'It's possible.' Lucy returned the card, closed the drawer,

and spun the combination to lock. She turned away from the drawer and reached for a huge chair on wheels, pulled it close, and sat down. 'One of our editors in chief was crooked. It must have been him – one of the men, surely, from the great era of drunken men. It's the only answer. Unless—'

'Unless what?' Grace sat on the edge of a desk.

'Last spring the police were here. They wanted a look-see, and could not tell me what they wanted.'

'The Montreal police?'

'I can't . . .' Lucy's hands were in her messy hair. She looked at the floor. 'Maybe RCMP? What's the Canadian version of the CIA called again? It's not on TV. If it were on TV we'd know. This damn country.'

'Was it men or women?' Grace made notes. 'Can you remember what they were wearing? What were they looking for? What did they say?'

'It was police business, they said.'

'Did you see what they were doing?'

For the next five minutes Lucy tried to describe the men and what they had done. Grace took down every word, but Lucy had turned small and regretful in her chair, mourning a shocking loss. She was vague and apprehensive. 'They told me not to talk to anyone about their visit. They said it could compromise . . .'

'The integrity of the investigation?' said William. 'Of course they did.'

In the elevator, on the way down, Grace asked William what he had said to Lucy to persuade her to help them.

He pushed his heavy glasses up his nose and crouching to look at his reflection in the elevator mirror he combed his black hair with his fingers. 'I told her she could help stop Anthony Craig.'

31

Elena and Anthony Craig looked out the window of Room 107 of the Hotel National. He was in the final stages of a cold and kept wiping his nose with a thin handkerchief he had bought at the airport in Berlin. It made him seem – to Elena – almost Slavic. Their assigned guide, Yuri, was officially from the state tourism agency but in her opinion he was far too knowledge-able about the whims of his American clients to be anything other than an entry-level KGB officer.

She knew the plan, what came next, and she didn't like it.

Back in New York Anthony would have told Yuri to fuck off a number of times by now, but here they were in the most prestigious suite of the most prestigious hotel in Moscow with a view of the Kremlin in the late afternoon sunshine, all of it courtesy of the Soviet government.

Friends had warned Anthony that the communists were easily insulted, so he pretended to be interested in Yuri's commentary about Lenin and his wife, Nadezhda Krupskaya, whose room they were staying in, pretended to know all about Pablo Neruda and Anatole France, who had also slept there.

'What year was it again, Yuri, the big show?'

'Our revolution was 1917. All leaders of the new government stayed in the Hotel National the following months because the Kremlin was damaged in fighting. Lenin himself. Trotsky, Dzerzhinsky . . .'

'Okay, okay.' Anthony waved the soiled handkerchief at him and looked back out the window at the Kremlin. 'I can't keep track of all the -*skys* but thanks, pal, it's a big help knowing this.'

Elena sat on the edge of the bed and laughed. She knew that men and women were listening to them in the ugly concrete Intourist tower next door. She imagined them wearing headphones, looking at one another. *This* is what a fancy capitalist sounds like? It had been a long time since she had been taught to find bugs in a room, fifteen or sixteen years ago, but even she found the listening devices in Room 107 crudely hidden: they were in the bathroom medicine cabinet, on the bedside lamps. The video cameras above the bed and in the salon were visible. All you had to do was look up.

'Is there anything else I can help with, Mr Craig?' Yuri placed his hands together, as though he were praying. 'Any facts?'

'What do you mean, facts? I'm a car guy, I love cars, they're all I ever think about, but this square – it's just a huge road and dumpy buildings. And those cars! Elena, they're even uglier than you said, belching diesel. Jesus. And Red Square? Where's the red you people are always blabbing about? And this is supposed to be the best spot. It's a capital city, Yuri. Have some pride. Live a little. You know what might help with this view?'

Yuri joined him at the window.

'A tree or two, that's what.'

'I see what you mean.'

'Look down there! Why isn't anyone smiling? It's summer. Don't you guys have winter ten months a year?'

Anthony opened the window and shouted over the seven or eight lanes of Mokhovaya Street, over an orchestra of engine noise, 'Live a little!' He closed the window again and wiped his nose. 'And what's with all the damn concrete? There's other stuff to build with, you know.'

Yuri looked over at Elena, for guidance. She shrugged.

'Tonight, Mr Craig, you will meet with very important people in politics and economics and manufacturing and automotive. I will brief you.' Yuri reached into the inside pocket of his jacket and pulled out an envelope. He cleared his throat and unfolded some papers. 'Many of these men and women are crucial in the Communist Party and very close to Mr Gorbachev himself.'

Elena's job at the dinner meeting that night would be to assure the Soviet leadership they would open an auto manufacturing plant in Russia if the terms were good enough and if the brand was entirely separate from Craig International. The conversation would move naturally in the direction of Anthony's political ambitions. Mayor of New York? Maybe. Governor? Maybe, but Albany? This was difficult to imagine. If only they could move the state capital to the Florida coast.

'How about president of the United States?' one of them would say.

It was not a state secret that the Soviets were unhappy with Ronald Reagan, who was no longer a young man. Sergei spoke of Gorbachev with a mixed tone. Communism in its current state would not, could not, last forever. Gorbachev and his staff were studying capitalism, and the possibility of a peaceful transition, earnestly and carefully. They had begun quiet conversations with the Americans on potential scenarios. There was only one dominant issue for everyone on the Soviet side of the negotiating table: *these changes could not humiliate and degrade the Russian people or the Russian soul.*

Yet in seeking *perestroika* and *glasnost* so transparently, Gorbachev had announced his weakness. Sergei had called it 'kneeling before America'.

What did Reagan do? He made arrogant demands, in exclamation points, from Berlin. Berlin! A city whose people would *rule America today* were it not for Soviet strength and sacrifice in the Great Patriotic War.

It demonstrated what Reagan knew. Enough intelligence had leaked out, through the sieve of KGB drunks and defectors: the Soviet war machine was an overhyped joke. The American strategy, to bankrupt the state through the arms race, had worked. Communism, what they called communism, had failed.

In Room 107 of the Hotel National, Anthony sighed and stepped away from the window. He put his arm around Yuri and led him to the door. 'No offense, but I'm good on meetings. There's a lot of things I'm good at. Wouldn't you say, Elena?'

She nodded.

'But my very best thing is meeting a bunch of strangers and making a deal. If anyone can make a deal with a room full of communists, I'm the guy. Okay? Really thankful for the chaperone duties and for organizing Elena's thing.'

'Her tour of the Kremlin,' said Yuri.

'That's it, chum. Really, really special. But now I'll get a nap in. Come back in four hours, all right, and I'll listen to you talk about all kinds of people, all the-*skys* and-*ovs* you can find for me. Great people. The greatest. Folks back home should know. But right now I just can't. Okay? What's your name again?'

'Yuri,' the entry-level spy said, for the twelfth time.

'Am I upsetting you, Yuri? It's not what I want to do here.'

'No, Mr Craig. Assuredly not.'

When he was out and the door was closed again, Anthony opened his arms in disbelief. 'They are so stiff.'

'Tonight they'll drink too much vodka and loosen up,' said

Elena. 'They're just nervous around you, Tony. Most of these people have never met an American, let alone a rich and famous American, a powerful one.'

He walked across the salon to the window again. 'That's a good point.'

'In Russia, there is only one kind of power. Political power. You represent another kind, and they're just not used to it.'

'I succeed using this beautiful thing right here.' He pointed at his head and blew his nose again. 'You're taking Alicia with you, to see the bodies of dead pinkos?'

'I don't think you can actually see them. It's a mausoleum.'

'No offense, but these Slavs are creepy.'

Alicia was Elena's assistant and, probably, her best friend. Anthony lusted after her, and he wasn't remotely sneaky about it.

'Does he have any strange fantasies?' Sergei had asked her, in his violin shop on West Sixty-eighty Street, as they planned the trip to Moscow.

'Like what?'

'Anything with body waste, with animals? Does he like to hurt or be hurt?'

'He is very conventional. Of course, Anthony likes to be told he is the greatest lover in the history of earth. Just as he is the greatest automaker. If he had only focused on it, he would be the world's greatest golfer as well.'

Would the room smell strangely, when she returned? While she and Alicia walked through Red Square and the Kremlin, three of 'Yuri's nice young friends' would arrive to entertain Anthony. The video cameras would record everything. The one consolation was he would certainly spread his cold virus to his visitors.

Now that Elena was in her late thirties, with a healthy and wonderful daughter, it did not matter so much that he did what he did. She had Kristína. In ten years of marriage to him, in a business partnership with him, she had learned how to build a company. She did not have love but she had ideas. She had influence.

Now that she was in Moscow, she could not believe she once imagined herself living here. Anthony was right. It was bleak and the people were uniformly miserable. Even with a weekend dacha on the Black Sea, there was no way she could have spent her life in Moscow.

Elena knew who was on the guest list tonight. They had talked about inviting Gorbachev himself, but that would have aroused too much curiosity back home.

When they learned about the trip, two men from the CIA had visited them in New York for a briefing. Don't talk about politics. Don't allow any money to change hands until you're back home and we can help you. Don't reveal anything personal about yourself.

Elena had insisted on joining the meeting with the CIA so she could steer the conversation away from how hot Russian girls could compromise naïve Western men.

There was a knock on the door. Elena looked through the

peephole to see Alicia in a simple white dress and a hat. She put on a light sweater and her sunglasses. 'Have a good time, Tony.'

'It's just a nap.'

'Maybe something interesting will happen while I'm gone,' she said, as she opened the door.

But he was already looking back out the window, his thoughts far away on what he might conquer.

32

'Baby It's Cold Outside' played from outdoor speakers on Sainte-Catherine Street as Grace and William made their way to Josef Straka's apartment. The Christmas shopping season begins officially on the first of November and shopkeepers were already putting up trees and garlands. And the early snow was becoming serious. They climbed Peel Street. A white transport truck slid into another white transport truck in front of Chez Alexandre et fils.

Both drivers stepped out of their vehicles. In New York they would have cussed at each other. Here, with their sweet union contracts, they sparked cigarettes and said local variations on *bien*.

Grace had paid the security guard at the *Herald* two dollars to borrow his cellphone for a local call. On Josef Straka's card there were two numbers. William dialed the landline and hung up when Straka answered.

They turned west on Sherbrooke Street, back into the wind and the worst of the blizzard. It was beginning to stick on the sidewalks now. Grace took William's arm instead of his hand. When they reached the Ritz-Carlton and the blue chemical ice melt, to cross the street, it was no longer slippery but William would not let her take her arm back. They walked like young lovers.

There was a black metal awning in front of the Acadia, Josef Straka's building. Under it, they shook and slapped the globs of wet snow from their hair and jackets. 'It's been so long.' Grace looked at the arms of her black wool jacket instead of William's eyes. 'Years and years, since I held a man's hand.'

'That, Grace, is a terrible shame.'

A gentleman in a fur coat opened the gold-plated door and led them to his desk. 'Madame Elliott and friend? I'll call up to Monsieur Straka so he knows you're coming.'

'We're not expected.'

'Monsieur Straka has many visitors.'

While he phoned, the doorman gave them two white towels to dry their hair. The towels smelled faintly of a swimming pool.

On the way to the elevator Grace told William more about Straka: how he was polite and formal, a minor donor and major fundraiser in the dusty European arts in Montreal. His apartment was on the top floor, and as the elevator rose slowly, Grace prepared her recorder. 'Somehow he got out of Czechoslovakia when she did, the hardest and most dangerous time to leave. And the files on him and Elena must be missing for a reason. I can only assume he had a government role before the fall of communism, a role worth concealing. What's your theory?'

'He wasn't in the Cibulka. I don't know where that takes us.'

Josef Straka stood at his open door. His white hair was freshly combed and he wore a crisp dress shirt with a black cardigan, tan chinos, a pair of slippers. 'Madame Elliott.'

'Monsieur.'

'What a pleasure to see you again.'

William said something in Czech and Straka agreed. They both translated for Grace. The snow in Montreal is real snow, unlike the nonsense that falls in Prague. Then Straka performed his Gilles Vigneault impression, singing, '*Mon pays, ce n'est pas un pays, c'est l'hiver.*'

Grace translated the classic Québécois song for William. 'My country is not a country. It's winter.'

In English it sounded banal.

They chuckled politely and shook hands while Straka looked at Grace's notebook and recorder. He had not yet invited them in. Through the open door, Grace could see bright white walls and dark wood floors and cabinetry, statues and abstract art. Through the big windows of his expensive condo, snow whorled and danced.

'What can I do for you?' Straka asked at last.

'I am writing a book about Ms Craig, her life story.'

He crossed his arms, the smile disappeared but he did not look surprised. 'She will not allow this. It will not be permitted.'

'Permitted?' she said.

'How does this affect your role at the *National Flash*, Madame Elliott?'

This was his way of telling her he knew she'd been fired. Grace turned on the recorder. 'I was surprised to learn that you and Ms Craig were once married, Monsieur Straka. I had never heard that before, despite all our conversations and all the interviews she has given.'

'This is false. We were never married.'

'But in the Montreal *Herald*, Elena herself said—'

'You were at the paper, yes? Please show me what you discovered.'

'How did you hear we were just at the paper, monsieur?'

Straka looked at his watch, evidently keen to get rid of them.

'Well, as you know, there's nothing in the archives.' Grace unlocked her phone and opened the email from Jean-Yves de Moulin. 'But I do have an image.'

Straka removed his glasses to look at the article. 'That's obviously a fake.'

'Why do you say that?'

'I lived here at that time. Elena lived here too. We weren't married. Someone created it to mislead you. Nine-year-olds can be graphic designers now.'

'There were hits, in the *Herald* system, for articles. Not just this one but lots of others. But the articles themselves have been removed.'

'Fake hits, to mislead you.'

William had his own notepad out now. 'We went to the provincial archives as well, Mr Straka. It showed there were files once about your marriage to Ms Craig, and that they too are gone.'

'There never were any files about my marriage to Madame Craig because we were never married.' Straka's angry voice boomed in the hall. 'We were childhood friends. To the best of my knowledge, the government of Quebec is not interested in such matters.'

'How did you escape Czechoslovakia?'

Straka turned slowly back to Grace and his smile returned, though this one was different from his *welcome-weather-song* smile. 'Carefully.'

'Can you expand on that?'

'No, I mean you, Madame Elliott. Tread carefully.'

'Monsieur Straka, Czechoslovakia doesn't exist anymore. Surely it doesn't matter how you left and came to Canada. It must have been terribly difficult and dramatic. All of the razor wire and the mines, the border guards with machine guns, the dogs.'

'This is mythology, Madame Elliott. Defecting was actually quite easy.'

'Were you working for the StB?'

Straka stepped back and reached for the door to close it.

'Was the marriage part of the strategy?' Grace stepped forward to keep the door open with her foot. 'I can't make that part out. How did it benefit you or Elena, to be married?'

'Enough, Madame Elliott.'

'Unless you were in love.'

'We looked for you in the Cibulka,' said William.

Veins had popped on Straka's forehead. As furious as he was, he also seemed to Grace a touch defeated. There was a new slouch about the way he stood with his hand on the heavy door. 'You disgust me, the way you try to smear good people. I've given so much to this city and this country. I have hurt no one.'

'I'll get the story,' said Grace. 'Depend on it. You can either control your place in it by giving us an interview or not.'

He took a deep breath and Grace thought for a moment that he was about to invite them in.

'You will not get the story,' he said, reaching down and turning off her recorder. Then he whispered so quietly she could only hear its edges. 'They'll kill you first.' He turned. 'Goodbye, Madame Elliott.'

William had already backed into the hall. Again, Grace stopped the door as he tried to close it. 'Who are they?'

Straka took a step forward and placed his hands on her shoulders, like he was going to lean in to tell her a secret. Then he shoved her into the hall. She fell back into William and rather gracelessly landed on her tailbone.

The door slammed.

It was, for a while, eerily quiet in the hall. Someone was using an electric drill. William eased Grace up and she righted the messed-up pages of her notebook. They stared at his door for a while, as though it were a dangerous object, and then Grace walked across the hall, pressed the down button on the elevator.

'Grace?'

'Yes?'

The elevator doors opened. 'Is it normal to be told you could be . . . killed for writing a story?'

Grace shook her head. Even in her jacket she was cold. As they walked through the generous lobby of the Acadia, the doorman saluted them. 'Madame Elliott? Monsieur Kovály?'

'How does he know my name?' William whispered.

The doorman gestured toward a man and a woman, both in black overcoats, standing up from the two chairs in the entrance hall. They were tall and fit, both of them with high cheekbones and skin the color of eggshells. 'These two have been waiting for you.'

33

MLADÁ BOLESLAV, 1990

As she stood over the grave of her father, her weeping daughter at her side, Elena watched her husband. The priest delivered the sermon in Czech, a language Anthony never bothered to learn: not even *hello* and *goodbye*, certainly not *thank you*. While in the beginning he always said her accent was cute, she knew he found the actual language coarse and disagreeable – the grunts of peasants, he called it. French was high class. Dutch and German sounded smart. The Slavic languages, which sounded all the same to him, were signs of a stunted culture, a stunted people. He would say this in front of her, in a crowd, at dinner. *Present company excluded, sweetheart.*

Anthony did that thing with his lips, curled into scorn and despair, and looked down at the casket. Elena imagined what he was thinking – *a good casket, the best casket money can buy in this fucked-up country*. When he looked at the quarterly results of Craig International, especially these days, this was the face he made.

Whatever he was thinking about, with a few flakes of dry snow swirling around him, Elena was absolutely certain it wasn't her father, it wasn't Kristína, it wasn't her.

Kristína had spent every summer of her young life at her grandparents' house on the river. Her grandfather was her father, far more than Anthony had been. Anthony was too busy to teach her anything, up until now, and wore it like a medal. *She learns from my example, from my business, from my work, and that has to be good enough. Her father's a great man, one of the greatest. You knew that when you married me. It's why you married me.*

Why she married him.

For years Elena had worried about her father, how he tortured himself. Petr Kliment believed he had sent his daughter, and therefore his granddaughter, into ruin. He said this to Jana, his wife. He said it to Elena.

Had he said these things, these truths, to others? This is what had driven Elena from sleep. When the phone rang in the middle of the night, her heart would go wild with worry, certain he had said too much to the wrong people.

Then it was over. Soon even the Soviet Union would dissolve. She was no longer a swallow. She was free. The dissident, Václav Havel, was now president of the federal republic.

The new motto of the country was *Pravda vítězí*: truth wins. Then she would think of Danika and her own dark days, the culmination of her life, and nothing seemed true at all.

Her first thought, when the Eastern Bloc began to fall apart a year ago, was that she could soon go home, take Kristína from Anthony and go home. Petr knew this plan. They had discussed it on a walk through the bush with Hektor, in the summertime, and he had been overjoyed. After twenty years of prison, his daughter could live a life of her choosing.

No one could hurt them now.

Kristína would be thirteen soon. Elena worried most of all that she would lose what Petr Kliment had taught her. Not, in Anthony's words, *to be a little communist* but to care for the rhythm of life around her, for other people and the spirit in the woods, whatever God had been to earlier generations of Czechs.

Elena was suddenly enraged, at her father's grave, to think that Anthony had never bothered to come to Czechoslovakia to meet him.

It had been more than a year since Elena had seen or heard from Sergei. She fantasized about them quietly trying and hanging him in the courtyard of a Russian state house, even though she knew there was no hanging a man like Sergei.

She had stopped expecting the phone call about her father, and then it came. In New York, on the airplane, in her mother's apartment, at the grave she could not stop thinking about her father's strong heart. He was young!

Jana was coming back to New York with them. Czechoslovakia was no place for her anymore, especially not now with people of stature under communism waking up in the middle of the night to bricks thrown through their windows. One of her mother's friends, a party official in Prague, had been accosted by a group of other women. They had slapped and spat on her.

Communism or capitalism had been irrelevant to Petr Kliment. No one had said a word against him. He died at sixty-three, putting up new shelves in his work shed. She imagined his final minutes, lying in the cold and dark.

A heart attack was only a heart attack if the doctor said so. And the doctor had not come to the funeral.

Beside her, Anthony sighed. It was too much for him, to listen to someone else speak – especially in Czech. The automotive division had never made money. They had reached the limits of what they could borrow and sometime in the next year or two they would have to begin selling off major assets. Management consultants from McKinsey had been called in to speak to the executive team, and Anthony called them cowards without imagination. He hated consultants and he hated banks. The deal with the Soviets, back in 1987, had fallen through despite all of her and Sergei's careful work. Anthony hated following regulations in Long Island and New Jersey.

'That's the problem to solve in America, and not only for Craig,' he told the men from McKinsey. 'We wouldn't need so much fucking capital if you geniuses could figure out how to get around taxes and regulations. Soon we'll be worse than

Moscow. Elena: tell them what it was like to build a factory in Moscow!'

She would start to tell them, and Anthony would interrupt. He could tell the story about all the dumb regulations in Moscow better, faster, and without an accent.

'Ow, Mama.' Kristína looked up at her in her black Prada overcoat, her big eyes red from crying. She had been squeezing her daughter's hand too hard.

The priest stopped speaking.

Anthony nodded with pretend sadness. 'Finally.'

Elena threw dirt on the coffin and so did Kristína. Anthony did too, conscious that a crowd was watching. Walking slowly to the black cars that would take them back to the hotel in Prague, Anthony put his arm around Elena.

'Who gets to be in those mausoleum crypts, the little stone mansions?'

'Before communism, whoever paid for them,' she said.

'You know what, fuck it. I'll have someone look into this. We can get one built for your dad, one of those light-colored ones like old churches. If we have to get him dug back up to put him in there, I say we go for it. What do you say? You don't want people walking past and thinking Anthony Craig is cheap.'

'It isn't important,' Elena said.

'You know what? I think it is.' He stopped her, turned her around, pointed to the distant hole in the ground where a small party of men was already shoveling. 'We're better than that.'

The mausoleum crypts were off to the side, on what amounted to an avenue of dead rich people.

'That's where someone of his stature belongs, Elena.'

'My dad never cared about stature.'

'You do. We do. Let's make sure he's remembered as the right kind of man.'

Kristína was on her own, speaking Czech with the priest. There would be a dour version of a wake in the rooftop restaurant of the Inter-Continental Hotel.

They had killed her father. Elena was sure of it. Where would men like this hide? Men who knew how to find people anywhere?

Anthony was not staying for the wake. He had chartered a plane to take him to Frankfurt, where he would meet with Deutsche Bank the next day. In the car he talked about how it was a great funeral but they had to build a beautiful mausoleum for Petr, with maybe enough room for old Jana when she died.

'You design it, Elena.' Anthony sat with his chest out, like this mausoleum idea had brought her father back to life. 'You tell me how you want it and it's done. It is fucking *done*.'

She sighed. 'All right.'

'A beautiful crypt that will last a thousand years. We can have a plaque on it: by the Anthony Craig family.'

Kristína, who had been listening to the conversation, interrupted. 'He'd like it better to be in the ground with the animals.'

'Who teaches her to talk this way?' Anthony motioned toward Kristína with his thumb. 'Is this what the kids learn every summer, here at commie camp?'

'Dad!'

At the hotel in Prague he had the porter load his bags into the car and he kissed Elena and his daughter. 'Great funeral. You looked great. Kristína: gorgeous. Your hair is gorgeous like that. You saw the press was there, right? You don't make eye contact when they take your picture. You look away and you look sad because that's what people expect you to be, right? Sad at sad things and happy at happy things.'

Two hours later, when the speeches were over at the wake, Elena led Kristína to the elevator, where a man in a dark suit and hat was waiting for them. She did not recognize him at first. He had gained even more weight and there were dark rings under his eyes.

'I am so sorry for your loss, Mrs Craig. Your father was a very good man.'

She simply nodded, as though he were a stranger, and allowed him to place a slip of paper in her purse.

Three hours later, when Kristína was asleep, Elena left the hotel. Sergei was in a pew in the middle of St Nicholas Church where no one would notice him.

Elena slid in next to Sergei and for the next ten minutes, as he whispered plans at her, she dug her fingernails into the palms of her hands.

'I want out.'

'Yes. We know. And as you know, that isn't how it works.'

'I don't care if that isn't *how it works*, Sergei. As long as there was an StB and a KGB, I did what was required of me. I'm taking my mother to New York. You can't threaten my father anymore.'

Sergei sat back in his pew with half a smile.

'Did you kill him?'

'Absolutely not. I visited him, last month. For some reason he was convinced – like you, Elenka – that it was *over*. That you were free of us. Your debts paid. You were leaving Craig, he said, and moving to Mladá Boleslav.'

'And?'

'Petr knew the rules, Elenka, and he benefited from them. He lived a life almost no one in this country could have imagined. All because of you. And he betrayed you. I can't tell you how many times I had to stop him from talking, protect him from himself. I was your father's protector, all these years. But last month I had to tell him the truth. Nothing is over. It is only just beginning for you, for our Anthony. Petr did not take it well.'

She stood up.

'Elena, your father did not have a heart attack. The coward hanged himself. Vrba did the right thing. She called me.'

'You're lying! And don't call him that.'

'You shouldn't shout in a church.'

Elena tried to slap him but he caught her arm at the wrist and squeezed. She tried to pry herself loose. 'I'm leaving him. I'm finished.'

'Oh Elenka.' Sergei took a deep breath and exhaled with a full smile, released her. 'You and Anthony and your pretty Kristína, you're finished when we say you're finished.'

34

The woman was one of the most beautiful people Grace had ever seen, with creamy skin and clear green eyes, bright copper hair.

'Mr Kovály. Ms Elliott. My name is Roberta McKee.' She gestured to the man next to her, in a camel cashmere coat. 'This is Bradley Tebb.'

The man nodded. It was slightly more than a nod, almost a bow. McKee presented Grace with a card, white with a maple leaf on it: French on one side, English on the other.

'We work with the Canadian Security Intelligence Service, Quebec Region.'

Grace inspected the card.

'We're following up on a message we received from our friends at the National Archives, in Sainte-Foy.'

The doorman leaned over his marble banquette and watched them.

'Might you have an hour to chat with us, Ms Elliott? Mr Kovály? We're not far away, near the Centre Bell.'

Bradley Tebb did not look or dress or stand like a Bradley Tebb. Grace was no expert on Canadians, but she had lived in Montreal long enough to recognize when something was off. 'We're pretty busy, actually. Maybe we can set up an appointment, later this afternoon?'

'Actually, Ms Elliott, we're rather pressed for time ourselves.' McKee swatted some of the melting snow from her black jacket. 'We have a car waiting outside. I promise it won't be more than an hour, transport included.'

Grace switched to French. 'It's where exactly, your office?'

'Not far at all,' said McKee, in French. 'Two steps away.'

Still, Bradley Tebb had said nothing. He led the way, walking sideways, his front arm out like a magician taking them to see the floating head. William and Grace walked behind Tebb and McKee followed. The car was a black Audi with tinted windows, its four-way flashers on.

Grace stepped out from under the awning. The temperature had dropped further and the snow was flying sideways now in the wind. She pointed up into the blizzard. 'Some weather, hey?'

'Some weather.' Tebb nodded. 'Yes.'

Sherbrooke Street had two lanes of traffic running in each direction. The walk signal, to cross, was counting down from six. Grace grabbed William by the jacket, yanked him to the crosswalk, toward the Ritz-Carlton, and pulled him across the street. McKee and Tebb were young and athletic but by the time they began running after them the walk signal had gone down to two. Grace counted on them knowing that Montreal drivers were not to be toyed with. McKee shouted something but with the wind and the cars Grace could not hear it.

The costumed valets of the Ritz-Carlton greeted them like royals. Grace turned to see the outlines of McKee and Tebb in the snow, their arms crossed by the Audi.

'What's happening?' Inside the white and gold lobby, William was so out of breath he could hardly speak. 'Who are they?'

'Canada's intelligence service is called CSIS, but her French accent's wrong, the card didn't have braille on it, and the man, Bradley, even his English accent is wrong.'

'So who are they?'

'Watch them.'

William went to one of the doors and looked out. 'It's hard to see. The car's going . . . gone.'

It was too noisy near the doors so Grace walked deeper into the lobby, under the chandeliers. It was not yet one in the afternoon and already it looked and felt like night had fallen. Grace called the number on McKee's card.

'That was very rash. What are you doing, Ms Elliott?' On

the phone, Roberta McKee no longer tried to conceal her Eastern European accent.

'I know you're not CSIS. Roberta McKee! What a stupid name.'

'You are going to get yourselves into worse trouble.'

'But we've done nothing wrong.'

McKee whispered something to her partner – driving instructions. Grace could not understand the language they spoke but it sounded Russian.

'Did you kill my cat?' she shouted. But it was too late. McKee had ended the call.

William led Grace deeper into the middle of the Ritz-Carlton lobby, where no one could overhear them. 'Russian spies,' he said, 'Russian mafia. There's no difference, I can tell you that. The FSB, the SVR, the GRU, they answer to the same institution as the gangs, to the same man, in fact: Aleksandr Mironov.'

'What?' said Grace. 'The president?'

'That's him, and he made them all. If those two are . . . Grace, they *will* just kill us. I feel terrible about Zip but I don't want to lose you.'

'Lose me?'

'Look, we can't call the police. We can't call anyone. Believe me, nothing and no one can stop them. You think the FBI hasn't tried?'

A tall and off-puttingly handsome black man in a suit walked over and spoke quietly, his hand on William's arm. 'Monsieur, madame. Is everything all right? Can I help you in any way?'

'No, monsieur.' Grace tried to match his *politesse*. 'Thank you, infinitely.'

'You're guests of the Ritz-Carlton this evening?'

'I'm afraid not.'

'Are you here for our afternoon tea service?'

'No, monsieur.'

The hotelier placed his hands together. 'Can we not serve you in any way this afternoon? Secure a reservation at Maison Boulud? Call you a taxi perhaps?'

'Everyone should be so polite about kicking people out.'

The hotelier bowed and gestured towards the exit of the hotel.

In the taxi on their way back to Saint-Christophe, neither of them spoke. Grace thought of her blind mother in Jason's Febreze-scented guest room in Coral Springs, responding to the doorbell in the middle of the afternoon: smiling at Roberta McKee and Bradley Tebb.

She asked the driver to go by the apartment and keep going a while, so she could check for cat assassins before going inside.

Just as she was about to ask the driver to stop, the Audi from outside Straka's building turned slowly onto Saint-Christophe. Grace stifled a scream with her hand, a scream of fear and rage and exhaustion. When she had first moved to Montreal, there had been an outbreak of cockroaches in her apartment. The landlord had to call an exterminator in the end, but for years she had a recurring dream where armies of cockroaches came up all of the drains at once and though she ran from room to room there was no way to stop them. They were too fast and too clever, too determined. There were too many of them.

Enough of the scream leaked between her fingers that both William and the squat driver jumped in their seats.

'Keep going,' said William.

'Keep going,' Grace repeated in French.

'Madame?'

'Drive, please.'

'Where?'

'Straight. Just go. Go!'

Roberta McKee and Bradley Tebb had stepped out of the Audi as it stopped in front of her apartment. Jean-Yves de Moulin was right. Now that they knew what she knew – whoever *they* were – no one was safe until her story was published. It could not wait until after the election.

She had to see Elena, now.

'You have your passport?'

William looked in his computer bag. 'I do. But my toiletries are—'

'The airport, *s'il vous plaît.*'

35

LONDON, 1992

The rebirth of Craig International began in a private dining room at the Connaught hotel in Mayfair. Elena was so nervous she could not think about food. She stared at the flickering candles on the table, now that the spring sun had set, while her husband looked out the window at Carlos Place. Anthony was nervous too, but Elena had never heard him admit it aloud and he did not now. Instead he adjusted his tie and touched his hair and sighed at his watch every thirty seconds. When their guests were officially fifteen minutes late, he stood up. 'Nobody shows up late to a meeting with Anthony Craig in New York. No one.'

This was entirely untrue. The mayor, who wanted to run again, had been forty minutes late for a dinner with them less than a week earlier.

'Tony, sit down. We need them.'

He did and slammed the table with his fist. The waiter arrived with a glass of pinot gris for Elena and a Diet Coke for her husband.

'Your guests will be arriving soon, Mr and Mrs Craig?'

'They goddamn well better be,' said Anthony.

It was obviously far too much emotion for the waiter. 'Very good, sir.'

The walls in the dimly lit private room were white stone. A fire crackled in the hearth. Apart from the vast table they had set up with four chairs, the room had a couch, a coffee table, and a bar. Anthony slouched and scowled, looked at the passing cars, noting ruefully that they weren't Craigs – *Beemer, Beemer, Mercedes, Range Rover* – and at his watch again.

It had been Sergei's idea to have the financiers arrive late, to establish dominance. He and Elena had been planning this evening for months, waiting until the last possible moment to set it up. Craig International's creditors were beginning to call in their loans, and Anthony was sleeping poorly. The *New York Times* had run a story and now the tabloids were beginning to cover it: unpaid bills, legal challenges, the end of the eighties and the end of 'American luxury'.

If it were to succeed, this meeting would be Elena's final act as Anthony Craig's wife. After this, Sergei had promised her she could do what she wanted, within limits. They could work out a new arrangement. She could even divorce him.

At 7:50 p.m. their guests arrived. 'We apologize,' said a bald man in his fifties with an earring and thick, blue-framed glasses. He looked like a hairdresser, an Elton John collaborator, not a banker. 'It was a very complicated day. It's such a pleasure to finally meet you, Mr Craig.' He extended his hand for a shake. 'I am David Sapozhnik.'

Anthony took his time uncrossing his arms. He said, quietly, 'How you doing, David?'

'I've been the one working with your team on the telephone, from Tel Aviv. This is my associate, Raphael Rivkin.'

Rivkin was the one they had come to see. He was wearing a dark, conservative suit and black tie, and kept his hair neat. Based on the newspaper stories about him, Elena had expected someone virile and charismatic. He was quiet and so short that he seemed childlike, as he sat in the heavy oak chair across from Anthony.

They finished shaking hands and exchanging manly greetings before turning their attention to Elena. Sapozhnik was courtly and expansive in his attention to her.

Rivkin did not engage in small talk, which annoyed Anthony. It displeased him that Rivkin insisted on meeting halfway in London and it displeased him that Rivkin was a thirty-one-year-old billionaire.

'I like your style, Raphael. I like it a lot. Back in New York, even here in London, young people dress like hobos. Grunge, they call it. Some of the new kids we're hiring out of Harvard, Stanford, Yale, Wharton. That's my school, Wharton, the best. They graduate and come to work for us and it looks like they're coming from prison – not the Ivy League. But you . . . you got the Craig look.'

Rivkin looked for a moment at his bald business associate, blankly, and then back at Anthony. 'Thank you.'

'If things ever go south and you need a—.'

'We have gone through your proposal a number of times, Mr Craig.'

'Straight to business.' Anthony leaned into Elena, as though he were telling her a secret. 'They say that about you people, that you don't stand for nonsense. I like it. I like it a lot. I should do more business in Israel. Hell, we all should. The deal you got, you and some of the other boys in the Russian market? It's legendary on Wall Street. Elena, you can buy a *trillion-dollar oil company* for ten bucks if you got the connections. You, Raphael, and your connections. You're just a front guy, right? A boy, really. Who owns you?'

Rivkin stared at him.

'Back in America we gotta build from the ground up. That's how I did it. You start with nothing, suck up to bankers, get a loan, secure it, pay it back with interest, build equity, take some risks, add value. It takes some time. Right, Elena?'

'Yes.'

'Now a boy like you can come to London and look like a real man of the world, a banker, a *capitalist* – not a young gangster, right? No offense, Raphael, I hope this isn't offending you.'

'As you say, Mr Craig. Straight to business.' Rivkin looked to the man beside him, to Sapozhnik, and nodded.

It was the older man's turn to speak. 'By any objective measure, Mr Craig, the automotive side of Craig International is a failure.'

'Only if you're objectively a fuckhead.'

'Mr Craig. It has never turned a profit.'

'We run a private family business. How can you say we haven't turned a profit? Who are you? What's your name again?'

'David Sapozhnik.'

'Now come on, David. I don't look profitable to you?'

'The debt you carry, Mr Craig, is—'

'It's beautiful, isn't it? Tell him, sweetheart. Have you ever suffered on account of the debt our beautiful company carries from time to time?'

Elena did not want him to ruin this, for his ego to overwhelm his ability to think himself out of bankruptcy. 'Tony, let's listen to what Mr Sapozhnik and Mr Rivkin have to say.'

The waiter arrived to take drink orders from Rivkin and Sapozhnik. Sapozhnik ordered for them both: two glasses of whatever Mrs Craig was drinking.

'I understand you will be joining us for dinner tonight.' The waiter turned his attention to the Russians. 'I know you two gentlemen have just arrived but might I take this opportunity to –'

Rivkin lifted his hand. 'I will not be staying for dinner. My associate will stay.'

'Yeah.' Anthony lifted his chin. 'Same with us. We have another appointment for dinner tonight.'

Elena sighed. Of course they had no other appointments.

When the waiter was gone, Sapozhnik pulled a stapled report from his briefcase and placed it on the table. 'We are prepared to extend this loan to you.'

'*To rescue you*,' said Rivkin.

Anthony spoke directly to Rivkin. 'Listen, fucko. We don't need rescuing. I've been speaking to Deutsche Bank, and if they offer better terms I'll be happy to tell you and Space Oddity here to head on back to Tel Aviv.'

'We know Deutsche Bank, Mr Craig.' Rivkin leaned over the table, so close Elena could smell his sugary hair gel. 'And we know they would not lend you a pfennig. Not without our backing. We are like parents, co-signing a loan for our untrustworthy son.'

'Who is this prick?' Anthony turned to Elena. 'Can you believe this? Has anyone ever talked to me like this?'

Sapozhnik cleared his throat and placed his hands, palms down, on the table. 'You may not like where Mustela Capital came from, Mr Craig. But the fact is, we know our business.'

'Well, you don't know shit about my business.'

Sapozhnik sighed. 'We know you are in distress. We know your automobile business is a disaster.'

Rivkin laughed. 'The absolute worst.'

'Let's be as clear as we can be.' Sapozhnik spoke slowly and quietly. 'You are on the path to bankruptcy, Mr Craig, your businesses and you yourself – personally. Bankruptcy and humiliation. Given the numbers you sent us, which are, sad as they are, themselves terribly inflated, our offer will be better than any other you will receive. I can absolutely guarantee this. Let us not play for the sake of playing. Do you want to lose your family business? Mr Craig?'

'Fuck you.'

'Answer the question, you child,' said Rivkin.

For the next silent minute, Elena watched Anthony transform from rage to resignation. Finally, he said, 'No.'

Sapozhnik reached for him, touched his wrist. 'Do you want to fail publicly? Shame your daughter?'

'No.'

'Do you want it to grow, to expand around the world?'

'Who doesn't?'

'Mr Craig. Do you want to be the man you always hoped to be? The man I read about in your autobiography? The man you claim to be in the gossip columns?'

'You're not a billionaire,' said Rivkin. 'That is absolute bullshit.'

'Mr Craig: we are not interested in your automotive business. We are not interested in your ball bearings.'

'Then what are we doing here? Huh?' Anthony looked at Elena. 'What is this?'

'Your cars and your ball bearings, your bankrupt jewelry concern and private jet and sports and television businesses, your junk bond nonsense – these are not the products we want. Mr Craig: *you are the product*. Just you. We are here tonight to give you everything you most want. Everything you most want to be.'

'For a price.' Rivkin was smiling now, like a lion tamer as the crowd cheers.

The waiter returned with the wine. Elena ordered another one and Anthony asked for another Diet Coke. His right hand was shaking. Elena had seen him angry in the past, but anger was a species of joy for him. This was different, and worse than she had imagined. She was worried he would get up and leave the hotel, walk through Grosvenor Square, and into oblivion.

She knew she had to restore the evening. 'Let's say it does not matter how we came to be here. Mr Rivkin, you have capital. We need capital. If we work together, Craig International can take Mustela Capital's investment and build something magnificent with it. We understand your terms, though we do not like them. If these terms were to become public it would be bad for us, because of your associations.'

Rivkin sipped his wine, then leaned over and rubbed Sapozhnik's back. 'This is fun, David.'

'I am only being honest, as you have been. And you are correct, Mr Sapozhnik, Mr Rivkin. We have lost the power to negotiate.' Elena took her husband's cool hand from his glass of Diet Coke and visibly squeezed it. 'But you, a thirty-year-old Israeli tied to a corrupt government in Russia and who knows what else . . .'

Rivkin laughed.

'You are our only hope.'

This time, the silence that hung over the table was better. Elena had filtered and improved it.

'I think he's thirty-one,' said Anthony after a while. He turned to Rivkin. 'I read you're thirty-one.'

Sapozhnik lifted his glass. 'To the future of Craig International.'

What did they celebrate? Elena thought about it as she lay in bed upstairs two hours later, how her husband understood what he owed Raphael Rivkin, understood who Rivkin worked for and represented, and how he came to be a billionaire at thirty.

'We may never call on you.' Sapozhnik touched Anthony's wrist, as they left the Champagne Room. 'But we may call on you.'

Elena could not make eye contact with Anthony. They always call.

If her soon-to-be ex-husband was unsatisfied with his new situation he did not say so, not in the Champagne Room and not later that night in their elegant suite upstairs at the Connaught. He slept soundly and woke up delighted to be recapitalized. The money would flow through the banks and his new partners would be cloaked behind a very modern system of private equity holding companies. His lawyers and their lawyers would go through everything, and absolutely no one would have access to the origins of anything.

'It's a beautiful deal,' Anthony said, in the morning, in the fine old lobby of the Connaught while they waited for his car to arrive.

'I'm so happy for you.'

'We did this together, remember? Those boys were your connections.'

'Not really, Tony. They were friends of friends. If it were not *you*, I never could have put it together. No one could have.'

'You can't ever tell anyone about that meeting.'

'I know, Tony.'

'No one rescues Anthony Craig.'

'Never.'

He looked out the doors of the Connaught. The car would be here any moment, to take them to the airport. Anthony could lie to her, knowing she knew it was a lie. She had felt him at the table beside her, trembling, when Sapozhnik outlined the terms of their arrangement. If he were to break this contract, Mustela Capital would use every financial and legal instrument at their disposal to destroy him and to destroy his family. They would seize his assets. They would release *details* about him. In the Champagne Room, Elena had waited for Anthony to squint and frown and lean over the table and ask, 'What details?'

But Anthony did not ask.

'Mr Craig.' The manager performed a little bow. 'Your town car has arrived, sir.'

A powerful man, a fully capitalized man, does not hurry. Anthony nodded to the manager. 'I never thought of it this way, the way what's-his-face thinks of it, the gay one.'

Elena waited.

'What did he say?' Anthony put on his version of an Israeli accent. ' "We do not care about cars. The only product we care about is you." I like that. It's true, you know. He's on to something, that bald fucker.'

36

MONTREAL, 2016

On a television in Houston Avenue Bar & Grill, at Gate 77 of Montreal-Trudeau International Airport, a bearded man in a bowtie said Anthony Craig would never be elected.

'Listen. This candidate never *wanted* to win.'

It was difficult to hear anything else over the other televisions playing a Montreal Canadiens hockey game, the bilingual airport announcements, and their neighbors' conversations at the bar. Grace and William had to read the closed-captioning.

'Imagine you own – you *own* – thirty-five percent of the American electorate, and a good piece of Canada and Europe. We're talking millions of angry and aggrieved people with money to spend, who believe every word he says. Cars? Who cares about cars? Only dictators and rock stars want his ridiculous bulletproof cars. It's his *ideas* they like, his simple crazy rage. They're breaking away from the rest of the country and Anthony Craig is building an asylum for them. He'll be CEO of Craig Broadcasting. It's already in the works.'

'Could that be true?' William held the rim of his beer against his temple, as though it helped him think.

Grace shrugged. 'He might not want to win. But a lot of other people want him to, powerful people.'

The CNN interviewer, a blonde woman in a peach jacket, expressed some cynicism. Why would anyone go to all this trouble to lose?

'Look at our current president: courtly, intelligent, careful. Like him or not, he couldn't achieve a thing! It's impossible. The presidency is designed to be the worst job in the world. When he loses in a few days, Anthony Craig and his army of angry white people from rural and suburban America, what media elites like you call "flyover states", will *own* this country. Now that is Anthony Craig's real power.'

The interviewer accused her guest of creating a conspiracy theory. Grace swiveled on her stool to look through the bar and into the US departures area.

'There is no point looking, Grace. It's their job to be invisible when they want to be.' William pointed up at the television set. 'I do hope that man is right.'

'Me too.'

'Your book won't be worth nearly as much if he doesn't win.'

'But fewer people will want to kill my mom.'

It was silent between them now, and there was only the Christmas muzak, hockey and CNN, cutlery-on-plates, and weather talk in the airport bar. Why did Canadians act surprised when it snowed in November?

Grace had sent an email to Elena, copying her two assistants. *I know you're busy but seeing you, even for an hour, is life or death.* Then she searched hotels and restaurants in midtown Manhattan. Her severance money would not last but she had never seen so much of it in her checking account at one time. She booked a late dinner at Upland, where the fancy writers ate, and hunted the Internet for a romantic boutique hotel. There was one in the Bowery she had always lusted for after seeing it in a travel magazine at the dentist's office.

They announced pre-boarding, seven gates away. William downed his beer. Grace abandoned hers.

Ten minutes into the flight to New York, William was gently snoring against the window. He had warned Grace that airplanes did this to him. While nothing about sharing a bed with a man who snored excited her, there was an animal quality to the sound he made that sent a shiver of anticipation through her. They would have showers after dinner. Then they would slip into the fragrant white sheets with a high thread count. What happened after that didn't matter a terrible lot. Middle-aged adventure and exploration behind a triple-locked door! The thought of a warm naked body in bed next to her made Grace feel faint with expectation.

Originally he had clutched his silver computer bag. Now

William shifted his body and released it and the bag looked as though it was about to tumble to the floor. Grace eased it off him. It was an international flight so she decided to order a Heineken, to make up for the beer she had not finished. Another woman had asked for one, and Grace could smell the soft skunk of it two rows away.

Buoyed by this decision, she unzipped William's bag and looked inside.

William had the latest, lightest MacBook. On one side of it was a beige folder filled with papers. Grace watched him for a moment, to be sure he was asleep, and then she pulled out the file.

The top page was in Czech. It looked like a printed news story from the web, with headlines and subheads, a photograph of Elena cut off on the right. William had underlined bits and he had made notes. Despite his messy handwriting Grace recognized the word *ledňáček*. Kingfisher. The next page and another four below it were similar: printed off websites.

At the bottom of the pile, clipped together, was a different set of papers. These were official-looking, like a corporate memo or a contract originating in a law office. Grace imagined it was the response to a Czech query for his book about the Arab Spring. The flight attendant in the aisle was taking orders one seat in front of her, in English. It was a Delta flight so the woman was not farting around with Canadian bilingualism.

The flight attendant was just about to ask Grace what she wanted and Grace was just about to say Heineken and slip the file back into his bag when she spotted her name on the bottom of the first page of the memo. It was there again on the second page, several times. On the third page was a photograph of her, from a failed gossip column she wrote for the *Flash* between 2011 and 2012. The memo was five pages long and her name appeared constantly: Elliott, Elliott, Elliott, embedded in the Czech. She found her mother's name. Austin popped out and Florida, *National Flash*, Elena Craig. *Elena Craig anonymní spisovatel.*

In brackets, in English: ghostwriter.

'Madame?' the flight attendant asked again. 'Can I get you something to drink?'

'Maybe just a tomato juice.'

'Ice? Squeeze of lemon?'

'Straight up, please.'

It was not a long flight: ninety minutes in the air. For a while Grace could not remember the word for this and then she did: dossier. Someone had created an official dossier on her, for this smooth man who pretended to be awkward, who had gone to some trouble to find bad eyeglasses and maybe-hipster sweaters to place him precisely in between adorable and unattractive.

She turned on the overhead light and took photographs of each of the pages of the dossier. Then she slipped it back in William's bag and watched him sleep a while longer. His mouth was open and a line of drool rolled down his chin and onto his neck.

There was a chance Elena would not speak to her. Grace

pulled out her own computer and opened the file she had started in Old Montreal and continued writing, inspired by fury and heartbreak. Though her news-writing muscles had atrophied, it did not take long to finish a first draft.

They were less than twenty minutes from LaGuardia when William began stirring. He opened his eyes and smiled at her. The smile seemed real. She closed her laptop.

'I dozed off.' He wiped the drool from his chin. 'Where are we?'

'On our descent,' she said, hoping he couldn't hear the disappointment in her voice.

'Sorry. I hate that I conk out. I was a fussy baby and my parents used to take me for a drive to calm me down. It's likely that simple.'

Grace reached up and pulled a piece of fluff from his shoulder. 'We are fragile creatures.'

He took her hand and kissed it, and then he laughed like it was the silliest thing he had ever done.

37

NEW YORK, 1994

The tabloid coverage of their divorce had made Elena Craig famous, not only in New York but all over the world. In the two years since she had 'caught' Anthony with one of MC Hammer's back-up dancers, she had launched her own spa business. She was still on the board of Craig International, oversaw the design facility, and remained something like a friend to her ex-husband; they spoke nearly every day, or at least she listened to him speak every day. Some women retreat into the comforts of anonymity, on some beach or in a mountain town, after divorcing a man like Anthony Craig.

Elena was not permitted.

So she was not initially surprised when a journalist ambushed her on her way to the ladies' at the Russian Tea

Room. He was overweight and sweaty. 'Sorry to do this here, Mrs Craig, but I've been leaving messages with your assistant and nothing.' The man, who spoke with a British accent, had sandy hair and blotches on his face. 'Jake Haynes. I'm with the *Daily Mail*.'

She took his meaty hand.

'I'm happy to wait here in the back, Mrs Craig, until you and your friends have finished tea. Then perhaps we could talk.'

The magnificent unveiling of the new Craig cars was in two weeks. The designs were supposed to be a secret until then. Her first thought was that someone had leaked photographs to him. 'About what, Mr Haynes?'

'Your past.'

In the ladies' room, Elena ensured she was alone and called Sergei on her cellular phone. He advised her to stay calm, to deny everything, and to keep the journalist in the restaurant as long as possible.

It was difficult to concentrate on her friends and their gossip. Elena was the only one among them to work, and they found it preposterous that she bothered. Volunteer boards of major artistic institutions they could understand: it was glamorous. There were openings and fundraisers. The messiness of running an expanding business, with employees to train and manage, real estate to contend with, and taxes to pay: why give yourself the headache?

When their lunch was finished, cheeks kissed, and the next date solidified in their calendars, Elena pretended to go back to the ladies' room one last time and joined the journalist at his table in the dark.

'What can I do for you, Mr Haynes?'

'*Ledňáček*. I'm sure I'm pronouncing it incorrectly but it's *kingfisher* in English, right?'

As soon as he showed her the files, it was obvious to Elena that someone had leaked them to him. He had a lot more than her code name and all of it was accurate: her recruitment, her parents' involvement, Jean-Yves de Moulin, her years in Montreal, page after page about Anthony and his relationships with leaders, his own political ambitions. She saw no mention of Sergei and nothing on the bailout of Craig International, but there were files on her mother, code name Vrba, that shocked her.

This was the first she had heard about Anthony's daughter, Alina, but she did the math. Alina had been born nine months after their visit to Moscow in 1987. Kristína had a half-sister in Moscow, the daughter of a prostitute.

'This is fiction, Mr Haynes.'

'Can you prove that, Mrs Craig?'

Elena laughed. 'I believe it is your job to prove this is real, Mr Haynes. I assure you it is not, and that whoever gave it to you is up to some dirty tricks. If you publish a word of this, my lawyers will destroy you and your newspaper.'

'That sounds like a threat to me, and right here in the land of the First Amendment.' He sat back, crossed his arms over his belly, and stared at her with a satisfied smirk. It seemed to Elena his neck had more hair on it than his face, so she focused on this and tried to guess his age – fifty-seven? – rather than give in to breathless panic.

He did not wear a wedding ring. 'Do you have children, Mr Haynes?' she asked, as calmly as she could.

'I haven't had that pleasure.'

'Married?'

'Three times. I'm currently a bachelor.'

'Just imagine, then, what it would be like to have a wife and a child who loved you. Imagine what a smear like this would do to them.'

'I've been writing for tabloids since I was twenty, Mrs Craig. It's not my job, frankly, to protect spies because it might hurt someone's feelings.'

Elena had to will herself to remain at the table, to hold his eye contact, to think clearly. She thought of Kristína, and what it would be like for her in her senior year of high school. How would she manage university, as the daughter of two people charged with treason? Elena thought of the lunch she had just finished, of La Cure Craig, of the car business, of her mother.

'Spies? Don't be ridiculous, Mr Haynes. All I mean is a little human understanding could not hurt.'

He watched her and said nothing.

'Your . . .' Elena had to stop herself from shutting down completely. 'Your newspaper, it's actually going to publish this nonsense?'

'I've not shown it to anyone yet. I wanted you to see it first.'

When her phone rang, it felt like someone had thrown her a

lifeline, a legitimate reason to look away from the journalist. 'Hello?'

'He's still there?' said Sergei.

'Yes.'

'We're outside. Now, Elenka, we're your lawyers. Yes? We're going to invite him to a meeting at La Cure Craig. All we have to do is get him into the car. Do you understand?'

'Yes.'

'Stay calm. You're interested in what he has found, where it has come from, but it's garbage. Garbage, yes?'

'Absolute garbage.' Elena looked at Jake Haynes and smiled.

'We're coming in one minute.'

'See you then.'

Elena took a deep breath. 'I was meeting my lawyers this afternoon, to go over some real estate transactions with my spa business.'

'La Cure Craig.'

'You know it? Would you like to join me? Join us? I would like them to see this, so we know who is out there trying to smear us. Since you'll get nothing else out of this, journalistically, maybe you can write about your first manicure.'

The journalist looked up. Sergei and his men had arrived.

Two weeks later, Elena learned that Jake Haynes had committed suicide in the Algonquin Hotel with a combination of good Scotch, antidepressants, and sleeping pills. Teams went through files in Prague, Moscow, and Montreal to erase what could be erased. They discovered the man who had sold the files to Haynes and he too succumbed to the ravages of alcoholism and mental illness.

With the relaunch of Anthony's business, foreign orders of bulletproof Craig sedans and SUVs exploded: first in Russia, then in the Middle East, in China, in Venezuela. A few hip hop stars bought them for their music videos, fans copied them, and it was all Craig International's automotive division needed to record its first profitable year.

At the Frankfurt Motor Show in 1995, Anthony Craig met a young model from Moldova, and when he called Elena to tell her about his new girlfriend she just said congratulations and took a long drink of wine.

38

NEW YORK, 2016

In the taxi lineup at LaGuardia, Grace canceled their dinner reservation and booked two single rooms at a Holiday Inn Express. She had gone over everything William had said and done since their first meeting in the lobby of the Institute for the Study of Totalitarian Regimes and now saw everything anew.

Their driver, whose ID on the dash said Lilesa, pulled into the mist and the rain. Glenn Gould played the *Goldberg Variations*, something that Grace did not expect to hear in a yellow medallion taxi.

'Is this the 1981 recording?' William leaned forward.

'Yes, sir,' said Lilesa.

'He hums as he plays in this one.'

'Yes, sir. I like it very much. It is very human.'

William put his arm around Grace. 'Very human,' he said.

Grace wanted to push him away, to slap him, to interrogate him, to scream in his face. Instead she reached up and touched his hand.

'When your book is finished, and in stores, maybe you can come with me to London,' said William.

Oh stop. Please stop, Grace thought. I trusted you.

'I mean, what's keeping you here in America? Your mum, I guess. Well, we could move her as well. Granted, the weather is not a draw in England. All right, it's terrible. But as we've just experienced it's not so great in Montreal either. We do have a decent health system. Even when it's occasionally indecent it's free. Maybe if we work together we could afford to put her in a better home than the one in Florida? If there's a garden or a park nearby, all the better; at weekends we could take her for walks. You mentioned you wanted your mother to see Prague while she can still see a little: a flight from London, on one of the discount airlines – it's nothing.'

Grace's mouth had gone completely dry. She could not look at him.

'You could find a job at a newspaper, or just go freelance or write another book. We could stay in my place or pool our fortune and get something a wee bit better, with more reliable plumbing. Oh – English plumbing. You won't like that!'

A tear ran down Grace's cheek and she wiped it away and looked out her window so William would not see. It took all of her strength to stop herself from confronting him about the dossier and who he really was. How dare he!

The cabbie turned down the piano music and said something about the traffic on the Grand Central Parkway. He asked a question and Grace could not answer because she did not want William to hear the emotion in her voice.

'I'm sure that's fine.' William dished Lilesa a thumbs-up. 'We defer to your instincts and expertise, sir.'

This was surely not in the book of excellent spy craft, Grace told herself, hiding one's teary eyes from the man pretending to be your almost-boyfriend.

'Is everything okay, Grace?'

'Fine, yes. Thank you. I'm just thinking about my mom.'

The cabbie was right about the traffic. A minivan had crashed into the back of a food truck which had a picture of the Taj Mahal on the side of it. Then, in the semi-darkness of the Queens Midtown Tunnel, William reached around and touched her face and kissed her. Grace let him. It is a long tunnel and the traffic was heavy and slow, so they kissed for a long time. Grace forgot where they were and what she knew about William; all she wanted was for the East River to go on forever. If they never arrived in Manhattan they could be lovers, drowning in the scents of charcoal and exhaust, in the hum and piano of Glenn Gould, until the end of time.

Eventually they passed through the tunnel, into the lights of the city. Under the Downtown-Crosstown-Uptown sign Grace couldn't take it anymore. His breath, his nose, his long fingers, the sound of their glasses touching: all was treachery. She pushed him away with so much force he cracked the back of his head against the window.

He rubbed his head and looked at Grace, his eyes transforming from shock to understanding. 'Wait. Grace . . .'

'Think before you speak, William, if that's your real name.'

West Thirty-ninth Street was narrow and chaotic. They passed a cocktail lounge, where Grace wanted to get drunk alone tonight.

'Grace. You have to listen carefully.' William's voice was high and panicked. 'I'll tell you everything.'

Just past the lounge a group of young men in T-shirts smoked cigarettes outside an Irish pub. The cabbie went wide around a man in a blue rain jacket with a silver cart under an umbrella selling hot dogs and they pulled up in front of the Holiday Inn. There was sidewalk construction and no easy way to get out of the taxi on the hotel side.

By now Glenn Gould was playing so quickly they could no longer hear his voice. William tried to pay and Grace reached past him with her credit card. 'I booked you a room, thinking I would be strong enough to pretend I don't care that you're a spy. I thought I could figure you out and protect myself, take control in some way, even *be with you* somehow. But I do care that you're a spy, that you only played at liking me. So you can go in and tell them you don't need the room and go wherever it is you people go. The Russian embassy?'

The piano was soft enough now that Grace could hear Glenn

Gould humming again. When she would not look at him William opened the door and stepped out. Cool wind blew into the car. The cabbie thanked her for the tip, hopped out, and tried to speak to William.

William ignored the cabbie and crouched. His face was white and his voice was urgent. 'Grace, you're correct. I've not been entirely honest, but I guarantee whatever you're thinking is wrong. Once you hear me out, everything will be different.'

'Isn't that what every betrayer says?' Grace backed deeper into the back seat of the taxi. 'I believed you . . . *liked me*. I believed you were trying to help me. My God, you helped me bury my cat. How can you do this to people?'

'Let's go inside. I'll show you some things. A proposition.'

'You fell asleep on the plane, William. I already saw your things.'

William extended his hand, to help her out of the taxi. 'You haven't seen this.'

'Back off, Ivan. I'm not touching you.'

'You just finished kissing me.'

'I changed my mind.'

William sighed and took a step back. Grace stepped out of the taxi without taking anyone's hand. The cabbie asked William why they had arrived in New York without luggage.

'It's a strange trip,' said William, sadly.

Time seemed to slow. Grace thought at first it was lack of sleep, or food, that was playing with her ears. The sound started as a rumble below the piano music and grew as she stepped out into the street.

'Hey!' It was the hot dog man.

A black sedan had pulled out from the scaffolding behind the food cart and was roaring up the street. Grace thought at first it was an unmarked police car missing its siren, on its way to some distant emergency. But there was no siren and it was on its way toward them.

The cabbie shouted and scrambled onto the hood of his taxi. William said her name and put his arms around her. She tried to resist him but he was too strong. 'Watch out!' he said, and Grace thought he was going to hurt her, and closed her eyes.

But he did not hurt her. Like a child, entirely powerless, she felt herself being picked up and swung around the rear bumper of the taxi and onto the pavement between two cars.

She fell back and her head hit the asphalt just as the sedan came alongside the taxi and sped into William.

39

William was turning away from the car as it slammed into him. His head and shoulders crunched into the hood and windshield, and then he was thrown into the air, his body loose and uncoordinated, as the car sped away. He landed on the street with a terrible sound.

Grace was bleeding from her ear. Screaming his name, she crawled from between the taxi and the car behind it, toward William. There was blood on his face too and his eyes were closed. Grace took his hands in hers and told him he was going to be okay. It did not matter now who he was. One of his shoes had come off, she noticed, when the car hit him, and his socks were mismatched.

Behind her, people were shouting. *911. Ambulance. A doctor.*

License plate. Then there were legs everywhere, and voices, and Grace wanted them to shut up because she was feeling for William's pulse. Then someone's hands were on her, someone calling her sweetheart. 'I'm a doctor,' said the woman.

Then another woman was kneeling on the other side of William. She seemed fine at first and then Grace realized they were everywhere.

'No,' she screamed. 'Get away from him!'

Someone was holding her back now as she tried to stop the woman pretending to be a doctor from hurting William. No one understood what she was talking about, that they were all being followed, all being watched.

'Ma'am, you're in shock,' a man said, his face too close to hers, so she shoved him away.

Now there were sirens, and she didn't want an ambulance because it meant he was not getting up.

'I'm sorry,' the doctor was saying.

Grace took William's hand again and put her ear, the one that was not bleeding, on his chest. *Shut up, everyone!* She could hear nothing over the sirens.

By now, the police had arrived too, and when she tried to move past them to be sure the medics were real, a man shouted in her face to get the *fuck* back.

Lilesa, their cabbie, was holding her purse and William's computer bag. He handed them to her and dabbed her ear with a tissue. 'They were trying to hit you,' he said. 'This car came when you got out, you.'

With the sidewalk construction crew, the ambulance and police, and people from the hotel the crowd was thick. Grace was sure the killer in the car was not alone. Some people were pointing at her now, and two police officers in uniform, a man and a woman, walked toward her.

They were both around thirty, both of them tall. 'We understand you were with the gentleman,' said the woman, 'when he was hit.'

Grace nodded. She tried to figure out if there was anything odd about them. The policewoman spoke with a convincing Brooklyn accent.

'We were working together.'

'What's his name?'

Grace looked around, and there were two men in suits leaning against the front window of the Holiday Inn watching her. One of them wore a fedora. 'William Kovály.'

'Can you spell that?' said the policeman.

Two other men squeezed through the crowd on the sidewalk and stood next to the police, one in jeans and a blazer and the other, with a trimmed goatee, in a blue suit that seemed too big for him. The man with the goatee flashed his badge at her and introduced himself. The other dismissed the uniformed police. Before he could say his name, Grace backed away and made her way through the crowd.

'Wait!' said the detective with the goatee.

Grace ran to the end of the block, crossed the street, and

turned right on Sixth Avenue. As she did, the detective in the blue suit caught up to her. 'Where are you going?'

She knew he was dangerous, another pursuer, so she hit him in the head with William's computer bag and kept running up Sixth Avenue, weaving through the crowds and, on the cross-streets, ignoring the red pedestrian lights and shouting warnings at drivers who looked as though they would not stop. She could hear the sounds of footsteps behind her and shouts, though in the wind she could not make them out.

Grace ran into Bryant Park, where a massive crowd had gathered at the winter market. School had ended for the day, and children and their nannies had joined the young lovers at the skating rink. There was no obvious place to hide, as the leaves had fallen from the trees, so Grace bought a black beanie at a kiosk even though it was $40. She pulled the knitted cap low and walked with the flow of tourists.

Turning back, she saw the apparent detective with the goatee and the uniformed policewoman walking through the winter market. Grace removed her jacket, tied it around her waist, and walked into the strangely lavish public restroom in the park. She locked herself in a cubicle and sat on top of the toilet. No real detective would chase her. There were plenty of witnesses to William's death. Someone had called out a license plate number.

The Bryant Park restroom was a popular spot. Women and girls came in and out, laughed and complained, talked about boys and men.

Grace sat back, closed her eyes, and replayed William's death. She thought of his one blue and one black sock, slightly pulled off. Where had his shoe flown? She thought of Katka and her father, and of Zip. If she had not been so selfish, if she had simply interviewed Elena about Christmas dinner etiquette and online shopping tips over a bottle of champagne on the road between Prague and Mladá Boleslav, everyone would still be alive. She started to cry, stopped herself and then she realized a public restroom in the middle of Manhattan is a perfectly legitimate place to cry so she let herself go.

For an hour she remained inside the Bryant Park restroom, crying, hating herself, hating Elena, worrying about her mother, her finances, her own inevitable murder. By the time she was ready to leave, she had found the address for the Midtown South police precinct. It was a fifteen-minute walk away. If the detectives were real, they would be there and she would have a perfectly reasonable excuse for them. She splashed some water on her red eyes and on her blood-caked ear and tucked her hair inside the beanie.

Perhaps the detectives would even offer suggestions for how to keep her mother safe. From her hotel room tonight she would expand her draft of the story as she understood it and in the morning she would take a taxi to One World Trade Center and sell it to *The New Yorker*.

It was over.

She opened the door into the darkness that had fallen while she was in the restroom. The cool air of the park hit her as her eyes adjusted. No one stood waiting for her, at the wrought-iron gate. Grace looked down at her phone, for directions to the precinct, and turned left.

Though he was in shadow, the man behind the stone arch seemed familiar. She abandoned the route to the precinct and walked deeper into Bryant Park along Forty-second Street, past the ping-pong tables and into the market kiosks. When she sped up, he sped up too. For an instant she turned and remembered where she had seen him: he was one of the men leaning against the front glass of the Holiday Inn.

Grace took deep breaths, the way her self-defense instructor had taught her. When we panic, we stop thinking. She wanted to choose the right moment to run. There was a group of tourists from China led by a guide with a small voice amplifier. She broke into a sprint and went around them, used them to interrupt the man's route.

They had killed William in daylight, on a busy street, and if he had not thrown her out of the way they would have killed her too. She walked quickly through the crowd watching the skaters, crossing the park diagonally, and turned right again to confuse the man if he had seen her. On the south side of the skating pavilion the lights were dimmer. She approached the children's carousel and scanned the park again for a place to hide, between the two gardens of plane trees, when she slammed into another man. Grace bounced off him and fell to the ground, her purse in one hand and William's computer bag in the other. It was the second man who had leaned against the front window of the Holiday Inn. The man with the fedora.

Behind her, his partner arrived breathless.

The chairs of the park were empty. Leaves blew over the paving stones. Children and parents were either at the skating rink or the carousel. The man she had slammed into, with the fedora, lifted a gun. 'You did well, Grace.'

'Wait. You can't do this.' She threw her purse up at the man and he batted it away. William's computer bag was so heavy that from a sitting position the best she could do was swing it at the assassins' knees. It flew between them in the leaves. Grace slid backward on the pavement as both men positioned themselves in front of her. Both had guns and did not seem to care who saw them.

'We can do anything we like,' said the man in a fedora. He looked to his left and right and aimed his gun.

Grace closed her eyes and though she had never been to church for anything but weddings and funerals she said a prayer. There were two pops, not much louder than what she had heard at the ping-pong table, drowned by the children's shouts of joy at the carousel and the distant rink. And they didn't hurt, not at first anyway.

She opened her eyes to two thumps. Both of the men in suits were on the ground, and the fedora was rolling in a semicircle. Roberta McKee stood over them. With a gloved hand she reached down for Grace's purse and then William's computer bag.

'Get up. Let's go.'

342

40

Elena watched the man wearing number 11, by far the slowest and smallest player on the ice. His teammates in red jerseys fed him the puck so he could shoot at the goalie. None of the defensemen on the white opposing team came anywhere near him when he had the puck, though they crushed anyone else who touched it. A robot video camera followed number 11's every move, whether he had the puck or not, and photographers from around the world bathed him in light whenever he shot on goal.

Aleksandr Mironov, the president of the Russian Federation, had prepared for the Sochi Olympics by dressing up and making himself the star of the $50 billion show. Although it was less than a month before the Opening Ceremonies, the Bolshoy Ice Dome was one of the few buildings that felt truly finished. But that was irrelevant now. Inside the dome, which resembled a glittering Fabergé egg, Mironov was Russia and Russia was back: grand, rich, mysterious, powerful.

When one of the best hockey goalies in the world allowed Mironov to score, a small crowd of VIPs and Russian journalists cheered. High above the ice, in a catered luxury box, Elena also applauded politely.

'If Anthony had run for governor of New York, he would have lost.' Sergei Sorokin popped a chocolate in his mouth. Unlike his boss, he did not play hockey, hunt, or practice judo, and over the past ten years he had, in Elena's opinion, grown into a walrus. 'It would have humiliated him.'

'You've spent so much time in America but still you don't understand it,' said Elena. 'He can lose and win at once, by building his brand.'

'We built his brand for him, Elenka. And yours. He'd be bankrupt if it weren't for us, even if he is only half aware of it. And I don't think his brand is about losing.'

Elena sighed. She did not like to think about Mustela Capital, let alone talk about it. 'Okay, Sergei.'

'Our Anthony may not be the greatest businessman in the world. But he is a brilliant marketer.' Sergei pointed down at Mironov, who accepted congratulations from his teammates and from his admirers in the stands. The game was over. 'Like Aleksandr. Some men instinctively understand the desires of regular people.'

'But Craig used to be a luxury brand.'

Sergei laughed. 'Oh please. Elenka, you're a European. It was never a luxury brand.'

Elena listened to Sergei tell her all about her ex-husband's business. The Craig customer and the Craig audience were the unsophisticated rich or those who felt they *deserved* to be rich but lacked the intelligence or motivation to do much about it. They were, in Sergei's definition, white, resentful, disenfranchised, and indebted. They bought a Craig on credit, almost never with cash. Craigs were the most leased automobiles in history – because this was by far the cheapest way to get one. Default rates were extraordinarily high.

'Our polling data show if he runs in 2016 he'll have a rump of between twenty-five and thirty-five percent of the American electorate. If he has the courage to give them what they want. And I tell you, Elenka, it has nothing to do with luxury.'

'What does it have to do with?'

There was a knock on the door. Sergei stood up and so did she. Elena had been searched three times, and they had taken her phone away. With a grunt Sergei made it to his feet and to the door.

Outside, there were between five and seven bodyguards, massive armed men with cropped hair and black suits laced with spandex. Aleksandr Mironov entered the luxury box in his hockey equipment and a pair of black oxfords. While Sergei had grown soft Mironov had become hard. He waited for Elena to walk across the box and to kiss him. 'Our wonderful Kingfisher,' he said, to Sergei.

Sergei applauded for a moment, ridiculously, Elena thought.

'I love a Czech woman.' Mironov removed his elbow pads as Elena and Sergei returned to their seats. 'I love Czech people. It's funny, what you call your transfer of power, the Velvet Revolution. This is my kind of revolution. Not one agent, yours or ours, was put in jail let alone taken into some alley and shot. Good souls, the Czechs. Close to my heart.'

Elena could not stand him. 'You mean we're subservient.'

'I mean you do not let emotion get in the way of the right decision. I have seen far too many people ruin themselves unnecessarily for an empty principle. You Czechs are too thoughtful for that.'

Elena did not want to thank him because this was in no way a real compliment. He was preparing her. Every word he said, every move he made, was designed to achieve something in the future.

She buried her feelings and smiled. 'Thanks to you two bad Russians I am forty years distant from my good Czech soul.'

'You are an American woman now, thanks to us.' Mironov pulled the bottle of white Romanian wine from its ice bucket and filled Elena's glass. He opened two bottles of beer, one for Sergei and one for himself, and lifted his own bottle. 'To America.'

Both Sergei and Elena repeated, 'To America,' and lifted their own drinks.

Then it was silent in the Bolshoy Ice Dome, a silence Elena did not want to break. Mironov had invited Elena to be part of

346

the VIP delegation to the Olympic Village at Sochi, as an unofficial ambassador of both the United States and the Czech Republic. La Cure Craig had locations in Moscow and St Petersburg. Why not Sochi?

Mironov himself seemed to be enjoying the silence and the tension in the room. Finally, he put down his beer and nodded at Sergei.

'The president and I have been talking about your situation,' said Sergei, reaching into his bag and pulling out a folder. He opened it to a photograph of a young woman in a fur coat. 'Alina will accompany the president to some of the events, here in Sochi.'

Despite all the years this still upset her. 'Does Alina know she's Tony's daughter?'

'No. But we think it's time to tell Anthony about her.'

'You will tell him ahead of the Olympics.' Mironov pointed his beer bottle at Elena. 'So when he sees her with me, here in the stadium, he will know what he owes us. It's more than money, you see.'

'Why should I tell him?'

Sergei leaned forward, with his elbows on his knees. He looked a little uncomfortable. 'This lack of discipline, it is both his greatest strength and . . . well, it frightens us.'

Mironov cleared his throat and gestured at Sergei to stop talking. 'Anthony is an unconventional thinker but in his secret heart he is just a man, a proud man,' said Mironov. 'He thinks in *any normal way*, even if he never speaks of it. Despite his

347

many wonderful flaws, our Anthony Craig is no imbecile. I understand what you are saying, Elena. Maybe we do it all with sugar, not threats. For now, we encourage him to run in 2016. We begin to help, in our way.'

'How?'

'Through your marvelous American institutions and inventions. Modern democracy, modern media, modern technology – they are your Trojan horses and we will use them against you.'

'Tony can't possibly win an election like that.'

'He will win,' said Sergei.

'My parents are in the Cibulka. People outside this room, they know where I come from, they know enough about me to have me arrested for treason. There are ten people in Mladá Boleslav alone . . .'

Mironov pulled up one of the soft chairs close to hers. Everything suddenly smelled of new paint and the off-gassing of unwrapped plastic: the wine, her chair, the building, the breath of the president of Russia. His voice was soft. 'Every day, someone publishes something about me and my past that could have me thrown in jail for treason. Every day, my Kingfisher. We come from KGB. I was head of the FSB.' He laughed.

'But what if they have proof, like Jake Haynes did? Proof of what I really did in university, what I was doing in Strasbourg, in Montreal? Tapes?'

'There is no proof. Even if something remains, it has been manufactured by our powerful enemies. Enemies of the people.'

The communist phrase – *enemies of the people* – popped in her head like an old song. Elena sat back. 'This is the way it works in Russia, maybe. It is different in America.'

Mironov finished his beer and got up to open another one. 'You shall see. Now, let us talk about the future. How can we help you help your ex-husband to become the most powerful man in the world?'

41

Grace looked out the window of a one-bedroom suite in the Plaza Hotel. It was too dark to enjoy much of the park view.

Behind her, Roberta McKee sat on the bed.

'I can see why you'd want to write it.' Roberta poured her half-bottle of mini-bar champagne into a water glass. 'You can imagine yourself on CNN, talking to Anderson Cooper. Yes? The tabloid writer turned investigative journalist. But it will never happen.'

Grace turned away from the window and sat in the cream chair next to the bed. Her hands were still cold and shaking, even though she had run them under hot water for five minutes when she arrived in the suite.

'If I go to the police—'

'They will send you away. And I won't be there to save you next time, in Bryant Park. I won't be there to save your mother, or your ex-husband. Or your friends in Montreal. I know this must be exciting for you, to have discovered something. Ms Craig's generation, they weren't so careful. They kept records, *physical records*. Most of it is gone now, as you know. Honestly, Grace, when you go to the precinct they will file you under 9/11 truthers and make fun of you as you leave.'

'The FBI could bring Ms Craig in.'

'Bring her in?' Roberta laughed. 'She'd have everyone in the Hoover Building signed up for free spa sessions in an hour. Grace, the FBI can't do anything for you. Every day, more of the evidence disappears. Those who come forward with stories, like you, will be discredited and disgraced. You're a paranoid and hysterical woman who was *fired from a tabloid*.'

Grace touched her sore ear. She did not trust Roberta but she saw no reason to trust the police or the FBI either. 'How do I know you didn't kill my cat?'

Roberta shrugged. 'You don't, I guess. But you *do know* I could have killed you, many times over. You do know I saved your life. Ms Craig wanted Bradley and me to keep you safe. The last journalist who tried to write this story, things did not work out well for him. Of course, he had documents. Not the garbage you found. But these are different times. You could put this on Facebook, the files, the Cibulka, what has happened to you. Most people will find it crazy. But some people . . .'

Grace had pressed record on her phone app in the car, as

351

Roberta dealt with valet parking. Her initial instinct, after Roberta had shot the men, was to run and keep running to the precinct as planned. But as they passed the carousel, arm-in-arm, Roberta whispering, 'Calm, calm, smiling,' she had also said something Grace had not expected: *William loved you.*

Although William had been working for Elena, he did not know that Roberta and her partner, Bradley Tebb, were working *with* Elena. Swallows and ravens answered to one boss, but they did not always agree on methods. They created alliances, and Roberta and Bradley were within Elena's orbit. She was their mentor.

Their bosses had wanted to eliminate Grace, once they saw what she had on her computer and on her phone, once they understood whom she had communicated with. Elena had a more elegant solution.

In the car, Roberta had shown Grace screen captures of texts William had sent Elena. When this was finished, his plan was to take Grace and her mother to England. In the Carnegie Park Suite of the Plaza Hotel, Grace asked to see the screen caps again. 'Why didn't he just tell me?' said Grace, as she read them, as she imagined the life she might have had with him.

'He was going to tell you today. The same thing I am here to tell you. Only he didn't get a chance.'

'But you're all, ultimately, the Russian secret service.'

'I am,' said Roberta. 'But William wasn't. He worked for Elena.'

'You mentioned the bosses. If Elena was William's boss, who is yours?'

'That's irrelevant to you.'

'Sergei Sorokin?'

Roberta put down her glass of champagne. 'Where did you hear that name?'

Grace told her about Katka and her father, about the fire in Mladá Boleslav.

'You don't have any documentation about him, do you? Any proof?'

Grace shook her head.

'Well, now I understand why they wanted you dead.'

'Who is he?'

Roberta lifted her hands in surrender.

'Bryant Park has cameras. They'll see you shooting those men.'

'Taken care of.' Roberta paused and took a mouthful of her champagne. 'Elena Craig became a swallow when, exactly? The early 1970s? Yet here she is, spitting distance from the White House.'

'But pundits say he can't win next week.'

'I'm sure even Monsieur Craig thinks he'll lose. But guess what, Grace? He won't. Did you watch the results of the Brexit vote on the BBC, by chance? The presenters began the evening with absolute confidence, because they all went to fine schools and the only people *they* know are voting to protect and sustain the status quo. Our people, our secret allies, fine men and women across America, they want to crush and destroy it because there's nothing to protect. You've figured it out too, haven't you? Was it your ambition, after uni, to work in Canada? For a supermarket tabloid? You're here to buy stuff, only you can't afford it and you never will. You're on social media, aren't you? For a lot of us there is nothing so exciting as *blowing it all up.*'

Grace had not thought of what Steadman Coe called their people, *her people*, as Roberta McKee's people.

'You're ten years older than me and you have nothing, Grace. No one remembers what you've written. You have no money. You own no assets. Your sick mother, nearly blind, lives in squalor. Yet you've worked hard. You've been obedient. You voted in all the elections, from afar, and you've volunteered for charities in two countries. Soon you'll enter the second half of middle age, filled with anxiety about your legacy, about death, and unless you're crazy – and you're not – you will begin to understand that this dream, this *lottery ticket* in the pocket of every decent American, has been a lie all along. Grace: you never had a chance.'

Roberta pulled a folder from the satchel next to her on the bed. Before Grace took it from her she knew what it was going to be. On the front of the folder there were photographs of lush gardens, a swimming pool, outdoor patios that resembled five-star resorts.

'It's called The Grove.'

354

Inside there were glossy leaflets outlining the lifestyle, the health services, and the community. It was in Florida, along the Everglades.

'There isn't a better facility in the world. You pay a one-time fee of $250,000, to become a lifetime member, and then $7,000 a month. For that you get the best food, the best medical care, a gorgeous one-bedroom apartment with every amenity imaginable. While nothing can guarantee happiness, in our senior years, this comes pretty damn close, Grace, wouldn't you say?'

'It's very nice.'

Roberta pulled out another folder. This one was plain white. Grace opened it to see a deposit statement in her name, from something called Zürcher Kantonalbank. The account seemed to have CHF 3,500,000 in it.

'What is this?'

'The Swiss franc does a little better than the US dollar, so maybe it's 3.6 million? You'll have to pay transfer fees, of course, to convert it to your currency. Unless you want to move to Zurich. Maybe Geneva would be better. It's a French-speaking town.' She leaned forward and pointed at the Zürcher Kantonalbank logo. 'It's one of the safest banks in the world.'

Grace looked up at her. 'All this for . . .'

'That's the best part. All this for *doing nothing*. Congratulations, Grace. You've bested us. We tried to stop you and we couldn't. And here you are, receiving your reward.'

'And they'll stop trying to kill me?'

'Ms Craig has influence with the bosses. She'll convince them you have more than we think, that you've squirreled it away somewhere, that your death will trigger its release.'

Grace looked at the number, at the zeroes, and imagined what she might do with it all: buy a condo in Miami South Beach, close enough to visit her mother but far enough to keep it to a weekly commitment. She could travel to all those places she had never been: France, Kenya, Thailand, Argentina. She could engage in meaningful journalism to assuage her guilt for taking this money.

'And if I don't take it? If I go to the FBI?'

'The Craigs will sue you. They're really, really good at that, and they have endless resources.' Roberta stood up off the bed and stretched. 'You'll go to sleep every night worrying about that phone call at 3 a.m., about your dear mother: a fall, a mix-up with her insulin injections, a coma. What will it be like for you on public transportation, in restaurants – if you can afford them – or even passing regular-looking people on the street? Who are these people, really, and what might they do to you?'

Grace shook her head. 'It must feel terrible, to threaten people with violence and death.'

'Tonight I'm here to make you a rich woman, a free woman, to give your darling mother a life of dignity and health and joy. Your own government cannot protect you. I can. This gives me enormous pleasure.'

'You can't quit either, can you? They own you like they own Elena.' Grace looked at the pictures of The Grove.

'My parents live well. I live well. This is a choice I have made, even if it's a life I did not seek.'

'You were recruited, like Elena.'

Roberta reached into Grace's purse and took her phone and her notebook. 'This is how we knew where you were, by the way. These lovely phones, your credit card.' With her other hand she grabbed William's bag.

'Hey!'

'A deal's a deal, Grace. Get yourself some new tech. Everything you need, to access the money, is in that folder. And tomorrow you'll receive an email confirmation about your mother's place in The Grove. It's hers as of Monday. Why not fly first-class to Miami and surprise her?'

'Where are you going?'

At the door Roberta stopped. 'This is your room. It's much lovelier than the Holiday Inn Express, and befitting of your new station.' She winked. 'Sorry to drink your champagne. Order yourself another one if you like, on us.'

42

Sergei Sorokin's driver had a hangover. Most of the city seemed to have a hangover, Sergei thought, as the morning traffic on the Rublevo-Uspenskoe Highway was light in both directions. The flying eagle of the Craig logo on the steering wheel pleased him so much that he moved to the right side of the back seat so he might see it better as they made their way west of Moscow. Most senior government officials rode in Craigs. When the car was first launched, people made fun of the Craig Ne Plus Ultra for having the worst name in automotive history, yet now it was a global bestseller. It was the largest, least fuel-efficient, and most opulent American car, and it was the first to be bulletproof. At just $145,000 it was cheaper than buying a less luxurious Mercedes and fitting it with aftermarket glass and Kevlar, steel plates, and ballistic nylon in the body.

At his early morning breakfast, in a quiet café next to a massive tavern, crews had not yet cleaned the bottles, cans, vomit, and other detritus of late-late-late-night partying. After so many years of Russophobia, the new president-elect of the United States of America was considered a friend of the Kremlin.

Mironov's president.

At seventy-one and irredeemably fat, grotesquely rich, and something like happy, Sergei considered what he was leaving behind. President-elect Anthony Craig *was* his legacy, but if it coincided with the Russian renaissance he had so longed for, a growing part of him wanted his grandchildren to understand and celebrate his role in it. He imagined a modest statue of himself at the Park Ville gate, in Rublyovka, five minutes from his home. Too many of the young oligarchs he helped make and mentor had abandoned their mansions in Rublyovka.

Today represented the day they began returning home, with their ambitions and their capital. A woman from the best flower shop in Moscow had met him at the café, and the bouquet smelled enchanting in the back seat. On his way home from this meeting Sergei would stop at the perfume stand in GUM and buy his new wife Svetlana a gift. He liked to buy Chamade, a Guerlain fragrance named for the drumbeat of Napoleon's retreat from Moscow.

They exited the highway and entered the forest near the

presidential palace. The driver asked if he could open the windows to clear the interior of the Craig of the scent of flowers. Though it was a cold morning, Sergei took pity on him. And he did not regret it. The forest air was cold and clean, in between the decomposition of autumn and the absolute death of winter.

The walls surrounding Novyy Rim were over six meters tall. The surveillance and security were outstanding. At the gate three men in suits and long black jackets inspected the car while a fourth man, his own eyes red with fatigue, spoke to his driver.

The palace itself was soft yellow with white pillars. To the right, as the car approached, two women walked with horses saddled for a ride. Sergei recognized one of them and waved. On the grounds there was a fine greenhouse and another structure for hens and chickens. President Mironov preferred to be at Novyy Rim because it was much safer than any residence or suite of offices at the Kremlin, and no one could listen in on his conversations.

It had always delighted Sergei to walk through the Kremlin, which for most of his career had been the seat of global communism. Purists might have pointed to the palace as the madness and decadence of the tsars but to Sergei's knowledge no one who ever controlled a square centimeter of the Kremlin had ever proposed ripping it down, melting the gold into coins, or selling it all for the glory of the proletariat.

Mironov was a cleverer politician than any of the previous

presidents or general secretaries. At least he made an effort to conceal his wealth and opulence, to make it seem the result of private cunning – not his due as the Russian Federation's leading public servant. If journalists dared look into the purchase and construction of Novyy Rim, they would discover at the end of a long string of shell companies a simple transaction in the name of Aleksandr Mironov, businessman and investor.

'Take three Aspirin and sleep,' said Sergei, as his driver opened the door for him. 'I may be an hour.'

'Thank you, boss.'

To the left of the palace, a technician fussed with Mironov's helicopter. At some point today, he would have to fly into Moscow.

Mironov did not come out to greet Sergei. An intelligence agent welcomed him at the front door and led him into the palace. Their shoes echoed on the shiny floor.

'The president is swimming. Do you mind meeting with him in the pool room?'

'Of course not.'

Sergei removed his jacket and entered the elevator as the agent whispered into a concealed microphone. Halfway down, chlorine overwhelmed the scent of the flowers. They passed through another manned security checkpoint and entered the gym. Then, with a swiped card, the swimming pool.

Mironov was finishing a lap. He stopped. 'Sergei. Care for a swim? I have extra trunks.'

'No, my friend. Thank you.'

'Are the flowers for me?'

'Congratulations.'

Everything Mironov said and did was, at its core, about power. He was in his mid-sixties, not much younger than Sergei, yet he looked and acted like an extraordinarily fit fifty-year-old man. It pleased Mironov to display the physical difference between them. In fact, Sergei was sure his old friend had orchestrated the nature of this encounter. Nothing with the president was random or happenstance.

Mironov pulled himself out of the pool. The intelligence agent placed a white towel on a chair, took a final look around, and left the sealed room. On his way to the hot tub, Mironov picked up the towel.

'This morning, when I heard the news from America, I remembered the moment you first told me about our King-fisher and her husband.' Mironov lowered himself into the steaming water. 'I remembered our first meeting together.'

Sergei smiled. 'The Inter-Continental in Prague.'

'A beautiful day. A beautiful woman. Escargots! Even with the divorce and her occasional transgression she has been a perfect asset and you have been the finest handler in history. Bravo.'

Sergei sat on the edge of the hot tub.

'When the American networks finally called the election for Craig, and I saw all those angry men dressed for a round of golf with their fists in the air, our own American soldiers, my first thought was that it was all too perfect, that it is the most elaborate plot in the history of statecraft – and that he will somehow destroy us.'

Sergei sat up straight. 'I don't see how, Aleksandr.'

Mironov was going bald when they first met. Now, after several transplants, he had a convincing head of hair. His skinny legs made his broad chest look strange, but in the hot tub the president was all torso.

'He is a monster of chaos. Completely undisciplined, and therefore an unreliable ally. He'll say or do anything.'

Sergei had never lost control of a possession but he could not tell the president the truth about his call with Elena, the previous night, and how she'd been in tears. 'We both have grandchildren,' she had said. 'Sergei, what have we done?'

Mironov wiped his forehead with the white towel.

'You do not have to worry about him,' said Sergei. 'Enjoy your gift. If he said anything about Elena, about us, it would be suicide. And besides, there is no proof.'

Mironov pulled a pistol from between the folds of the towel, pointed it at Sergei, and pulled the trigger twice. He stood up out of the hot water as Sergei fell in.

'No. Not anymore.'

43

Unless she was traveling for a story, Grace drove up from Miami once a month to have dinner with her mother. Friday nights were taco nights at The Grove. In the beginning, she came every week and they shared a table for two. Over time, however, Grace had to find a place for herself at a table for eight or ten and realized she was preventing her mother from a jollier and freer evening with her friends.

That evening a mariachi band from Ocala was playing on the small outdoor stage. The staff poured good sipping tequila for anyone who was interested, a follow-up from a presentation on *reposado* and *añejo* back in August. The dining room was on a gorgeous terrace which led to a lush garden and a pond.

Every now and then an alligator showed up in the pond and her mother's retirement community in Central Florida made the local news.

Grace watched her mother singing along to 'Cielito Lindo' with her friends. In the years since the election, Elsie Elliott had become a different person. A staff doctor at The Grove took an interest in her and in only a few months he managed her diabetes to the point where her eyesight began to improve, enabling her return to one of her dearest loves: reading mystery and romance novels.

For her birthday in September Grace had flown Elsie to Prague, as promised, and they stayed at the Four Seasons.

Grace's phone hummed with a new call just as the mariachis began playing their encore. They had invited her mother and two of the other women up to sing along. Grace ignored the call and watched her mother sway in front of the microphone, buzzed on Tapatio Añejo, singing in front of her new best friends: good, attractive, wealthy people in pretty white dresses, in tan chinos and button-up shirts, fine jewelry, brand-name watches.

At the end of the song they all applauded and a man named Barry, who she worried might be her mother's boyfriend, stood up to lead an ovation. Grace did not recognize the number of the caller but she hoped it would be one of the editors she was in touch with, desperate on a Friday night to dole out a killer story to a not-so-desperate freelancer.

Grace walked into the garden to listen to her voicemail. 'I am in Miami tomorrow on business. Can we have dinner?'

It was Elena.

They agreed to meet at La Vaquera, an Argentinian restaurant in South Beach a half-hour walk from Grace's little orange ranch house on Michigan Avenue.

When Grace arrived the following evening, the maître d' asked her for picture ID and then he led her through the restaurant and up a set of stairs. She had only been there for brunch and did not know about the private room, with an open-air view over the beach and the ocean – dark now. There was Elena, sitting alone in the vast room, looking down over the action on the ground floor terrace below.

She stood up. 'Duše moje.'

A bald, white giant of a man politely asked if he could check Grace for weapons or listening devices. He took her phone.

The pat-down was uncommonly thorough, nothing like airport security. When the man was finished, he apologized for the inconvenience and left them.

A server immediately appeared with champagne.

'I took liberties.' Elena inspected the bottle. 'It's a Larmandier-Bernier Terre de Vertus Premier Cru.'

Grace knew she should be impressed. 'Oh.'

'A great year, 2009.'

'Thank you, Ms Craig. And what a beautiful spot.'

'For you, duše moje, anything.' While the server fussed

366

with the bottle and popped the cork, Elena stood up and kissed Grace's cheeks. In her out-of-season beige linen, Grace thought she would have fit in beautifully at The Grove. The warm breeze moved through her loose slacks and her hair. It had been two years since they had last spoken, in the back seat of the Craig sedan in Mladá Boleslav. Elena looked tired and older than Grace had ever seen her, and a bit puffy, almost her age. There was a new tremor in her left hand. When their glasses were full the server prepared to excuse himself.

'You can begin bringing us food,' said Elena.

'Oh. Right, ma'am. What . . . sort of food?'

'We are two.' Elena placed her hand on Grace's. 'Ask the chef to impress us.'

'Wonderful. Wonderful, ma'am.'

Elena had not been visible in Anthony Craig's transition to power. From time to time Grace had read about her, about how she remained a trusted, informal advisor to the president.

What Grace most admired about her was still there: her confidence, her poise, her elegance, and her charm.

But there was something new.

'It must be so exciting, to see your family . . . ruling the free world.'

Elena did not smile or nod. 'The man who searched you, my security man, he works for the government. I asked him to sweep the room, for listening devices, so we can speak freely. Your little house, duše moje, it is pretty?'

'It is, thank you.'

'And your mother? She is happy?'

'Very happy. And healthy. She's absolutely transformed.'

Elena took a drink of the expensive champagne. 'Do you understand now why we did what we did?'

Grace thought of her mother's comfort and safety, of her own prosperity and the lonely sort of contentment in her life now. She could trade it for an explosive worry every night – that her mother could be taken from her, that her own life could end with a spiked drink or meal, a pinprick in an airport she hardly felt that would grow into a demon of pain and suffering and darkness. She understood clearly why *we did what we did*.

'I imagine the choice is even simpler when you have a daughter.'

'It is simpler and more complicated, duše moje. It is no longer a question. You submit because you will do anything for your child. Do you understand?'

'I do.'

A *chacarera* song with a dance beat underneath it played while they sipped their champagne and looked out over the couples on dates below.

'Does anyone know what you achieved, Elena?'

She shrugged. 'My close friend Josef Straka, of course. By now you know about my relationship with Sergei.'

'I know he exists. I don't know anything about him.' Grace felt like she should be taking notes but why and for what? It was over.

'He's dead.'

Grace did not know if she should apologize.

'You are in my prison with me.'

'I'm living a life I never would have lived.'

'It's a curse. You'll come to see that. A slow infection that devours everything. You see, to them we are nothing. Sergei called us his possessions. These men, who possess us, they really only have one goal, and they would like to achieve it while they are still alive.'

'What's that?'

'To turn all of this upside down.'

'What do you mean?'

'To destroy us, duše moje, so artfully that we do not know it is happening. We do not feel the dagger go in. We just slowly bleed.'

'We?'

'They have you and me, my daughter. And they have him too.'

Grace thought of all that had happened, since the election. It felt like a coup d'état in slow motion.

Elena gestured at the terrace full of lovers below, even the dark beach where the courageous nighttime joggers ran silent and barefoot. 'They have us all.'

Grace thought of her mother in the lobby of the Four Seasons in Prague sipping a glass of Moravian wine, winking at her daughter, proud of her. Her mother thought the money for this new life had come from a book deal, something secret. A ghostwriting job.

'Someday someone will find out.' Elena slid her champagne flute in a gentle circle on the table. 'You found out.'

'But Roberta McKee, she told me there's nothing left. Not a trace.'

'Do you know my code name?'

'They're so pretty, kingfishers. A good name for you.'

'I suppose they are. That is why they recruited me, why Sergei recruited me. I was so pretty.'

'And an athlete.'

'A mediocre athlete. Just smart enough, just dumb enough. I had friends, smarter friends, who did not make it.'

'What do you mean?'

'I mean they are dead. They could not endure what I endured.'

'Living the life of a fabulous multi-millionaire?'

Elena shook her head. 'Grow up, duše moje.'

Their first courses arrived: little hunks of meat with chimichurri sauce, some chorizo, and a kale salad of some sort. It all smelled delicious and they complimented the server, as he topped up their champagne glasses, but Grace wasn't hungry anymore. The security man stepped in and looked around, apparently to be sure a ninja had not sneaked in under the server's black apron.

When they were alone again, Grace saw that Elena wasn't any hungrier than she was.

'How many of them are there, women like you and Roberta? Swallows?'

'There were twenty or thirty in America in the 1970s.' Her voice was dour. 'Now there are probably five hundred.'

'Ms Craig, doesn't this mean you've won?'

She chuckled, but not because anything was funny. 'I'm on pills for depression. It makes my face big.'

'Why did you ask to see me?'

Elena looked down on the terrace again. 'You know, before the election, I was trying to help you. But I had to be careful.'

'William.'

'You could not even speak Czech. He knew how to find what had to be found. I wanted you to write it, to write something, before the election. Then I changed my mind. I was afraid.'

'He completely fooled me.'

'Falling for you, believe me, duše moje, that was not part of his job.'

Grace felt her eyes fill with tears. She thought of a life she nearly had, in a small apartment south of London, the weekend strolls through parks with her mother.

'You wanted to write a book.' Elena leaned forward over the untouched food. 'Let's write it. A true book.'

Grace was shocked. This was not what she was expecting. 'But we can't. They'll . . .'

'Kill us? Maybe. Maybe not.'

There was a black safe in Grace's closet, where she kept her notes on Elena and her story. She had been using an old Mac clamshell laptop without Internet access. 'Ms Craig, I already started.'

'I knew it.' Elena lifted her champagne flute. 'I knew this about you, duše moje. That you are brave enough. I will tell you everything.'

'Wait, wait.' Grace's appetite was returning suddenly. 'How would it work?'

For the next two hours, over several more plates of meat and sauce and the rest of the champagne and a bottle of Malbec, they plotted. There was nowhere to hide so they decided not to hide. They would meet in the spa and in the Hamptons, where they used to meet. Elena would tell her story.

In the morning, every morning, Grace wakes up and wonders if this will be the day. When she returns home from a walk with her new puppy, she inspects the safe in her closet to be sure it's still there, that the old orange computer is still inside, that the previous night's writing is saved. She calls her mother twice a day to say 'I love you.' Once a month she drives to St Petersburg to spend three days mentoring young journalists. She goes to rallies and she signs petitions. Every night she goes to sleep hoping she will wake up.

Grace knows all of this can end any day, before we reach the end of the lazy fragment of a final sentence. She wants you to know why.